He stood so close that she could see the thick lashes framing his eyes, the light stubble on his chin, and the sprinkling of hair above the open collar of his shirt.

If she was honest with herself, she *was* curious. About him. The man who pushed his grandmother out of his life one moment and doted on her the next. The man who scolded Beth for leaving their party at the gardens but held her hand beneath the fireworks. The rogue who had a reputation for pleasuring London's most beautiful women but seemed to be flirting with a renowned wallflower—*her.*

I DARED
the
DUKE

I DARED *the* DUKE

ANNA BENNETT

St. Martin's Paperbacks

This is a work of fiction. All of the characters, organizations, and events portrayed in this novel are either products of the author's imagination or are used fictitiously.

I DARED THE DUKE

Copyright © 2017 by Anna Bennett.
Excerpt from *The Rogue is Back in Town* Copyright © 2017 by Anna Bennett.

For information address St. Martin's Press, 175 Fifth Avenue, New York, NY 10010.

ISBN: 978-1-250-10092-4

Our books may be purchased in bulk for promotional, educational, or business use. Please contact your local bookseller or the Macmillan Corporate and Premium Sales Department at 1-800-221-7945, ext. 5442, or by e-mail at MacmillanSpecialMarkets@macmillan.com.

Printed in the United States of America

St. Martin's Paperbacks edition / April 2017

St. Martin's Paperbacks are published by St. Martin's Press, 175 Fifth Avenue, New York, NY 10010.

10 9 8 7 6 5 4 3 2 1

For Dana
Love you like a sister, always.

Chapter ONE

Alexander Savage, the Duke of Blackshire, was known throughout the ton for three things: the horrific burn scars on his neck, his distinctly ornery disposition, and his undisputed skill at . . . that is, his innate ability to . . . er, a certain knack for pleasing—

Blast it all, the duke was good in bed.

None of which was *any* concern of Elizabeth Lacey's. In fact, just two months ago, Beth would have bet her best bonnet that she'd go to her grave without ever setting foot inside the duke's town house.

And now she lived there.

It was a temporary arrangement—a favor to her dear uncle. His friend the Dowager Duchess of Blackshire had mentioned, repeatedly, that she longed for a companion—someone to escort her to various functions and ease her loneliness now that her niece had married and moved to Somerset.

While the thought of a full social calendar made Beth

break out in a rash, the truth was she needed . . . well, she needed to be needed.

Her sisters lovingly teased her for her habit of embracing every cause—whether it was tending to a bird's broken wing, standing up for a bullied child, or collecting books for the foundling home. Beth couldn't help it—she liked to fix things, right wrongs, and restore harmony.

She supposed that's what came from enduring a childhood where little seemed fair or orderly. After the sudden death of her parents, she and her sisters had been like frail leaves caught up in a whirlwind, their lives spinning out of control. She'd learned at a tender age that the world wasn't always a fair or decent place . . . and she'd resolved to make it so.

When she'd considered that acting as companion to the duchess would place her in proximity with the brooding, if reportedly talented, duke, she *had* hesitated briefly. But Beth doubted her path and the duke's would cross often, if at all.

Indeed, the dowager had assured Beth that the duke preferred to spend his time at his estate house outside of London. She'd blinked rapidly and her thin voice had cracked as she'd admitted she suspected her grandson preferred the company of younger people and naturally did not wish to have his bachelor activities curtailed by the presence of a feeble old woman.

Incensed by the duke's callousness, Beth had agreed to play the part of companion on the spot.

And now, there she was. The duke's sumptuous drawing room was a far cry from the cozy parlor with the threadbare settee in the house where she'd lived with

Uncle Alistair and her sisters. Humming to herself, she laid a whisper-soft quilt across the duchess's lap and fluffed the silk damask pillow behind her back.

The white-haired woman sighed contentedly and sipped her tea.

"Shall I inquire about this evening's menu?" Beth asked.

A look of alarm flitted across the duchess's heavily powdered face but vanished so quickly Beth wondered if she'd imagined it. "No, no." The tightly spiraled curls at the duchess's temple bounced as she shook her head. "I'm sure Cook has dinner well in hand." Her shrewd blue eyes roved over Beth's simple morning gown. "But would you be a dear and fetch my paisley shawl from upstairs?"

"Of course." Beth started toward the door.

"While you're looking in my armoire," the duchess added breezily, "perhaps you'd like to pick out a shawl for yourself."

"You're very kind," Beth said. "But I'm not at all chilled." Sunlight streamed through the drawing room's tall windows, and a cozy fire crackled on the hearth. Furthermore, it was *July*.

The duchess raised her thin brows. "I forget that young people are impervious to the cold. Still, I find there's nothing like surrounding oneself with cheerful colors to brighten the mood." She sighed forlornly. "A bit of rose silk would complement your fair complexion."

Beth absently raised a palm to her cheek, fairly certain she'd just been given fashion advice by a woman well into her seventies. But it couldn't hurt to indulge the duchess. Too many of Beth's peers dismissed the opinions of their elders, scoffing at their hard-won wisdom. She'd witnessed the same prejudice directed at her uncle scores of times.

"Very well," Beth said brightly. "You've convinced me. I shall take you up on your generous offer and borrow something colorful."

"Excellent." The duchess leaned back in her chair, pleased to have her small wish granted. It wasn't difficult to make older people happy. They simply wanted the same as anyone—to be heard and respected.

Beth made her way to the duchess's elegant bedchamber and located the paisley shawl, as well as a lightweight pink silk for herself. She paused in front of the vanity to drape the scarf around her shoulders and admire the effect.

Goodness. She had to admit, it was a marked improvement. Perhaps if she consulted the duchess about her gown before her next ball she'd finally shed her reputation as being the middle—and therefore the least notable—of the Wilting Wallflowers.

Either that, or she'd become notorious for wearing a rich purple turban and prematurely securing her spot among the gray-haired set.

She shrugged. There were worse fates, after all.

Whisking herself out of the bedchamber and down the stairs, she rounded a corner just as the front door burst open. A pair of footmen laden with trunks, boxes, and bags dashed up the porch steps and shouldered past her. The butler, Mr. Sharp, strode into the foyer, then chased the footmen up the staircase, issuing orders as to where each parcel should be placed.

Beth contemplated the odd scene. The duchess hadn't

mentioned she was expecting guests. And whoever had arrived was causing rather a fuss. Moreover, the front door gaped open, inviting a warm but strong breeze that would no doubt drift down the hall toward the drawing room. The duchess would feel it as surely as the princess had felt the pea nestled beneath her hundred mattresses.

Clucking her tongue, Beth rushed across the foyer and swung the door shut.

Only to have it bounce open again, revealing the tall, muscular, and vexingly breathtaking form of the Duke of Blackshire.

Drat.

He glared down his slightly crooked nose, not bothering to hide his displeasure. "Good God," he intoned, crossing the threshold. "Have you taken leave of your senses?"

Beth's jaw dropped and heat crawled up her neck. How *dare* he? She longed to issue a blistering response—a witty yet cutting retort to put him firmly in his place, a clever remark to make him realize how wrong he was, a metaphorical slap across his chiseled cheek.

But her throat squeezed shut, and the words wouldn't come, blast it all. Even worse, her eyes burned.

"Never mind." The duke rolled his eyes as he slammed the door behind him. "I believe I have my answer."

He tugged off his gloves, tossed them onto the small table in the foyer, and strode past her as though she were a potted plant. Or rather a person with the intellect of one.

Her blood boiled. She couldn't allow him to dismiss her so, wouldn't let him treat her with such indignity.

Summoning courage, she cleared her throat. "My

name is Miss Elizabeth Lacey." Though she'd tried to match his haughty tone, her traitorous voice cracked.

The duke's boots froze on the marble floor. "Miss Lacey," he repeated in a tone that suggested he felt a headache coming on. "Why are you roaming the halls of my house?"

"I was hardly roam—" She closed her eyes briefly to collect herself, then raised her chin before she continued. "I am your grandmother's new companion."

He snorted. "She said nothing about you."

Beth shrugged. "As it happens, the duchess has said very little about *you*." A small fib. The duchess loved nothing more than droning on about her grandson, fairly beaming with pride each time his name crossed her lips.

The duke planted his hands on narrow hips, as though exasperated by Beth's insolence. Well. If she was rude, it was no more than he deserved.

"Where is she?"

"Your grandmother is in the drawing room."

He stalked up the stairs and down the corridor, and Beth followed on the heels of his polished boots. If he meant to confront the duchess about taking on Beth as a companion, she intended to be there.

Ignoring her, he walked through the drawing room, directly to his grandmother's side.

"Alexander! What a pleasant surprise!" the older woman cooed.

He placed a perfunctory kiss on her cheek and sat on a stool opposite her settee so she needn't crane her neck to look at him. Beth stood beside the duchess, who perked up, as though the mere presence of her grandson was more potent than a drink from the Fountain of Youth.

"You grow more handsome each time I see you," the duchess proclaimed.

"Your eyesight is failing, Grandmother," he teased, causing her to giggle like a debutante.

"Nonsense." But she adjusted her spectacles just the same. "I assume you met Elizabeth?"

"Yes, she was in the foyer when I arrived. Does she always guard the front door?"

The duchess's smile faded a fraction. "Why, heavens no. She was fetching my shawl."

Realizing she still held the shawl, Beth clumsily laid it over the duchess's sloped shoulders.

The duke leaned forward and reached for the duchess's frail hands, enveloping them in his. "Grandmother, your lady's maid could have handled the task."

"Oh." Her brow creased. "I suppose you're right. But Elizabeth didn't seem to mind."

"Of course I don't mind," Beth interjected, incredulous.

"My point is," the duke continued to address the duchess without sparing so much as a glance for Beth, "that you are not in need of a companion. But if, for some reason, you felt that you *did* require one, you should have consulted with me."

Beth gripped the back of the settee and pressed her lips together. Honestly, the man's arrogance knew no bounds. Though it wasn't her place to respond, she couldn't idly stand by while he scolded the duchess.

"Your grandmother is quite capable of making all sorts of decisions on her own, your grace. Furthermore, even if she *had* been inclined to consult with you, circumstances made that quite impossible, as you were not here. In fact, I gather you are *rarely* here. Which is why my presence is necessary."

The duke dropped his grandmother's hands and stood, launching the full force of his glare at Beth. She hadn't liked being ignored, but perhaps it was preferable to this—his unapologetic scrutiny. Her skin tingled with the knowledge that a fight was imminent, and she swallowed the knot in her throat. She might as well have been facing Goliath with a slingshot.

"Necessary?" He folded his arms across the considerable width of his chest, and his expression turned bemused. "I have made sure that the duchess has everything she could possibly need. You are approximately as *necessary* as the ostrich feather in that vase." He inclined his head at the pretty, if superfluous, plume displayed on the fireplace mantel.

The duke's words cut her to the quick—probably more than he knew. She'd thought the duchess needed her, but maybe Beth had only been desperate to believe she did. That *someone* did.

"Alexander!" The duchess pressed a hand to her chest. "You mustn't insult Elizabeth. She is here as a favor to me."

A moment of awkward silence ensued before the duke finally spoke. "Forgive me, Grandmother."

However reluctant his apology might have been, the duchess relaxed, instantly mollified. But then, *she* hadn't been deemed as useless as a discarded feather—of a flightless bird, no less.

"It's quite all right. I'm certain you're weary from your travels and eager to freshen up," the duchess said.

Travels? For heaven's sake. His country house was less than an hour away by carriage, and even a journey from Northumberland in knee-deep snow couldn't have excused his bad behavior. Besides, he didn't appear weary to Beth in the least. He was all lean muscle and coiled strength. He fairly exuded power.

"I do have some pressing business to attend to." He glanced at the gold clock that was also on the mantel— ornate but infinitely more utilitarian than the ostrich plume beside it.

Beth bit her tongue. He'd been gone a fortnight, and yet he couldn't afford to spend a quarter of an hour conversing with his dear, adoring grandmother?

But the duchess smiled, unperturbed. "I trust you'll be dining with us tonight?"

"If I'm able," he said noncommittally.

"Wonderful." The duchess clasped her hands. "I think Elizabeth and I should rest so that we'll be at our very best."

Beth sniffed. The duke was hardly deserving of her *best*. Given his churlishness, he'd be fortunate if she managed to refrain from hurling her peas at him for the duration of the first course.

"A fine plan," the duke said smoothly. "Why don't you retire for a nap, Grandmother? In the meantime, I require a word with Miss Lacey."

A chill ran the length of Beth's spine.

"Oh?" The duchess looked from the duke to Beth and back again. "Whatever for?"

The duke smiled, revealing white, even teeth. "We seem to be off to a rocky start. I wish to make amends."

"Then I shall leave you." The duchess stood with an alacrity Beth hadn't known she possessed and made her way to the door. "You are two of my favorite young people," she said over her shoulder, "and nothing would make me happier than to see harmony restored to this house. I shall see you at dinner," she added cheerfully.

And with a wave of her hand, she left Beth alone—with the notorious Duke of Blackshire.

He stared at her for the space of several heartbeats, with the same cold detachment one usually reserved for examining a hem in need of mending. Not that the duke would concern himself with a torn gown hem. No, if rumors were to be believed, his interest in gowns was strictly limited to their ease of removal. Still, she refused to be intimidated by either his scandalous reputation or his intense masculinity.

"Elizabeth Lacey." He gazed at the ceiling as though searching his memory. Beth wanted to tell him not to waste his time. While they'd attended a few of the same balls, he was unlikely to remember a thin girl in an unfashionable gown propping up the wall near the refreshment table.

"Aren't you one of Lord Wiltmore's—?"

"Wallflowers?" she provided. "How kind of you to mention it," she added dryly.

He raised a dark brow. "I was going to say 'nieces.'"

She shrugged. "Perhaps. But you were *thinking* 'wallflowers.'"

"I am fascinated by your uncanny ability to know what I'm thinking. If you can predict what I'm going to say before I say it, this whole conversation is rather pointless."

"I couldn't agree more," she said, smiling too sweetly. "Are we through?"

"Not quite." The feral grin that lit his face did not reach his eyes. "I've no doubt you know what I am about to say, and yet I feel the need to state it explicitly: your services are not needed here. Go home, Miss Lacey."

Chapter TWO

Alex sat and poured himself tea—into an empty cup clearly meant for Miss Lacey. But this was *his* domain, damn it. And he'd returned this morning for the sole purpose of removing people from his house, not taking more in.

Miss Lacey's blue eyes grew round as saucers, but despite his unambiguous order that she leave, she did not flee the room in a flurry of tears.

Instead, she strolled around the end of the settee and slowly, deliberately, sank onto the seat directly across from him.

"I assume you have some items you need to pack," he said, leaning back in his chair. "I'll send up a footman in a half hour to assist you with your bags."

Miss Lacey did not respond, but rather, reached for the folded napkin on the silver tea tray, snapped it open, and laid it across her lap. She then proceeded to claim the single unused dish—*and* the last blueberry scone.

A bold move. He had to give the wallflower credit.

A smug smile lit her face as she proceeded to bite into the pastry. He watched, oddly mesmerized, as she ate the entire scone and licked the crumbs from her lips. "Now then," she said smoothly, "you should know that I intend to stay on as your grandmother's companion. I believe you said something about making amends."

He stretched out his legs, crossing them at the ankles. "I lied." He had no intention of apologizing . . . but he was not above paying her off. Anything to get her out of his hair—and his house.

He'd heard rumors that her uncle, Wiltmore, was in dire financial straits. His oldest niece had married Lord Castleton, but perhaps the earl wasn't keen on sharing his wealth with the eccentric—some said mad—Lord Wiltmore. Part of him admired Miss Lacey's resourcefulness.

He set down the teacup and folded his arms across his chest. "How much do you want?"

She blinked prettily, the picture of innocence. "I beg your pardon?"

"I haven't time for games. Name your sum."

A pink flush stole up her cheeks. "Are you talking about . . . money?"

"I presume that's why you're here."

"No," she said, frowning. "I have no expectation of payment for my services."

No wonder his grandmother had been taken in. Miss Lacey played the part of the generous, charitable ingénue to perfection. But such selflessness was always an act, as Alex knew all too well.

"You agreed to be my grandmother's companion out of the goodness of your heart?" he asked skeptically.

"Is that so difficult to believe?"

"I believe a pretty young woman has better things to do with her time than fetching fans and listening to complaints about aching joints." His offhand compliment seemed to fluster her. God help her if he ever attempted to be truly charming.

She swept an errant curl behind her ear and composed herself once more. "You do not give me very much credit, your grace. And you give your grandmother even less. Perhaps if you took the time to converse with her on occasion, you would know that she is a delightful conversationalist."

He shrugged off her barb. "She does like to talk about *me*," he boasted unapologetically. "Has she told you the story of how I fell off my horse at the age of five, broke my arm, and insisted that my father place me back in the saddle so that I could attempt the jump again?"

Miss Lacey rolled her eyes. "She might have. I don't recall the particulars."

He shot a smug smile at her. "It's one of her favorites. But entertaining tales of my childhood escapades are not sufficient incentive for someone like you to voluntarily agree to shop for gout remedies and read tedious poetry to a seventy-year-old woman who isn't even related to you."

Gazing directly into his eyes, she said, "My reasons for agreeing to help your grandmother are personal, but they are not sinister. Perhaps you assign evil intent to my actions because that is what is in *your* heart—but I can assure you, it's not in mine."

The barbs kept coming. She must have a quiver full of them.

"Very well," he said. "Let's set aside the issue of your motivation, for now. The fact of the matter is you simply cannot stay here." The truth was he held no grudge against Miss Lacey. She was beautiful and bold—a swath of wildflowers brightening an otherwise drab field. But he couldn't be responsible for her well-being—not in light of recent events.

"I don't understand." She blinked rapidly, as though fending off tears.

He swallowed and reminded himself this was for her own good. And that the less she knew, the better. "My grandmother's circumstances will soon be changing, and she'll have no need for a companion. I would rather she not form a deep attachment to you in the meantime, as it will only make the inevitable separation more difficult for her. You see, Miss Lacey, I'm not the ogre you believe me to be."

She sniffed indelicately. "If you say so."

"You have some place to go, I presume?"

"After you turn me out on the street?" Her blue eyes seemed to look through him. "Never fear, your grace. I shan't be reduced to serving pints to drunken sailors, if that's what's troubling you. I can return to my uncle's house. My sister would no doubt take me in as well. Having a place to live—*that's* not the problem."

But her answer, sarcastic as it may have been, suggested there *was* a problem. He exhaled slowly. Whatever her underlying issue might be, it was not his concern. The sooner Miss Lacey was out from under his roof, the better off she'd be. "I'm glad to hear you have options."

She rolled her eyes dramatically. "And I'm glad I could help to ease your conscience. I'll pack my things while your grandmother is napping. I'm not sure what I'll say to her, but I do want to say good-bye in person."

"You can stay until tomorrow." The words had tumbled out of his mouth, unbidden.

"Tomorrow?" she repeated.

A short reprieve couldn't hurt. It was one night, and he'd be extra vigilant. "We'll inform my grandmother at dinner this evening that you'll be leaving. You can send word to your uncle or sister to expect you in the morning."

"Excellent. That will give me a few more hours to formulate a plausible explanation as to why I was tossed out on my ear."

"You could always tell them that my untoward behavior made it impossible for you to stay."

She seemed to consider this, then blinked. "Are you suggesting that I allow my family to believe that you made improper advances toward me?"

"Why not? They would believe it. I've scared off sturdier maidens than you, Miss Lacey."

She stood, slowly, and from beneath thick, sooty lashes, cast a haughty look at him. "First of all, you should know that I'm far *sturdier* than I look. Furthermore, neither my uncle nor my sister would believe that I was intimidated by the likes of you—ogre or no."

He stood as well, forcing her to raise her chin if she wished to continue glaring at him. "A complete lack of fear may make you courageous, but it does not make you wise. A young, attractive woman living within the same walls as a notorious bachelor has good cause to worry."

"Is that a threat, your grace?"

"No," he answered quickly. For God's sake, he wasn't *that* depraved. "You have no reason to fear me. I only meant that people will talk, rumors will spread. You might as well make the gossip work in your favor."

She pressed slender fingers to her temple. "I am trying to figure out how rumors of impropriety could possibly work to my advantage."

"I'm sure you're aware of my reputation."

"Hmm?" She raised her eyebrows in question even as a telltale blush stole up her cheeks.

"I'm afraid there's no delicate way to say it, but I'm rather known for—"

She raised a hand and closed her eyes. "No need to state it," she blurted. "I can imagine."

"Can you?" He was enjoying her discomfort far more than he should have. Maybe he *was* that depraved.

"Now that you mention it, I believe I may have heard a rumor." She fanned herself with her hand. "Not that I put much stock in gossip."

Touché. "And you are obviously aware of your own reputation."

"As a wallflower? Yes, your grace, we've covered this ground—remember?"

"Consider this. If the ton believed that a confirmed rake was interested in a wallflower . . ."

She shook her head, incredulous. "You think that your interest in me will cause other gentleman to hold me in esteem?"

"A dog always wants another dog's bone."

Miss Lacey gasped, clearly horrified by his attempt to explain. "How dare you compare me to a dog?" she snapped.

For the love of—"*I'm* the dog. You're the bone."

"Your charming little metaphor was not entirely beyond me, your grace."

He shrugged. "Apparently, it *was*."

Narrowing her eyes to slits, she stepped toward him. Close enough for him to see the subtle rise and fall of her chest.

"I followed your meaning. Now allow me to explain something to *you*." She spoke slowly, anger dripping from each word. "I am *not* the bone. But if I were, I wouldn't be caught dead in your mouth."

He arched a brow but didn't respond immediately. Better to let her embarrassment stew in the awkward silence that ensued.

Miss Lacey closed her eyes as though chiding herself for her indelicate choice of words. "Blast," she muttered, then clamped her lips into a tight line.

But she needn't restrain herself on his account. He found her candor refreshing. Borderline arousing.

"I'm glad we've cleared up the matter," he said smoothly.

She heaved a frustrated sigh. "I should go." She hurried toward the drawing-room door as if the hounds of hell snapped at her heels.

"Dinner is at eight sharp," he called after her.

Her muffled reply sounded suspiciously like a curse.

But he, for one, already looked forward to their next

meeting. He would enjoy her company—and perhaps sparring with her again—for this one evening.

Tomorrow morning, he could turn his attention to more pressing matters.

Like figuring out who the hell was trying to kill him.

Chapter THREE

Tonight she, Elizabeth Lacey, would dine with the Duke of Blackshire.

Perhaps tomorrow she could poke a sleeping bear or swim across the Thames naked. Just for sport.

Beth couldn't imagine why she'd agreed to stay another night under the duke's roof. Her two small bags were already packed and waiting by her bedroom door. She should have requested a private audience with the duchess after her nap and simply informed her that her insufferable grandson had decreed that she leave. She could have left it to the duke to explain why he deemed it necessary.

But she supposed she wanted to hear his explanation with her own ears. She could hardly wait to discover the colorful falsehood he would fabricate to justify sending her away. She was fairly certain he would spare his dear grandmamma talk of dogs and bones. One hoped.

What had really tipped the scale in favor of staying for dinner, though, was the knowledge that the duchess might be distraught by the news. She wasn't precisely the stoic sort, and if the duke's edict upset her, Beth wanted to be there to console her as best she could.

But at the stroke of eight, as Beth escorted the duchess to the drawing room for a pre-dinner glass of sherry, the older woman nearly bubbled over with excitement. "Alexander is so droll, is he not? All the young ladies are drawn to him."

Not *all* the young ladies. And though Beth hated to dwell on the matter, it wasn't his *wit* that made women flock to him, but something rather more scandalous. "I'm sure he has his fair share of admirers," she said diplomatically.

"I trust your conversation with him earlier was agreeable? He can be devilishly charming when he sets his mind to it." The duchess cast an assessing glance at Beth, as though looking for signs that she'd fallen under the duke's spell. In truth, it was a wonder she'd refrained from slapping his chiseled cheek.

"Our conversation was . . . illuminating." And infuriating at the same time. "He doesn't mince words, does he?"

"He had a difficult childhood." The duchess said, as if that were a legitimate excuse for poor manners. Her eyes clouded over for a moment, then turned sunny again. "But he's made of strong stuff."

Beth recalled the rumors of the burns on his neck. All she'd noticed was a patch of lighter, puckered skin behind his left ear. His cravat and jacket collar likely covered the worst of the scars—at least the physical ones. Both of his parents had died in that fire, and Beth understood that unspeakable pain all too well.

She'd been a girl of fourteen on the bleak winter day that her parents' coach had careened off an icy bridge and plunged into the frigid river below. With one freak-ish accident, Fate had robbed Beth and her sisters of everything: Mama, Papa, happiness . . . and the only home they'd ever known. Left penniless, they'd had to beg the kindness of relatives. And the only relation who'd offered to take in their heartbroken trio had been dear Uncle Alistair.

Beth understood loss. She knew grief so raw and blinding that one could easily drown in it, never to surface again. But she had. And so, apparently, had the duke.

He'd emerged a darkly attractive, wildly rich, and powerful man. Beth doubted he needed her pity—or wanted it, for that matter.

She and the duchess glided into the drawing room, where the duke sat with one muscled arm draped across the back of the sofa, staring into his glass of brandy.

"Alexander!" the duchess cried, as though she couldn't quite believe her good fortune at seeing him twice in one day. While they greeted each other, Beth accepted a glass of sherry from the footman and took a healthy swallow before joining them.

The duke's gaze drifted over her slowly, almost in-solently, heating her skin in its wake. If she'd taken a bit more care dressing for dinner this evening, it cer-tainly wasn't for *his* benefit. She'd been saving her blue

gown—the one she'd worn to her sister Meg's wedding—
for another special occasion.

Being tossed out of the duke's house seemed to qual-
ify. After all, it never hurt to look one's best during the
most trying of times. When the impending humiliating
scene repeated itself over and over in her head, as it no
doubt would, she'd be able to muse, *at least my hair
looked somewhat fetching.*

"Good evening, Miss Lacey." The low timbre of his
voice vibrated through her.

She raised her chin and sniffed. "Your grace."

"Impressive." He nodded thoughtfully.

Beth blinked. "What's impressive?"

"Your ability to make a simple greeting sound like
an insult. Not everyone can manage it, you know."

The duchess frowned, confused by the storm cloud
that had suddenly drifted into her idyllic evening.
"Alexander, is this the way young people are conversing
these days? I must say, I don't care for it a bit."

A muscle in his jaw ticked. "Forgive me, Grandmother. It was meant to be playful banter. Wasn't it, Miss
Lacey?"

Beth rolled her eyes at his audacity. "If you think that
qualifies as—"

"Oh my." The duchess's hand fluttered to her throat,
and Beth bit her tongue. If this was to be her last evening
as the duchess's companion, keeping peace was the least
she could do.

"That is," Beth choked out, "I'm certain the duke
meant to be charming."

"*Meant* to be?" he challenged.

Beth shrugged. "I cannot help it if I wasn't swept off my feet."

"True," the duchess chimed in. "But the two of you have only recently been introduced. Once you spend more time together, you'll each become accustomed to the other's sense of humor."

Beth felt guilty about allowing the duchess to think that she and duke might, over time, develop the capacity for civil conversation. Time had already run out—and that was no doubt for the best.

She glanced sideways at the duke, then looked directly into the duchess's bespectacled eyes. "There's something we must tell you," she began.

"Oh?" The older lady beamed as though she anticipated a grand surprise, and Beth's heart sank.

"Well, I'm afraid—"

"I'm famished," the duke announced, cutting her off. "I trust this momentous news of yours can wait until after we've eaten?"

Beth narrowed her eyes at him. "*My* news? I rather thought it was *your* news."

He shrugged impossibly broad shoulders. "I'm going to require sustenance if I am to properly debate pronouns with you, Miss Lacey."

"Oh dear. You really are peckish, Alexander." The duchess clucked her tongue. "Did you stop for luncheon earlier today? Heavens, did you even break your fast this morning?"

He frowned, and a dimple dented his cheek. "I can't recall."

Beth planted a hand on her hip. "He's hardly on the verge of wasting away." Nay, he was the sort of physical specimen that sculptors surely drooled over. Women too, apparently—though she personally failed to see the appeal of an ornery, self-absorbed aristocrat who was too handsome for his own good.

"Let us go through to the dining room," the duchess suggested. "Alexander, you may have the singular honor of escorting both me *and* Miss Lacey."

"No, no," Beth balked. "You must have him all to yourself this evening. I insist."

The duke nestled his grandmother's wrinkled hand in the crook of one arm and offered the other to Beth—along with a wicked smile. "There's plenty of me to go around, Miss Lacey. We can't have you walking unescorted to the dining table."

"I don't see why not," she retorted breezily. "I daresay I managed the journey perfectly well last evening. Your grandmother did as well. Somehow, we navigated that great distance without the assistance of a man."

"And you didn't end up in the library?" he teased.

"Oh," the duchess giggled as though his inane quip were the wittiest thing she'd heard in an age. "There's that droll sense of humor. How I've missed you, my dear boy." She patted his arm affectionately. "Come, Elizabeth. We shall have the entire evening to converse."

The duke proffered his arm once more and shot Beth a look that dared her to refuse him twice. Fine. For the duchess's sake, she would play along tonight. Tomorrow morning, she would wipe her hands of him, forever.

Gritting her teeth, she curled her fingers around his sleeve, startled by the hardness of his forearm. Mentally, she scoffed. So, he had a few muscles. She'd wager her favorite parasol he was flexing for her benefit.

The unlikely trio shuffled all the way to the dining room and were seated, with the duke at the head of the table, his grandmother on his right, and Beth on his left. The setting might have felt intimate and cozy if it weren't so impeccably elegant. The marble fireplace mantel, intricate plaster moldings, sparkling crystal chandelier, and stately framed landscapes bespoke wealth and privilege.

Hardly a wallflower's natural habitat. However, adapting was often necessary for survival. As the footmen served a variety of dishes, she located what she hoped was the correct fork and ventured a bite of salad.

And though the food was excellent, Beth hardly tasted it. She was too preoccupied with the knowledge that her sudden departure would likely crush the sweet old duchess.

"We received an invitation for Lord and Lady Claville's ball on Saturday," the dowager announced. "I replied that we would attend, naturally."

"Naturally," the duke mumbled in agreement. Like Beth, he appeared to be preoccupied, but not with his dear grandmother's well-being. No, rather he was preoccupied with the *roast*. He gazed at it almost lovingly as he speared a hunk with his fork and shoveled it into his mouth.

"I'd hoped that you might escort Elizabeth and me, Alexander."

The duke coughed as though the beef were suddenly difficult to swallow. "This Saturday, you say?"

Beth sat back and sipped her wine, eager to watch the duke try to squirm his way out of his grandmother's simple request.

"Yes. They are dear friends, Alexander." The duchess blinked behind her spectacles. "And it wouldn't kill you to put in an appearance."

But the pained look on the duke's face suggested quite the opposite. "I'll have to see if I can clear my schedule," he said noncommittally.

The duchess opened her mouth as if she'd say more, then pressed her thin lips together and, for her grandson's benefit, managed a tight smile.

Really. Was it too much to ask that he forego a few hours of debauchery this Saturday in order to make his grandmother happy? Beth felt like a teakettle on the verge of boiling over.

But she kept her temper in check through all four courses of dinner, right up to the last bite of her pineapple ice cream.

Then the duke leaned back in his chair like a medieval king settling himself into his throne. He laced his fingers together and rested his hands on a stomach that was impossibly flat, given he'd just eaten three times as much as she and the duchess combined.

"Now then," he drawled. "I believe Miss Lacey had something of import she wished to tell us."

Beth dragged her traitorous gaze away from the duke's taut abdomen and shook her head. Perfect physique or no, she refused to be his puppet. If he wished to sack her, he could tell his grandmother himself.

"Why no, your grace. I've nothing to share. Nothing at all."

Chapter FOUR

Alex turned to his left and shot Miss Lacey a look that would have made most men shake in their boots. She simply batted her eyes and smiled sweetly.

"Are you quite certain you have nothing to say?" he prodded.

"I am."

He was in no mood for games. "I believe you had some news concerning your own situation," he said meaningfully.

She sipped her wine, her blue eyes thoughtful. "*Situation* is such a vague word, is it not? It could refer to any number of topics. I'm afraid you'll have to be more specific."

"Don't be obtuse, Alexander," the duchess scolded.

Miss Lacey could hardly keep the self-satisfied look off her pretty face. "Honestly, your grace," she said as though slightly exasperated, "if you have something to share, you are at liberty to say it."

He narrowed his eyes. "How kind of you to grant me permission to speak at *my* dining room table."

She waved her hand as if to say, *the stage is yours.*

Alex cleared his throat and prepared to inform his grandmother that Miss Lacey would return home to her uncle in the morning. But the sight of his grandmother's sparkling eyes and rosy cheeks stopped him cold. He couldn't recall the last time he'd seen her so vibrant and happy. It seemed Miss Lacey had already wormed her way into his grandmother's affections, and if he announced he was sending her away . . .

His grandmother might well be devastated.

Damned if he could break her heart. She was the only real family he had left, and while he wasn't particularly adept at showing it, he adored her.

The fire that had killed his parents had almost claimed him too. His grandmother, though grief-stricken over the death of her only son and daughter-in-law, had stayed by Alex's bed night and day, refusing to let him die. She'd followed the doctor's instructions to the letter, changing bloody bandages and applying salve to burnt flesh, even as he'd thrashed and cried out in pain. And for every tear he cried, she'd shed ten.

And *that* was why he wouldn't hurt her.

So he changed the subject. "I've decided to purchased a new coach."

"How exciting," his grandmother cooed. "I'm certain it will be the height of elegance."

Miss Lacey was less enthused. "Is something wrong with the old one?"

It had hit a rut, broken an axle, and flipped over, leaving one side of the cab resembling an accordion—but that was none of her concern. Still, he might have related the tale if his grandmother wasn't present. As it was, he preferred to spare her the details. He'd been in the coach when it rolled off the road—and was damned lucky to have walked away with only a bump on the head and a few bruises.

He shrugged. "Suffice it to say that the time has come to invest in a new coach."

"I see." Miss Lacey pursed her pink lips, giving him the distinct impression she was judging him. "I suppose that means you had grown tired of the old color."

Yes, she was *definitely* judging him.

"I am quite fond of the forest green," his grandmother said, frowning. "What color shall the new one be?"

"Whatever color you choose, Grandmother," he said, glad he could indulge her.

"Oh, that is a momentous decision." She clasped her hands together. "I shall have to think on it. Elizabeth, I shall solicit your opinion as well."

She sniffed. "I'm not certain I *have* an opinion on the prospective color of a coach. As long as it conveys me safely from one point to another I am perfectly content."

Alex snorted. "So, it's frivolous for us to debate the merits of possible colors of a coach?"

"Please don't put words in my mouth, your grace. However, I'm sure you agree there are weightier matters to consider."

Honestly, her hypocrisy bordered on the comical. He shot a pointed look at the cerulean blue silk hugging the curves of her body. "Would you mock your sisters for deliberating over the color of a new gown?"

"Of course not!" Miss Lacey raised her chin, indignant. "But then, my sisters are truly grateful for such opportunities. Until recently, we had very few gowns."

How had she managed to turn the conversation around and make him sound like some sort of sheltered, pampered aristocrat?

"Well," his grandmother said smoothly, "I, for one, think that the gown you're wearing tonight is perfectly lovely. Don't you agree, Alexander?" She blinked innocently, as though she were completely oblivious to the undercurrent of the previous conversation. Alex knew better.

"It is a fine gown." In truth, he noticed the gown far less than the graceful column of her neck, the smooth skin of her shoulders, and the delectable swells of her breasts. But he'd sooner tie himself to a whipping post than admit he found Miss Lacey attractive.

"You see?" his grandmother said, smiling. "It's not so difficult to find common ground." With a happy sigh, she placed her napkin on the table and scooted her chair back as though she wished to stand. Before he could rise, Miss Lacey leaped out of her seat and dashed over to help her.

"Shall we go through to the drawing room?" Miss Lacey asked.

"I'm for bed," the duchess said. "I fear the excitement of the day has worn me out."

"And it's no wonder," Miss Lacey said. "Come. I'll see you to your room."

Damn it. She was about to escape without turning in her resignation, and first thing tomorrow he had half a dozen leads to investigate. He needed this matter settled—tonight.

"Grandmother," he said, giving her an affectionate kiss on the cheek, "I wonder if you could you spare Miss Lacey for a few minutes."

"Oh?"

"I thought perhaps she could fill me in on anything I've missed while I've been out of town." Pure rubbish.

Miss Lacey made a sour face. "I don't keep up with—"

"Of course you must stay and chat with Alexander. It's far too early for young people like you to retire. I can make my own way to my bedchamber, and my maid will take over from there."

As his grandmother left the room, Miss Lacey folded her arms, making no secret of her displeasure. When they were alone, she spun on him. "You should have told her you were letting me go."

He raked a hand through his hair. "I intended to . . . but I realized she's quite fond of you."

She blew out a breath slowly. "And I am fond of her. Still, most of the time you are unfailingly blunt. Rude even. Why is it so difficult to admit you're sacking me?"

"She'll be disappointed." Crushed.

Miss Lacey threw up her hands. "Then why do you insist on making me go? Do you fear it will reflect poorly on you or your grandmother to have me hanging about? Do you have someone else in mind for the position? Or do you just want everyone else to be as miserable as you are?"

Hellfire and damnation. "Do you really want to know?"

She blinked prettily. "Yes."

"Come with me." He unceremoniously grabbed her

hand, pulled her down the corridor to his study, and steered her to a chair flanking the fireplace. "Sit."

Surprisingly, she did. While he poured them each a drink, he debated how much to reveal. Not so much as to frighten her. Just enough to make her his ally.

As he turned away from the sideboard and offered her a glass of brandy, he relaxed his shoulders and flashed his most charming grin. "May I confide in you, Miss Lacey?"

Beth accepted the drink, valiantly trying to act as though it were perfectly normal for an unmarried miss to be sitting in a bachelor's study, swirling a glass of brandy. "Of course you may confide in me. But please do not waste my time with half-truths or excuses. Tell me precisely why it is you wish for me to leave."

The duke leaned back in his chair, directly opposite her. "I need my grandmother to move out of this house— out of London entirely—and into the dower house on my country estate."

Beth tried valiantly to bite her tongue—and failed. "Your grandmother is not an old piece of furniture to be moved out of the way just because you no longer find it useful."

His eyes flashed with anger. "You go too far, Miss Lacey. My grandmother is the most important person in the world to me."

An impassioned little speech, but she wasn't about to apologize. Not when his actions belied his words. "You have an odd way of showing it, your grace."

"Let me assure you, I have her best interests at heart. The move is necessary, for her own well-being."

She sipped her brandy and shot him a skeptical look. "How so?"

"I cannot divulge the particulars. But I am hopeful that, eventually, circumstances will allow her to return."

"To her home, family, and friends, you mean?"

He glared at her, then stood and began to pace behind his chair. "I'll admit that the situation is far from ideal. I'm not happy that I have to—"

"Banish her?" Beth provided helpfully.

With a withering look, he said, "Be apart from her for a while." He threw back the rest of his drink and set the glass on a table with more force than was necessary. "I do not wish to hurt her," he said, his voice raspy with emotion.

It might have been that hitch in his throat, or it might have been the haunted look in his eyes that touched her.

And made her believe him.

She stood and faced him, toe to toe. "You must do what you think is right," she said softly. "And you must tell her yourself."

"Will you help me?" He gazed at her, his eyes pleading. "Not to tell her you're leaving, but to persuade her that the move to the dower house is necessary?"

She pinched the bridge of her nose, incredulous. "Why would I do that?"

"Because you care about her too. And she likes you. She'll listen to you."

"She might." Beth was nothing if not persuasive. "But I'm not convinced that it's what's best for her. Your grandmother loves the social whirl—soirees, dinner parties, balls, and shopping on Bond Street. There will be precious little of that in the country."

"She has friends there . . . and you could go with her."

Beth nearly choked. "A scant few hours ago, you *fired* me, your grace. Have you forgotten?"

"No. But I've determined you might be useful after all."

She leaned toward him and clenched her fists to prevent herself from throttling him with his perfectly tied neckcloth. "I must say, tales of your charm have been greatly exaggerated. If you truly wish to bend me to your will, you might at least attempt a bit of flattery."

The duke leveled a brooding look at her. "I've miscalculated then. I thought you far too levelheaded to fall prey to a few pretty words."

Oh, he was good, and she almost fell for it. Almost.

"On second thought, I don't require flattery. Respect would be preferable." Bold words, spoken by a soon-to-be-sacked companion, to a duke known for his prowess in the bedroom. But she had the upper hand—at least for the moment.

And she intended to use it.

"Respect must be earned," he said. "And I will need to know you better before I can assess your character."

"Fair enough. But I should tell you that I'm formulating an opinion of you as well—to determine if you are deserving of *my* respect."

He chuckled—a deep, surprisingly genuine sound that warmed her blood like too much wine. "I know better than to ask how I'm faring at the moment. But I hope I shall have time to make my case." Thoughtfully, he rubbed the light stubble along his jaw and sat on the arm of a chair, bringing his eyes level with hers. "I would like to return to something you said earlier," he said. "About bending you to my will. What will it take?"

Heat crept up her neck. But she would not give him the satisfaction of knowing the vexingly heady effect of his suggestive words.

His interest in her lay in her ability to convince the duchess to move to the country, nothing more.

And if she could accomplish the feat, he was willing to give her something in exchange.

Beth scrambled for an idea. Not so long ago, she and her sisters had been desperate for money. But Meg had recently married Will—a handsome, wealthy earl who not only adored her, but provided for the entire family.

Their fortunes had changed, and Beth required neither money nor favors from the duke. But there *was* something valuable he could give to someone else.

"I am willing to lend my assistance," she said, absently twirling an errant curl around her finger. "But you may find my price too steep."

The duke leaned forward and propped his elbows on his knees, so that their faces were mere inches apart. "Name it."

Chapter FIVE

Alex was far more intrigued by Miss Lacey than he should have been. He could practically see her mind racing, trying to leverage all she could out of him. And his own mind strayed to all the wildly inappropriate, yet oddly appealing possibilities. Perhaps she'd ask him to teach her to properly kiss or to take her to his bed and school her in the art of lovemaking. Or maybe she'd ask him to—

"Grant your grandmother three wishes."

What the *devil*? "I beg your pardon?"

"That is my price," she said.

"My grandmother doesn't *require* three wishes," he said, scoffing. "She has everything she could possibly want."

Miss Lacey propped a shapely hip on the arm of the chair beside him. The mysterious smile that lit her face sent a shiver down his spine. "These are very specific sorts of wishes," she said. "You must indulge your grandmother on three separate occasions of her choosing."

"In case you hadn't noticed, I'm not a leprechaun."

"Oh, I noticed," she said, sounding more like a skilled courtesan than a prim companion. "Have no fear, these wishes shall be well within your powers. All that is required of you is time . . ."

Hell, he didn't like the sound of that.

". . . spent in your grandmother's company . . ."

"What?"

". . . engaged in activities that please her."

Dear Jesus. He glanced longingly at his empty brandy glass and raked a hand through his hair. Apparently Miss Lacey wanted to teach *him* a lesson—and not the tantalizing kind he'd hoped for. She'd incorrectly assumed he wanted to avoid his grandmother's company, when all he truly wanted was to keep her safe.

Still, a few wishes were a small price to pay in exchange for Miss Lacey's help . . . and his grandmother's happiness.

"Very well. I spent time with my grandmother tonight, at dinner. Shall we count that as fulfillment of the first wish?"

She laughed. And laughed. Miss Lacey had the audacity to laugh until she was wiping tears from her pretty eyes. "You misunderstand, your grace. A greater commitment of time and effort will be required."

He crossed his arms and waited for her mirth to expend itself. "This payment of yours borders on manipulation. I don't like being told what to do."

"I can't say I'm shocked. However, that is my price," she said, blue eyes flashing, "and it's a fair one. It requires

you to prove your dedication to your grandmother before you send her away."

He clenched his jaw, biting back a curse. "I don't have
to prove anything to you, Miss Lacey."

"That is true. And *I* don't have to convince your
grandmother to relocate to the country."

Damn it, he *needed* his grandmother to move out. It
wasn't safe for her to be living with him—not when
there'd already been two possible attempts on his life.
The farther away from him she was, the better off
she'd be.

Miss Lacey had him by the metaphorical bollocks—
and she knew it. But her price wasn't terribly steep . . .
and he *did* like spoiling his grandmother. Besides, how
long could granting three simple wishes take?

"How certain are you of your ability to persuade her?"
he asked.

"I'm confident I could help her find the silver lining
in moving. I promise to do my best if you'll do yours."

"And you won't make me out to be the villain?"

She batted her eyes sweetly. "Never."

"Well then, Miss Lacey"—God help him, he must be
mad—"I believe we have a bargain."

She thrust her slender hand forward to shake on their
agreement, but he shook his head. This called for something more momentous than a handshake. "We shall seal
the deal with a toast."

He strode to the sideboard, grabbed the decanter of
brandy, refilled his glass, and topped off hers before handing it to her.

He guided her to a settee in front of the fireplace
where they both sat, the blue silk of her gown almost

touching his trousers. He thought for a moment, and then raised his glass. "To ostrich feathers, which are far more utilitarian than most people realize."

Grinning, she raised her glass as well. "To leprechauns. Who are far more real than most people realize."

He clinked his snifter against hers and met her sultry gaze as the brandy slid down his throat. Damn, but those blue eyes of hers bewitched him.

She certainly wasn't *acting* like a wallflower. And in that moment, as a saucy smile played about her pink lips, he knew without a doubt that he'd rue the day he'd foolishly labeled her and her sisters the Wilting Wallflowers. Yes, his offhand, jocular quip had saddled the Lacey sisters with the epithet they hadn't been able to shake for three seasons—and it would come back to haunt him. Maybe it already had.

Miss Lacey set her glass on the table in front of them and smoothed her skirts, as though signaling she meant to return to business. Pity, that.

"There are a couple of terms we should clarify," she announced.

Holy hell. "Such as?"

"For one, our little deal must remain a secret. I would not want your grandmother to know I had to coerce you to spend time with her. That would rather defeat the purpose."

Why must she always make him feel two inches tall? "Agreed."

"Some subtlety on your part shall be required. A bit of finesse."

He shot her a wicked look. "I've no shortage of finesse. Perhaps you've already heard."

Her cheeks pinkened, and she brushed an imaginary speck of lint off her shoulder. "What I mean to say is that you cannot be too obvious or rush your grandmother to make a decision with respect to her wishes."

He draped an arm over the back of the settee, his fingertips tantalizingly close to a curl that dangled from her nape. "I do understand, Miss Lacey. However, I must remind you that time is of the essence. I feel confident that we shall be able to accommodate one another's needs."

The blush on her cheeks deepened and spread down her neck over the delectable swells of her breasts, triggering a highly inconvenient wave of desire.

Dragging his gaze away from her neckline, he arched a brow. "Have you any other last-minute rules you wish to impose?" he asked dryly.

"Yes, as a matter of fact. It's not a rule so much as a request." She bit her lip as she glanced up at him, her expression uncharacteristically hesitant and—unless he was mistaken—vulnerable. The shrewd negotiator in him should have smelled blood, and yet, it was all he could do not to blurt, *I'll give you anything you want. Anything. Everything.*

Attempting a droll tone, he merely said, "Go on."

"I don't know if you've noticed, but your grandmother becomes distressed when we argue. I think that—for her sake—we should refrain from bickering when in her presence and strive to treat one another kindly."

It was hardly an unreasonable request, but he couldn't resist the urge to tease her. Rubbing his jaw thoughtfully, he let his gaze linger on her plump lower lip. "How kindly, exactly, should I treat you?"

She narrowed her eyes suspiciously, then shrugged. "Somewhat more kindly than you'd treat a mangy stray dog, and somewhat less kindly than you'd treat your . . ."

"My *what*, Miss Lacey?"

"Your mistress."

Good God. He leaned forward, wanting to read every nuance of her expression, every emotion written on her face. Her eyes held a flash of defiance and a spark of pride, neither of which was particularly surprising. But beneath her bravado lay a blush of something raw and wholly unexpected—longing.

Then again, maybe he'd simply had too much brandy.

"You made two assumptions just now," he said smoothly, "both of which I feel obliged to correct."

She batted her thick lashes mockingly. "By all means, please enlighten me."

"First, you implied that I wouldn't treat a stray dog with kindness. The truth is, I'd be more inclined to treat a mongrel well than I would most men of my acquaintance."

"That is good news for dogs throughout London and rather unfortunate news for your friends."

"Indeed," he conceded. "I must also correct your second assumption—that I have a mistress. I do not."

"Forgive me, your grace," she said dryly. "I did not mean to impugn your character."

Alex relaxed against the plush cushions of the settee and flashed his most charming smile. "No offense was taken, Miss Lacey. I just thought you should know."

Beth could not imagine how the conversation had devolved to talk of mistresses, but perhaps the brandy toast was partially to blame for that—and for the headiness she felt from sitting so close to the duke.

"I'm delighted that we've cleared up the matter of your nonexistent mistress," she said primly. "And I do hope that in the future we shall be able to keep civil tongues in our heads—at least while we're in the duchess's presence."

"Oh, I don't know," the duke drawled. "Surely we can do better than mere civility. I thought we were striving for kindness."

"True, but I've since realized the folly of it."

He leaned forward and propped his elbows on his knees. "No, I think we're quite capable."

Beth wasn't so sure. The duke seemed to bring out the worst in her. But perhaps if they aimed for kindness, they'd manage to achieve civility. "Very well then. Our goal shall be kindness."

"Excellent. Let us practice."

"You want to practice being kind?" she asked, incredulous.

"It may come naturally to you, but I suspect it will require rather more effort on my part." He tented his fingers beneath his chin, then mused, "How to start? Perhaps I could begin by paying you a compliment."

Her cheeks heated. "That's not necessary. Besides, you should save your kindness for when we're in the company of your grandmother. No sense in using it up now."

"But kindness is not a limited commodity, is it, Miss Lacey?"

"It isn't for most people," she muttered uncharitably.

He shot her a mildly scolding look. "Tsk, tsk. I think you could use some practice too."

She bristled and set down her glass. "Believe it or not, I'm practicing right now. I'm refraining from all manner of retorts and, instead, bidding you a good night."

As she rose from the settee, he grasped her hand, making it suddenly hard to breathe. She could have easily pulled away. It's what she should have done. But she didn't.

"Wait," he protested. "If you leave now, you won't hear my compliment."

She savored the warmth of his hand and the fluttering in her chest. "Nor will I hear further insults."

"I wouldn't insult you." He shook his head as though truly offended.

"An empty compliment would feel worse than an insult." She was amazed by her ability to keep her voice cool, even as her skin heated from his touch.

He moved closer and clasped her hand between his, looking earnestly into her eyes. "I will always be truthful with you—to the extent that I can."

"Fine." She couldn't endure much more of this closeness, dismayingly enthralling as it was. "Pay me a compliment, if you wish."

His gaze traveled over her face and lingered on her mouth before dropping to her breasts and hips. As she braced herself for something wholly inappropriate and wildly titillating, she could already feel the heat climbing up her neck.

"There are a great many things I could compliment you on, Miss Lacey, but the thing I admire most about you . . ."

She closed her eyes, not certain she could bear it if he should mention a body part south of her chin.

". . . is your devotion to my grandmother. Your loyalty to her is commendable."

She opened her eyes to see if the duke mocked her, but he seemed quite sincere. The breath she'd been holding rushed out of her. "Thank you. She is a rather amazing woman."

"And so are you."

Beth swallowed. They'd both had too much to drink. She shouldn't have allowed him to hold her hand. Blast, she shouldn't even have come to his study. He needed her services—such as they were—and as a certifiable rake, he was not above using pretty words to achieve his aim. Something she'd do well to remember.

"Tomorrow, I'll start to determine what the duchess might choose as her first wish," she said. "But for now, I think it is well past time I retired."

Almost regretfully, he released her hand and stood. "I appreciate your assistance, and I have a feeling we shall make an excellent team."

Beth wasn't so sure about that. If she was on anyone's team, it was the duchess's. But her knees were too weak to spar with him further. "Good night, your grace," she said, rising and making a beeline for the door of his study, which suddenly felt more like a dragon's lair.

"Good night, Miss Lacey. And please do me one favor, if you would."

Drat, she'd almost made her escape. She halted and looked over her shoulder at his dangerously handsome face. "What might that be?"

"Make sure you lock the windows and door of your bedchamber tonight—just as a precaution, of course."

A chill ran the length of Beth's spine. Good heavens.

What dangers lurked the halls of the duke's house—
besides him? "Don't worry," she choked out. "I will."

And if she could manage it, she might just block the
door with her dresser for good measure.

Chapter SIX

Seated at a worn wooden table outside of the Goat and Goose, the fickle sun warming his face as he nursed a pint of ale, Alex could convince himself all was right with the world.

That morning, he'd persuaded his friend, the Marquess of Darberville—Darby to Alex—to accompany him to a reputable shop on Crawford Street where he placed an order for a new coach. Mr. Dodd's conveyances were widely touted as the finest in all of London.

And yet the coach Alex had commissioned from the same man a mere three years ago was likely being used for kindling at that very moment. Little had been salvageable after his accident—only a heap of splintered wood, bent wheels, and broken axles remained. It was a miracle that he, the driver, and one of the horses had survived. Alex had to put down the other animal—a memory that would forever haunt him.

But the possibility that someone else could have been

traveling in the coach with him that day troubled him even more. Darby could have been accompanying him, or his grandmother . . . even Miss Lacey.

He'd joined his grandmother and her feisty companion for breakfast that morning and nearly scalded himself with coffee when his grandmother announced that his new vehicle should be a vivid shade of purple, a royal and therefore supremely respectable hue. She ultimately—and fortunately—had a change of heart and settled upon midnight blue. Miss Lacey may have helped him dodge that particular bullet by commenting that she thought dark blue to be both classic and perfectly masculine.

In any case, the coach was ordered, and the least he could do was buy Darby a couple of drinks.

As Alex rolled his shoulders and took a long draw on his pint, he contemplated telling his friend about the intriguing Miss Lacey—that she was his grandmother's new companion and that he'd made a devil's bargain with her. But doing so would likely spark a host of questions Alex wasn't sure he wanted to answer. It wasn't that he kept secrets from Darby—in fact, he trusted no one more.

But he didn't feel like sharing Miss Lacey just yet. Especially not with an affable, highly eligible bachelor who'd probably never suffered the humiliation of a minor blemish, much less ghastly burn scars.

As it turned out, Darby launched the conversation first—in an entirely different direction.

"Have you figured out who the hell's trying to kill you?" His friend grinned as he swiveled his torso and looked around the otherwise empty courtyard. "Or should I don my armor and raise my shield while in your company?"

Alex shrugged. "Do what you must. It's every man for himself."

His friend guffawed. "Until you require help."

Alex nodded. "Exactly." Alex stared at the thin ring of foam floating on his ale. "I've been thinking. What are the chances that my illness and the coach accident were mere coincidences?"

Darby snorted. "Not bloody likely. First, you're poisoned at the club. Then, your coach axle mysteriously breaks a few weeks later? Something sinister is afoot."

"Maybe I wasn't really poisoned. The brandy I was drinking might have turned bad, or I might have simply taken ill."

"Balderdash. A valiant attempt to explain away unpleasant facts. You're as healthy as an ox, and the symptoms came on too suddenly to blame sickness. Besides, my drink came from the same decanter as yours."

"Maybe. Maybe not."

Darby leaned forward, elbows on the table. "You were green and convulsing, for God's sake. Face it. Someone slipped something foul into *your* drink."

"I remember." He didn't, actually, but he'd take Darby's word for it. Alex had felt like death for three straight days, and the doctor had said he was lucky to have survived.

Alex thought he was rather *unlucky* to have been poisoned.

Once he'd finally managed to haul his ass out of his sickbed, he'd gone back to his club, searching for witnesses and possible clues—but turned up nothing.

"I'll admit poisoning is the most likely cause," Alex said, "but the coach accident—"

"Was no accident." Darby stared thoughtfully into his ale. "You saw Dodd today. I thought the vein in his forehead was going to burst at the mere *suggestion* that an axle on one of his coaches could have been faulty. His reputation is solid. If there was a problem with your axle, someone must have tampered with it."

Alex cursed. "My staff would never allow such a thing."

"Anyone could have sneaked into your coach house at night," Darby countered. "Or, some miscreant could have taken a hacksaw to it while you were at a house party or the opera or some bloody ball. There's no telling how long you were driving around with it on the brink of snapping."

"True. Alfred, my driver, inspected it regularly, but his eyesight's not what it used to be."

"Jesus, Alex. You have a driver with bad eyesight?"

"I recently saw him offering a bowl of fish scraps to a rat in the stables—he called it Kitty. But he's been a loyal employee for years. I can't cast him aside just because he doesn't see as well as he used to."

Darby raised his brows, disbelieving. "You might consider a different position for him—or buy him some damned spectacles."

"I offered, but that only got Alfred's feathers ruffled."

Darby swallowed the last gulp of his ale and signaled the barmaid for another. "I'm glad we took my coach today."

Alex had bigger worries than his driver's stubborn-

ness, however. Until he figured out who was trying to
kill him, he was going to be looking over his shoulder
every time he left the house. And worrying about the
safety of anyone who was with him.

"I can't understand why someone would want me
dead," he mused. "Whoever it is should just challenge
me to a duel and be done with it."

"Maybe he fears you'd put a bullet through his head."

Fair point, although Alex was more likely to aim for
a shoulder or knee. "So he's a coward."

"Unless he has a good reason to remain anonymous,"
Darby said. "Who are your enemies?"

"That's a loaded question." Alex dragged a hand
down his face. He'd rankled his fair share of the ton, for
a couple of reasons. First, he detested small talk. Standing around and exchanging pleasantries was akin to
torture. Still, his lack of social graces, in and of itself,
shouldn't incite the kind of anger that drove someone
to *murder*.

Second, his reputation as an unapologetic rake had
infuriated—even threatened—many a husband. Yes,
jealous husbands were probably the logical place to
start.

"Lord Newton doesn't like me much." An understatement, to be sure. The viscount was under the impression
that Alex had seduced his wife. Understandable, since
Lady Newton herself had whispered throughout London's
ballrooms the salacious stories of Alex's expertise at
lovemaking. She claimed she'd been powerless to resist
his charms—that no woman could.

Which wasn't quite true.

But facts mattered little to the ton. What mattered was that the tale had been circulated and that it was *believed* to be true.

"I'm surprised he hasn't called you out already." Darby smiled appreciatively at the barmaid as she thrust her impressive cleavage close to his face and set a fresh pint on the table in front of him.

"And publicly admit he's a cuckold? He's too proud for that."

Darby nodded thoughtfully. "Newton could be the one trying to kill you. Although, I can't see him getting his hands dirty. He'd hire some lowlife to do the job."

"Not exactly comforting."

"Whoever the scoundrel is, he's already proved he's not the cleverest bloke. He's botched the job twice."

"Right. You know what they say about the third time."

The smile slipped from Darby's face, and his expression turned sober. "We'll keep an eye on Newton. Who else wants you dead?"

"Haversham owes me five thousand pounds. A friendly game of vingt-et-un at his house party last month turned nasty. He played too deep one night, lost, then accused me of cheating. I reached across the table and punched him."

"You didn't."

"I did."

Darby let out a long whistle. "Must have made for an uncomfortable scene at breakfast the next morning."

"I left that night—out of respect for Lady Haversham."

Darby snapped his head up and quirked a brow. "Did you and she . . . ?"

"God no. But not for a lack of trying on Lady Haversham's part." Alex shrugged noncommittally, and Darby chuckled.

"Five thousand pounds. That's a lot of money."

Alex snorted. "The bastard has plenty in his coffers." Or at least he made a good show of pretending he did.

"So, Haversham hates you too," Darby said, adding him to a mental list. "Wait a minute." He blinked as though mentally scolding himself. "We're overlooking the most obvious question of all."

"Which is?"

"Who has the most to gain from your death? Who stands to inherit your title and wealth—which must rival Midas's by now?"

Alex shook his head. "My second cousin, Richard Coulsen. He's a stand-up fellow. Doesn't even live in London."

Darby squinted as he reached into the recesses of his memory. "Ah, yes . . . I know him. Claville's steward. Decent sportsman. I met him at the marquess's house party. But living away from London doesn't mean he isn't capable of orchestrating a murder."

"Could we avoid using the word *murder*?" Alex said, cringing. "It's putting a damper on my uncharacteristically good mood. Besides, I've never known Coulsen to be anything but honorable. In fact, he might be a little *too* decent for my liking." Every man should have a *few* vices.

"Duly noted," Darby said thoughtfully. "I'm merely pointing out that you are the only thing standing between him and a dukedom. Some might consider that motive enough to commit mur—er, to commit a crime.

If you think him such a paragon, however, we won't include him on the list. Even so, you've no shortage of detractors, have you?"

Alex smiled like he didn't care in the least what people thought of him.

But sometimes, having people constantly assume the worst about him grew tiresome. Even Darby thought him an unrepentant seducer of innocents. It wasn't his friend's fault—Alex had never bothered to correct the assumptions or quell the rumors.

Because playing the part of the villain had perks. His formidable reputation served him well, and more often than not, people left him to his own devices. No one got too close or asked too many questions. No one saw beyond the carefully cultivated image of a cold, heartless rake.

And that was precisely the way he wished it.

Chapter SEVEN

Alex strode through his front door later that evening, rifled through the mail on the table in the foyer, and froze. From down the corridor came laughter—women's laughter.

After spending the morning at the coachmaker's and whiling away the afternoon at the Goat and Goose, he could no longer neglect the contracts and ledgers on his desk. He'd planned to spend a couple of hours holed up in his study before meeting Darby for dinner at the club—where they could further investigate the poisoning.

And yet, his feet carried him to the drawing room. Only one person could be to blame for this sudden, uncharacteristic urge to socialize: Miss Lacey.

He approached the door quietly—not spying, exactly, but not announcing his presence, either. He found the companion perched on an ottoman, while a maid pinned her hair into a ridiculously tall mound atop her head.

The maid stepped back cautiously, as though she feared the tower of hair would topple any moment. "How do you like it?"

While his grandmother adjusted her spectacles and tilted her head to the side, the maid offered Miss Lacey a hand mirror. She held it in front of her face, then moved it from side to side, viewing the hairstyle from all angles.

"I think it's a vast improvement over the previous attempt," his grandmother said diplomatically. "And it would certainly make you appear taller. What do you think, dear?"

Miss Lacey reached up and tentatively patted the mass of hair. "I think it looks like I'm hiding a pineapple in here."

The maid covered her mouth with her hand but couldn't stifle a giggle. Neither could his grandmother. "Don't walk beneath a chandelier unless you wish your coiffure to catch fire," she managed between fits of laughter.

As Miss Lacey chuckled, the thick tresses coiled atop her head sprang free from their pins, and a torrent of curls tumbled around her shoulders.

Leaving Alex quite mesmerized.

Jesus. He couldn't tear his eyes away from her. He should clear his throat or say something to announce his presence, but then the laughter would stop and Miss Lacey would no doubt revert to her prim, proper, buttoned-up self. Which would be a damned shame.

"I'm sorry to have spoiled your work," she said to the maid.

"Never mind, miss," the maid said, smiling. "Gravity was bound to win out sooner or later."

The remark unleashed a fresh fit of laughter, and Miss Lacey's cheeks turned pink as she fished a pin out of her gloriously tangled curls. Alex's palms itched with the urge to spear his fingers through that silky hair and cradle her head in his hands as he—

"Alexander!" His grandmother uttered his name like a mild scolding. "Why are you skulking about the doorway? Come in, and give a proper greeting, for goodness's sake."

Bloody hell. In the blink of an eye, the spell was broken. The maid scrambled around the ottoman, scooping up hairpins and shoving them in the pocket of her apron. Miss Lacey wound her hair into a tight coil and held it at her nape, blushing as though she'd been caught not just with her hair down, but disrobing. An image that was damned arousing.

He schooled his face in a bored look and ambled toward the ladies. "Forgive me for intruding," he said drolly. "I did not expect to return home and find my drawing room converted into a ladies' dressing room."

Miss Lacey nearly fell off the ottoman but caught herself.

The maid gasped and muttered apologies as she fled the room.

"Why do you sound so stern, Alexander?" his grandmother asked with a shrug. "I'm certain Elizabeth is not the first woman you've seen in a state of dishabille."

Miss Lacey coughed, as though she wished to remind everyone she was still present and capable of speaking for herself. "I feel obliged to point out," she said through gritted teeth, "that I am fully and quite decently dressed. I regret that my pins did not hold and that the sight of my unbound hair distressed you, your grace. It will not happen again."

A pity, that. He wouldn't mind if her hair were loose all the time. He could imagine those lustrous curls swaying as she walked, glistening in the sun . . . even fanned across his pillow. "I am relieved to hear it. Now, if you'll excuse me—"

"Before you go," Miss Lacey interrupted, "there is a small matter your grandmother wishes to discuss with you."

His grandmother waved a dismissive hand. "It can wait till later—when Alexander's mood has improved."

"I hope you're prepared for a long wait," Miss Lacey muttered.

His grandmother squinted behind her spectacles. "What was that, dear?"

"I think *now* would be a most opportune time." Miss Lacey shot him a pointed look.

Taking the hint, he shrugged and lowered himself into a chair. "I am at your disposal, Grandmother. What do you wish to discuss?"

"Elizabeth inquired as to whether I'd ever seen the fireworks at Vauxhall, and I realized that I have not. It's been an age since I visited the Gardens," she said with a wistful sigh.

He hazarded a glance at Miss Lacey, who had apparently located a stray hairpin and was attempting to spear it through the thick coil behind her head. Her gaze locked with his as she gave a subtle nod.

So, this was to be his grandmother's first wish: to see fireworks. Harmless enough and easily accomplished. At this rate, he'd have his grandmother and her beautiful, meddling companion out of his house by week's end.

"We must remedy the situation at once," he said magnanimously. "If you have no plans for tomorrow night, I would be happy to accompany you to the Gardens."

"That would be delightful!" The sheer, unadulterated joy on his grandmother's face made him feel almost . . . guilty. It had been a long time since he'd made her smile like that.

"As long as you're going," Miss Lacey added, "it might be nice to dine there, too."

"Oh, you'll be there as well, Elizabeth," his grandmother said. "I wouldn't dream of going without you. In fact, since we're hiring a supper box, we should make a small party of it."

Damn, but this was quickly turning into an elaborate production. "The smaller the party, the better," he announced, ignoring the withering look Miss Lacey sent his way.

"It shan't be too large, Alexander. Six or eight at the most. Elizabeth, you must invite your uncle and sister Juliette."

Miss Lacey frowned as though the suggestion did not sit well. "Why, that's very generous of you. Are you certain that—"

"I am," his grandmother insisted. "I've been meaning to thank your uncle for sending you to me—my own veritable angel."

Miss Lacey blushed, clearly ill at ease with the label

of angel—as well she should be. She'd all but black-mailed him into doing her bidding.

"Your sister will prevent the outing from becoming too dull," his grandmother said. "A party is always improved by the company of lively younger people. Not that you and Alexander are ever boring," she quickly added. "Far from it."

Alex chuckled. "No offense taken, Grandmother."

"Excellent. And while we're discussing the guest list . . ."

Alex scratched his head, wondering how in the hell a jaunt to Vauxhall had evolved into an event requiring a guest list.

". . . you must invite your friend, Lord Darberville." Alex's grandmother clapped her hands together, inordinately pleased at the prospect.

Alex knew his friend well, and Darby would sooner run the gauntlet than endure a dinner party where the average age of the guests neared sixty. That settled it. "I'm sure Darby would be thrilled to attend. I'll extend the invitation."

If Alex was to be miserable, he saw no reason Darby shouldn't suffer alongside him.

"While we're at the Gardens, your grandmother mentioned she'd like to hear the orchestra play in the rotunda."

Alex stuck a finger inside his cravat in an attempt to loosen it. "Fine."

"It's a two-part concert," Miss Lacey said sweetly.

"It sounds enchanting." Alex glared at the companion so she would know just how thin his patience had been stretched.

"My dear, dear boy," his grandmother cooed, "I would never ask you to spend the entire evening in the company of a feeble old lady like me. A night of fireworks and dinner will be an unexpected treat—and more than enough to make me happy."

Good God, he truly was a heel. "First of all, you are not feeble. You wear out the soles of your slippers at every ball you attend *and* climb stairs with the agility of a school girl. Second, no visit to Vauxhall would be complete without hearing the orchestra play." He smiled at Miss Lacey before returning his attention to his grandmother. "Both parts."

Unable to contain her glee, his grandmother leaped from her chair and hugged him, her powdered face soft against his own. "I know you disapprove of displays of affection," she murmured, "but I simply cannot restrain myself. Thank you, for it shall surely be an evening to remember."

"I couldn't agree more." Alex glanced over his grandmother's thin shoulder at Miss Lacey, who essentially held court from her velvet ottoman, smiling as though inordinately pleased with the scene—which she'd directed from beginning to end.

Worse, he suspected she was only getting started.

Chapter EIGHT

"We should have come by coach to Kennington Lane," the duke grumbled in Beth's ear.

"That does seem rather obvious *now*," she retorted.

Blast. How could she have known that a squall would pop up and the heavens would suddenly unleash a torrent of rain? If she *had* known, she never would have insisted that passing through the water entrance to the pleasure garden was part of the experience that the duke's grandmother should not be denied.

Unfortunately, the boat he'd hired to transport their small party across the Thames to Vauxhall Gardens rocked like it was making a transatlantic voyage. Chilly raindrops pelted them, and while the duchess sat beneath a velvet canopy, Beth attempted to shield her from the blowing rain with her parasol—which promptly lost its battle with the wind and flipped inside out.

"Good heavens!" the duchess cried. Beth struggled

valiantly with the wretched parasol and barely refrained from cursing.

The duke's friend, Lord Darberville, held the side of the boat in a white-knuckled grip and moaned each time the boat crested a wave and dipped.

Beth's sister Julie, on the other hand, embraced the wicked weather. Raising her face to the sky and closing her eyes, she laughed. "What a grand adventure this night is turning out to be."

"The excitement is only beginning," the duke announced dryly. "If another whitecap broadsides our boat, we'll all be going for a swim."

Lord Darberville clutched his stomach and groaned.

The duke stepped in front of his grandmother's seat, protecting her from the worst of the wind. Then, facing Beth and pointing to her parasol, he barked, "Give it to me."

Reluctantly, she handed it to him and watched as he efficiently wrestled it into its former shape—if one discounted a few broken spokes beneath the torn silk. Heaving a sigh, she closed it as best she could and resigned herself to a thorough soaking.

"Here." The duke shrugged off his jacket and draped it over Beth's shoulders. Warmth enveloped her, and a clean, slightly spicy scent filled her senses.

Gathering her wits, she shook her head. "I can't wear your jacket."

"I beg to differ," he said curtly. "You're wearing it now."

True. The duke's torso, meanwhile, was clad in only a waistcoat and his shirtsleeves. Both garments grew wetter by the second.

"That's not what I meant, as you're well aware." And yet, Beth didn't remove the duke's jacket. She should shrug it off and thrust it back at him. Nay, she *would*. Just as soon as the chill left her bones or the rain subsided a little.

"So, you'd rather be drenched and risk catching your death's cold than be seen wearing a gentleman's jacket?"

Well, it *did* seem rather ridiculous when he put it that way. But the issue wasn't her pride so much as it was pure self-preservation.

He had to know it wasn't proper for a young miss— or even a young*ish* one, as the case may be—to wear any gentleman's jacket. But to wear the Duke of Blackshire's jacket was far, far worse. Entirely beyond the pale. She might as well place an ad in the *Lady's Magazine* announcing to all of London that she was the duke's latest conquest. Beth could practically feel the lorgnettes of nearby boat passengers trained on her, burning a hole in her back.

"It was a kind gesture," she said, aware that both his grandmother and her sister looked on, keenly interested in the exchange. "But I'm afraid that it might be interpreted by some as . . ."

Water dripped from a curl on his forehead, and he slicked it back with one hand. "As *what*, Miss Lacey?"

Swallowing, she slipped off his jacket and held it out to him. He didn't take it. "Some might erroneously think that we are . . . that is, they might assume, quite falsely, mind you, that you and I . . ."

Good Lord, her face was burning up in spite of the rain.

He raised a dark brow, challenging her to complete her sentence.

Beth forged ahead. "Some people might reach the wholly incorrect conclusion that you and I are involved. With each other." There. Not her most graceful speech, but she'd made her point.

A shadow darkened the duke's face, making her heartbeat trip in her chest. She had the distinct impression she'd wounded him.

"How absurd," he snapped. "Heaven forbid anyone would think such a thing."

"My thoughts exactly," Beth agreed.

The duchess clucked her tongue—at whom, Beth couldn't be sure.

But she did sense that she'd done something wrong.

Before she could determine her error, the duke accepted his jacket and stuffed his arms into it. A charming grin erased the pained look, making her wonder if she'd imagined it. "We're almost to the dock," he said. "Miss Juliette, I hope our safe passage isn't too great a disappointment."

"It's a shame the boat didn't capsize," Julie quipped, instantly lightening the mood.

Beth stared at the toes of her soggy slippers, wishing she could be more like her younger sister—cheerful, witty, and fun-loving. The type of person who could walk into a room and make it seem warm and sunny.

By contrast, Beth was a gray fog. Chilly. Difficult for others to read. Sometimes even off-putting. Maybe her hard, thick shell had developed after she and her sisters had been on the receiving end of one too many barbs and had been the butt of one too many jokes. All she knew for certain was that the minute she let down her guard, someone would betray her. They always did.

"We've made landfall, Darby," the duke said. "Pry your fingers off the side of the boat and disembark so we can enjoy a quart or two of burnt wine."

Lord Darberville grimaced at the mention of wine but clambered onto the dock, while the duke helped his grandmother to her feet. Together, the men assisted each of the women off the boat.

"I'm glad Uncle Alistair decided to take the coach and meet us here," Julie said. "I don't think he would have fared well in the choppy waters."

"Pshaw." The duchess removed her spectacles and dried them with the corner of her shawl. "I've seen bigger waves in my bathtub."

Everyone laughed, the rain subsided, and the merry sound of minstrels' music floated on the waning breeze. Perhaps the evening could be salvaged after all. For the duchess's sake, Beth hoped so.

The duke offered his arm to his grandmother, and their party strolled away from the dock toward the garden entrance. "What would you like to do first?" Oddly, he directed the question not to his grandmother, but to Beth.

"We're to meet my uncle in the rotunda for the concert at eight o'clock."

"Very well, my grandmother and I shall lead the way." He paid their entrance fees and ambled down a pebbled lane, pausing patiently at an artificial ruin that his grandmother admired. It pleased Beth to see him doting on her. Perhaps the memories of this night would bring the duchess joy after she'd been banished from her grandson's house.

Beth, Julie, and Lord Darberville followed them, enjoying the sights and sounds of revelers. Beth was eager to experience Vauxhall. She'd never been but had read her share of gossip papers and knew that the pleasure gardens had earned the name in more ways than one. She'd already resolved to avoid the famously potent arrack punch. Still, the fragrant orchard, glowing lanterns, and winding walkways quickly charmed her.

As they approached the rotunda, the crowd grew denser. The duke turned and called over his shoulder to his friend, the marquess. "Stay close to the ladies, Darby. Don't let them out of your sight."

Beth tossed her damp curls. "We are not children who need minding, your grace."

The men exchanged an odd look. "I would prefer that we not become separated in the crowd," the duke said sternly.

She bristled a little, but even if she had a sufficiently clever retort—which she didn't—bickering with him would only spoil the duchess's special evening. "Don't worry," she said, "I have no plans to abandon our group."

Before long, they were inside the rotunda, breathtaking in its size and magnificence. Beth tilted her head back and stared at the elaborately painted domed ceiling.

"It's lovely," Julie sighed.

"Let's secure a spot near the stage," Lord Darberville suggested, and he immediately began weaving his way toward the center of the room, with Julie in tow.

"Keep an eye out for Uncle Alistair," Beth said to her

sister over the din. Spotting him in the throng would be difficult, but Julie's height gave her an advantage.

For her part, Beth searched the sea of fancy hats and tousled curls for two tufts of wild white hair. Though highly intelligent, her uncle was easily distracted, and she could imagine him wandering aimlessly, his senses overwhelmed by the venue and scores of people. He could be disoriented and confused right now.

She craned her neck around the room as they migrated toward the stage, and through an open door behind her, she saw a head of white hair that wafted in the breeze.

"Julie," she called out. "I think I see him."

Julie cupped a hand to her ear. "What did you say?"

"I'm going to retrieve Uncle Alistair. I'll return shortly and find you near the stage."

Before her sister could protest, Beth spun around and headed for the door, walking as fast as good manners would allow—which was not nearly fast enough for her liking.

The gentleman shuffling down the path must have been her uncle, and it would only take her a minute to find him and reunite with the group.

Or so she thought.

It seemed everyone was entering the rotunda at once and walking in the opposite direction as she. When she finally made it through the door, she scanned the hedge-bordered walkway for any sign of her elderly uncle. An assortment of couples strolled by, as did a half dozen young men who staggered across her path as though they were foxed.

"Uncle Alistair!" she called, not caring if she looked foolish to passersby. "Are you out here?"

A young man approached, cravat askew, while his friends snickered behind him. "You look like you need an escort," he said suggestively.

"You're mistaken." She brushed past him, irritated that in the past quarter hour no less than two men had assumed she was incapable of going anywhere without a male to guide her.

The drunken group jeered. "She's clearly smitten, Roscoe. Don't let her escape."

Beth's heart beat frantically, but she ignored the men as she continued down the gravel path. They were just drunken boys, she told herself. A nuisance, but hardly dangerous. If she refused to take their bait, they'd look for trouble elsewhere.

Still, the more distance she put between her and them, the better, so she walked faster and, before long, noticed a stream of people heading toward a misty grove. Thinking Uncle Alistair might have been swept up in the flow, she followed the crowd. Beneath a canopy of leaves, a large circle of onlookers had gathered around five minstrels wearing feathered hats and playing pipes and percussion instruments.

Beth walked around the spectators, searching for her uncle's favorite hat and his perpetually wrinkled dark green jacket. She'd almost given up hope of finding him when she spotted him on the perimeter, clapping merrily to the beat of the drum.

"Uncle Alistair," she said, mildly scolding. "We've been searching for you!"

He blinked as though dazed, but then the corners of his eyes crinkled warmly. "Elizabeth! I've been looking for you too. Or, I was, before I stopped briefly to watch these immensely talented performers. See, they're each playing two instruments." His lined face lit with child-like wonder, making it impossible for Beth to be cross with him.

"It's quite a show," she said, raising her voice to be heard over the clang of cymbals. "But the rest of our party is expecting us. We must go to them at once."

He looked crestfallen but dutifully shuffled away from the minstrels. "It would never do to keep the duch-ess waiting."

Beth neglected to tell him that he'd already kept the duchess waiting and that Julie was probably half out of her mind with worry. She curled a hand around his arm and slowly guided him back to the walkway leading to the rotunda.

They were halfway there when the drunken mob she'd encountered earlier blocked their path. The rogue who'd spoken before stepped to the front, swaying on his feet. "Don't tell me *this* is your beau," he slurred, gesturing at her uncle.

The hairs on the back of her neck stood on end, and she gripped Uncle Alistair's arm a bit tighter.

"What is that young gentleman talking about?" he murmured in her ear, clearly confused.

"He's not a gentleman," she whispered back. "Don't mind him."

Then, with far more bravado than she felt, she ad-dressed the unruly group. "Step aside and allow us to pass."

"Wait a minute," one of the men sputtered. "I recognize that bloke. He's Lord Wiltmore, which means *she*"—he pointed rudely at Beth—"must be one of the Wilting Wallflowers."

"I beg your pardon." Incensed, Uncle Alistair wriggled his arm free from Beth's grasp and took a menacing if wobbly step toward the men, who were easily four decades younger than he. "How *dare* you ridicule my niece—the epitome of loveliness and grace?"

Blast. Beth wanted to melt into the ground. Her dear uncle meant well but was only making matters worse. She tugged on his sleeve. "You are very sweet to defend me," she said, "but you mustn't listen to their taunts. Let us go back the opposite way, so we can meet our group."

"I will not leave this spot," he said, "until these men have issued you an apology. I shall not tolerate their defamation and salamander."

Oh dear. The sodden fools stared mutely for a second, then burst into laughter. The one who'd insulted her shoved Uncle Alistair's shoulder. "You're as mad as they say, old man."

She shook with rage momentarily, then something inside her snapped. "You daft . . . ill-mannered . . . drunken brute!" She swung her broken parasol and hit his arm—but he didn't flinch.

Cursing, he wrested the handle from her grasp and tossed what was left of her parasol over his shoulder.

"You little *shrew*," he spat. "I should teach you a lesson." He yanked her by the wrist and pulled her so close that she smelled the alcohol on his breath.

Uncle Alistair tried to step in, but one of the scoundrels pushed him to the ground.

Beth looked around, desperate for help. Passersby walked faster, most avoiding the scene altogether. She tried to twist her wrist free from her captor's clammy grasp, but he only squeezed harder.

"Uncle Alistair," she said firmly, "you must get up, if you can, and go to the rotunda. Find Julie and the others and tell them where I am." She couldn't see any other way out of their predicament.

"I won't leave you, my dear," he said gallantly—even if he was still sprawled on the ground. "In fact, I insist that this gentleman release you at once."

"You're in no position to insist anything, you crazy old codger."

"Very well." Uncle Alistair pushed himself to his feet, wheezing from his exertions. Then he stood toe to toe with the beast who held her wrist. "You *will* let her go," he said bravely, "or I shall demand satisfaction."

Dear heavens, this couldn't be happening. Beth's throat constricted and her eyes burned.

The villain snorted. "You're challenging me to a duel, grandpa?" he asked, incredulous.

"No, he's not. *I* am." The reply, low and lethal, came from a man behind Beth. She craned her neck and caught a glimpse of him. With his impossibly broad shoulders, clenched fists, and flared nostrils, he might have been the Devil himself.

Beth rather wished he *was*.

But their rescuer was none other than her vexingly handsome nemesis—the Duke of Blackshire.

Chapter NINE

Alex recognized the cretin holding Miss Lacey—Roscoe, if he wasn't mistaken. He was one of the young bucks who frequented his favorite gaming hell. And the sight of his grimy hand on her slender wrist made him want to punch something—or someone. Hard.

"I believe there's been a misunderstanding," Roscoe stammered, releasing her at last.

Miss Lacey stifled a sob and flew to her uncle's side. "Were you hurt?" she asked, brushing grass and mud off his jacket.

"No, my dear. I am fine. But I am deeply troubled that, because of me, you were placed in such a precarious premonition."

When a couple of the drunks snickered, Alex stepped forward and cracked his knuckles.

The snickering stopped.

"Miss Lacey," Alex said while glaring at Roscoe, "you and your uncle will go to the rotunda at once. I shall join you shortly, but first, Roscoe and I have some business to conclude." There was no need for her to witness the aforementioned business. It wasn't going to be pretty.

"Are you certain?" She asked, as though she were concerned for his welfare, which was nice, but also slightly insulting—as if he weren't capable of handling a half-dozen drunken whelps on his own.

"I am quite certain," he replied, and yet she made no move to leave. Was it too much to ask that she cooperate with him—just this once?

"Your grace," the coward groveled, "we did not realize that Wiltmore and his niece were friends of yours. Besides, we were only jesting. Having a bit of fun."

"Name your weapon," Alex told Roscoe.

The color drained from the younger man's face. "I have no quarrel with you, Blackshire."

"Oh, but I have one with you. It began the moment you laid your hand on Miss Lacey," Alex said, clenching his fists. Why in the hell was she still standing there beside her uncle, looking on anxiously, instead of returning to the rotunda as he'd asked?

"She suffered no harm," Roscoe stammered, "and I've no wish to meet you at dawn."

Alex stepped forward until his chest nearly bumped his opponent's. "So then, you'd prefer to settle it now?"

"Your grace," Miss Lacey interjected. "I fear that if we don't leave immediately, we'll be late for the concert."

"Punctuality is overrated." Alex grabbed two fistfuls of Roscoe's jacket, hoisted him off the ground, and shook him until his eyes were practically popping out of his head. "Apologize to the lady," he ordered. "And I *might* not kill you."

"Forgive me." The bastard gasped as though fighting for air.

The muscles in Alex's forearms shook under the strain of Roscoe's weight. "You'll have to do better," he ground out.

Roscoe's hands and feet flailed as his eyes pleaded with Alex. "Miss Lacey, you have my deepest apologies." He gurgled as though his cravat was choking him, then continued. "My behavior earlier was inexcusable, and if you would be so generous as to forgive me"—he coughed and hacked some more before finishing—"I would be forever in your debt."

"I accept your apology," Miss Lacey blurted anxiously. "Please, your grace, put him down at once."

Alex shrugged. "As you wish." With that, he tossed the bounder directly at his friends and watched them topple like bowling pins.

It didn't feel nearly as good as it would have to plow his fist into Roscoe's chin or bloody his nose, but he didn't want Miss Lacey to suffer nightmares of the violence.

Even if it *would* serve her right for refusing to follow his orders.

Roscoe laid on the ground, moaning, as his friends slowly righted themselves, scratching their heads in a drunken daze.

Alex stepped over a sprawled leg and grabbed his grandmother's companion by the hand. "Wiltmore," he called over his shoulder, "follow us closely, and make sure no one else bothers Miss Lacey."

The old man stood a little straighter and raised his chin like he was reporting to Wellington for duty. "You may count on me."

"I'm glad to hear it." If Wiltmore thought he was protecting his niece, perhaps he'd manage not to get himself lost again.

And at the moment, all Alex could think about was Miss Lacey. Upon discovering that she'd left the rotunda, he'd felt a surge of panic—closely followed by a wave of anger. But when he saw the rowdy band of men taunting her and Roscoe touching her . . . he'd felt pure, hot rage.

As he pulled her along in his wake, he willed his pulse to slow. She was safe now—at least for the moment. The problem was that *no one* was truly safe with him. He was a target, and that meant everyone around him was in constant danger too.

He'd told himself that Vauxhall would be safe enough. Whoever was trying to kill him, wouldn't dare do so in such a public place, and Darby would help him protect the women and keep an eye out for suspicious behavior.

Besides, Miss Lacey's unfortunate encounter had nothing to do with him. She shouldn't have ventured out of the rotunda on her own, and Alex intended to make his displeasure with her known—at the appropriate time. For now, he simply savored the feel of her hand in his— soft, warm, and feminine. He didn't give a damn if it was improper for him to hold her hand in public.

He wasn't letting go.

She halted beside a fountain with shell-shaped basins, pulling him to a stop.

"I thought you wished to hear the concert," he said impatiently.

"I do. But I fear my uncle is having some difficulty keeping pace with us. I thought we might wait for him."

Alex craned his head around, and sure enough, Wiltmore shuffled along several yards behind them, never taking his gaze off his beloved niece.

"At this rate, we'll be here till Christmastide," Alex muttered.

She frowned and opened her mouth as if to issue a retort, then clamped her lips shut. He found himself vaguely disappointed.

"Was there something you wished to say, Miss Lacey?"

"Yes, actually." She closed her eyes briefly as though summoning courage. "In regard to the incident with those men, I feel I must explain—"

"Not now," he said curtly.

"But I only wanted to say—"

"Not. Now." He was still too tightly wound to discuss what had happened. He had no wish to lose his temper with her—especially when it seemed that half of London was enjoying the pleasure gardens this evening. They'd succeeded in creating quite the spectacle already, and he'd consider it a small miracle if a full accounting of his fight with Roscoe and his friends didn't appear in tomorrow morning's gossip rags.

"Very well," she sighed.

Though he'd spoken sharply, she seemed wholly unperturbed. Almost bored.

As he stood there, waiting for Wiltmore and holding

Miss Lacey's hand, it occurred to him that she was one of a select few people who wasn't intimidated by him. The combination of his notorious reputation and surly manners scared off most proper young misses—and rightfully so—but not her. It was as though she could see past the brooding, rakish duke to the person who lay beneath.

But she couldn't—thank God. No one *truly* knew him or what he'd done, except perhaps his grandmother. And Alex intended to keep it that way.

Throughout dinner later that evening, Beth fretted about the earlier scene with Mr. Roscoe and his drunken friends. Of course, the altercation never would have occurred if she'd remained with her party in the rotunda, but the duke hadn't allowed her to apologize earlier, and now she felt like a naughty child who must wait for her father to mete out her deserved punishment. Blast.

Fortunately, the duchess, Julie, and Lord Darberville were blissfully unaware of the incident. The duke apologized for their temporary absence and merely said they'd been delayed watching the minstrels perform. Even Uncle Alistair seemed to have forgotten that he'd impulsively challenged a man forty decades his junior to a duel.

Now, comfortably ensconced in an elegant supper box, they all exclaimed over the wafer-thin ham slices, freshly mixed salads, and the savory dishes the waiters presented. Lord Darberville entertained the group with slightly off-color tales from a house party he'd recently attended, and Julie recounted the events of the one and only ball they'd ever hosted—which had led to their sister's hopelessly romantic engagement. The duchess sat in a padded chair with a shawl tucked around her, interjecting her characteristically shrewd observations and beaming with happiness.

Only Beth and the duke remained relatively silent—but perhaps for different reasons. She was contemplating what might have happened if the duke hadn't stepped in. Uncle Alistair could have been forced to defend her honor and forfeited life or limb on the dueling field. She could have been mauled by an inebriated reprobate.

"I believe it's almost time for the fireworks." Julie's cheeks glowed with excitement. "I can't wait to see them, but I wish they didn't signal the end of the evening's festivities."

"The night is still young," Uncle Alistair said. "Let us take our wine and repair to the lawn, where we'll have a clear view of the show, which is spectacular by all amounts."

"A fine plan," the duchess said, graciously ignoring Uncle Alistair's flub and taking the arm he offered. "And we are fortunate—it seems the heavens have cleared just for us."

The older pair led the way to the lawn, and Lord Darberville and Julie followed suit, which left Beth and the duke bringing up the rear of their little procession.

He offered his arm and leveled a look at her that said *don't even think about refusing*. Shrugging, she tucked her hand in the warm, hard crook of his elbow and resolved to enjoy the fireworks.

The duke directed the group to the edge of a clearing, near a row of tall hedges, and they looked up in time to see the first rockets streak through the black-velvet sky and explode in a burst of red.

Julie laughed and covered her ears with her hands.

The crowd cheered, delighted that the show was finally underway, then quieted and settled in to enjoy it.

Beth released the duke's arm and clasped her hands behind her back. His sideways glance said he didn't trust her to remain in one spot for more than two seconds—and after the night's earlier scuffle, she supposed she couldn't blame him.

They gazed at the sky in companionable silence, but Beth was very, very aware of the duke, standing beside her, his muscled arm only inches from her shoulder. When the duchess applauded, delighting in a brilliant white rocket, the duke caught Beth's eye and shot her a knee-melting grin. Dangerous, that. But he was genuinely happy to see his grandmother happy.

And that made Beth happy.

As the show continued, however, the duke seemed to grow agitated. The direction of the breeze had shifted, and a cloud of gray smoke floated above the crowd. He rocked his weight from one foot to the other and raked a hand through his thick hair, grabbing a fistful.

Beth stepped closer to him and whispered in his ear. "Is something wrong?"

"No," he whispered back, but a sheen of perspiration covered his forehead. Frowning, he admitted, "I dislike the smell of smoke."

Ah, yes. She'd forgotten about his burns. According to the rumors, he'd almost died in the fire that had claimed the lives of his parents. It was no wonder he found the acrid smell of the smoke and the crack of the fireworks unsettling.

"If you'd like to skip the second half of the show, you could leave and meet us at the coach afterward."

"If I didn't know better, Miss Lacey, I'd think you were trying to rid yourself of me."

"No," she said honestly. "I just want to help."

"You are helping." He wiped a sleeve across his brow. "Keep talking to me."

"Very well. I shall say what I attempted to say earlier—that I appreciate you defending me and my uncle earlier tonight. And that I'm in your debt."

"It was nothing," he said shrugging. "I would have done the same for any young woman cornered by a band of dissolute drunks."

His words, surely meant to downplay his chivalry, wounded her a little. Not that she imagined she was anyone special to him. But he had seemed more than a little incensed on her behalf. Perhaps she'd read too much into his actions.

Some of the color had returned to his face, so Beth kept talking. "It may have seemed like nothing to you," she said softly. "But it was *not* nothing to me."

"It's a good thing you're a companion and not a governess. Your grammar is horrid," he teased.

"I've never claimed otherwise," she countered. "My talents lie elsewhere."

He arched a wicked brow at her. "I'd be very interested in hearing more about your talents, Miss Lacey."

Ignoring his obvious innuendo and the fluttering in her chest, she rolled her eyes. "If you must know, I'm rather good at gardening and sewing." There. He couldn't *possibly* make those activities seem improper. Although if anyone could . . .

"I feel certain that your talents extend to other areas as well. However, I think we can safely conclude that you lack skill at parasol combat."

Beth blinked. "Parasol combat?"

"Roscoe barely felt your blow to his arm. Actually, it was more like a tap."

"My weapon had been compromised." She waved her battered parasol as evidence.

"It could have served you well—if you'd used it properly."

Beth refrained from rolling her eyes. He certainly seemed to be feeling more like himself, in spite of the ongoing firework show and the haze of smoke surrounding them.

"And I suppose you're an expert on parasol combat?" she challenged.

He shrugged. "The parasol is certainly not my weapon of choice, but sometimes we must make do with whatever's on hand." He took the sorry contraption from her hand and demonstrated. "Instead of swinging it like a cricket bat, you should have gripped it with both hands and jabbed it like a fire poker."

"Jabbed?" she repeated, skeptical.

"Precisely," he said. "And you should have used the point to hit Roscoe where he's most vulnerable—in the eyes, neck, or . . ."

Beth snatched the parasol out of his hands. "No need to elaborate." Though they spoke softly, anyone nearby could have heard them between the explosions overhead.

She moved a bit closer. "You would have liked me to maim him—right in the middle of Vauxhall Gardens?"

"It would have been no more than he deserved." More seriously, he added, "Sometimes you only have one opportunity to defend yourself. If you do, you should not waste it for fear of making a scene. Your only thought should be of protecting yourself."

"I shall keep your advice in mind," she said, touched by his concern. "But I am unlikely to ever find myself in that position again."

"One never knows," the duke replied soberly. "It's good to be prepared, in any event."

Beth smiled to herself. She never would have believed that the formidable Duke of Blackshire would deign to teach his grandmother's companion the finer points of self-defense—and demonstrate with a lace-trimmed parasol.

In front of her, Uncle Alistair pointed to direct the duchess's attention to a tightrope walker in the distance, illuminated by the glow of the fireworks. The duchess watched, captivated, and soon everyone in the crowd watched as well. The acrobat moved slowly along a rope suspended between two poles that looked like ships' masts.

Beth relaxed. The duchess seemed to be enjoying herself immensely. The earlier rainstorm hadn't spoiled her special evening, and neither had the incident with Roscoe—which, thankfully, she knew nothing about. In another half hour, the show would be over, and they'd return home, and the duke would be able to cross off one wish.

Which meant the duchess—and Beth—had only two

wishes before their time in London was over. Not that Beth wanted to prolong it, but she did want to be sure that the duchess thoroughly enjoyed her last couple of weeks in town—with her grandson.

Through the mist, Beth held her breath as she watched the tightrope walker inch across the wire. Everyone was transfixed on her silhouette as she seemed to walk between the stars.

But suddenly a flare fired sideways and streaked toward the crowd. Toward *them*.

Beth felt the heat as a missile whizzed by and landed in the tall hedges behind them.

"Look out!" the duke shouted, rushing Beth and the rest of their party away, just as the rocket exploded.

Chapter TEN

Alex hauled his grandmother and Miss Lacey away from the blast as fast as he could. Darby dragged Wiltmore and his other niece behind them. When everyone in the group emerged from the cloud of smoke, Alex checked each of them to make sure no sparks from the explosion had landed on their clothes.

Damn, but he hated fires.

His heart pounded out of his chest, his nostrils burned, and the boom still echoed in his ears. It was just like his nightmares—where he was a boy, unable to breathe, clinging to his father while flames licked his neck and singed his flesh.

"What on earth happened?" his grandmother asked meekly.

"One of the rockets must have misfired," he said. "Is everyone all right?"

The ladies and Wiltmore answered in the affirmative. Darby nodded. "None the worse for wear."

"You have some embers on the back of your jacket, your grace," Miss Lacey said, frowning.

She pressed her closed parasol firmly against one of his shoulder blades and a spot on his side.

"There," she said, brushing ash off his sleeve. "The sparks are out, but I fear your jacket may be ruined."

He didn't give a damn about his jacket. "Was anyone hurt?"

"I don't think so," Darby said. "The hedges took the worst of it, and they were still damp from the storm. If they'd been dry, the whole garden might have turned into a tinderbox. We're fortunate."

Alex arched a brow. It didn't *feel* like luck was on his side tonight.

And yet, above them the fireworks display continued. The acrobat walked on her tightrope.

Meanwhile, he still tried to tamp down the panic that had flooded his veins.

Miss Lacey placed a hand on his arm and spoke softly in his ear. "Shall I tell the duchess it's time to leave? I'm sure she wouldn't mind missing the end of the show, and we've certainly had our share of excitement for one night."

Alex wanted nothing more than to get the hell out of that place, away from the whizzing rockets and deafening explosions and suffocating smoke. But the sight of Miss Lacey's pink cheeks and sparkling eyes had him shaking his head. She was obviously dazzled by the tightrope walker and the fireworks display, and if he was honest with himself . . . he was a little dazzled by her.

"No. It will be over soon. Enjoy the show. We'll leave immediately after." And within the hour, he'd be in his study with a glass of brandy—or three—in a futile attempt to ward off the terrifying dreams that would plague him tonight.

Miss Lacey shot him an assessing glance, and her pretty eyes narrowed with concern. As though she *knew*.

He pretended to turn his attention to the tightrope walker, but in actuality, he was doing two things: periodically checking the hedges in case a few remaining sparks caused them to burst into flames and planning an escape route for his party in case another rogue rocket should suddenly hurtle their way.

Miss Lacey stood close—as though she wished to keep an eye on him. Completely unnecessary, of course. But nice. Her mere presence caused his demons to retreat—for a while, at least.

He reached for the folded parasol she held and inspected it, frowning at the broken spokes and burnt silk. "I don't know why you haven't disposed of this by now—it's beyond ruined. Order a new one and bill it to me."

"I intend to keep this one. I rather like the black spots and its jaunty angle when it's opened." She took it back, pointed the tip at his side, and arched a brow. "And it still could be of use—as a weapon, of course."

"Touché." He closed his fist around the top of the parasol while she held the handle, initiating a mock tug-of-war. And when their gazes locked, the air between them crackled.

For the space of several heartbeats, neither of them moved. Then they heard a woman behind them whisper loudly—as though she'd had too much wine. "Seems the Duke of Blackshire has a new paramour."

"I'm not certain whether we should offer her our congratulations or condolences. He can't be content with one miss for long," her companion replied.

On the opposite end of the parasol from him, Miss Lacey's smile faded a tad.

"Who *is* she?" asked the first woman.

"I'm not certain, but I believe I saw Lord Wiltmore with their party, which means she must be . . ."

". . . one of the *Wilting Wallflowers*? With the *duke*? One can only surmise he lost a wager."

"Or perhaps someone dared him to flirt with her." An unladylike hiccup escaped her, and both women fell into fits of laughter.

But all the sparkle was gone from Miss Lacey's eyes . . . and it gutted him. She released the parasol and looked away.

"Pay no attention to them," he said to her. "They're foolish *and* drunk."

"I know," she said, despondent. "But they're simply saying what everyone else is thinking."

"Would you like me to speak to them? I will, if it would make you feel better."

"No. It would only create more of a scene."

God, he felt helpless. She'd comforted him earlier, and he could think of nothing to say. "Would you like to leave? I'll gather everyone so we can go."

"No. Do not worry about my feelings. I'm used to the insults. I'm just relieved that Julie and Uncle Alistair didn't hear them."

Damn. He felt like the villain in a bad play. He'd carelessly labeled her and her sisters the Wilting Wallflowers before he even *knew* them. And now he was catching a firsthand glimpse of the suffering those thoughtless words had caused her. How could he have been so callous?

"I know what it's like to be the subject of gossip," he said. It was true. Not the gossip, but the fact that he was the subject of it. "The best course is to pretend like you don't care."

"You probably don't even have to pretend."

If she only knew. "You might be right. Or maybe I've just become very good at pretending."

She sighed forlornly. "I suppose it's been a trying evening for both of us."

"It hasn't been a complete loss." Impulsively, he reached for her hand, laced his fingers through hers, and gave a little squeeze.

She blinked in surprise and looked up at him.

He held his breath, wondering if she'd pull away. Hoping she wouldn't.

Because holding her hand was the best part of his whole damned day. Hell, it might be the best part of his year.

Beth didn't pull away, even though she should have. A few seconds ago, she'd felt sad and miserable and angry about a stranger's snide remarks. Now, all she could think about was the warm pressure of the duke's hand and how her whole body tingled from that simple touch.

Of course, she was just providing more fodder for nasty gossip, but she wasn't sure she cared. Their hands were mostly hidden by her skirts. The duke brushed his thumb over the back of her hand, sending delicious shivers up her arm and making her pulse race.

Perhaps he wasn't as cold-hearted as she'd thought. He seemed truly sympathetic, and he certainly had nothing to gain by comforting her. It wasn't as though he was interested in her in a romantic sense . . . or *was* he?

Impossible. Just yesterday, he'd seemed to detest her.

When she'd recovered her senses sufficiently to speak, she attempted to change the direction of the conversation. "This night did not go as smoothly as I'd hoped, but I feel certain that the duchess's next two wishes can be accomplished with less drama, your grace."

He winced at her use of formal address. "You should call me Alex."

"No, I shouldn't." She could hardly imagine it.

"And I should address you as Elizabeth."

"What's wrong with Miss Lacey?" she asked.

"Nothing's *wrong* with your surname. It's perfectly fine."

"I'm glad you approve," she said dryly.

"I shall use it when we're in the company of others," he said, "but when we're alone . . . I like Elizabeth."

"My sisters call me Beth. So did my parents, when they were alive." She wasn't quite sure why she'd shared that fact.

"Fine, then I shall call you Beth too."

Oh, but he was good—making it seem like he was accommodating her wishes. Still, she couldn't allow it. "I don't think that would be wise. I'm practically a member of your staff."

"No," he countered. "You don't work for me."

He was correct, if one discounted the deal they'd made. But there was no sense in splitting hairs. After all, once he'd succeeded in sending his grandmother away, Beth was unlikely to see him again.

And the truth was that she found it difficult to argue with him as long as he caressed the back of her hand like he was . . . flirting.

"Fine. Address me however you like." God help her, she was weak.

He grinned like he'd won big at the gaming tables. "Thank you . . . Beth."

She attempted a cool nod, as though she were quite accustomed to having handsome gentlemen hold her hand and whisper her given name under a sky lit with fireworks. "You made your grandmother happy tonight," she said. "I thank you for that."

"She does seem happy," he agreed. "But I find myself curious. Are *you* happy?"

Beth blinked. She'd never really stopped to consider the question. In the years after her parents' coach had careened off an icy bridge and left her and her sisters orphans, she'd been busy simply trying to survive. But then her sister Meg had fallen in love and married an earl, and they no longer had to worry about money. *Meg* was certainly happy, and Beth was happy *for* her. But she suspected the duke was asking her something altogether different.

"I don't know," she said honestly. "It seems that I am always worried about something." It was true. From the time she was a girl, she'd worried about everything from scarlet fever, to catastrophic storms, to the once-very-real possibility that she and her little family would land in the poorhouse. Beth had always had a knack for spotting potential trouble and latching onto it until the threat was resolved. How else was she supposed to protect her sisters and her uncle?

"What are you worried about right now?" He looked at her earnestly, as though her answer mattered very much.

She thought about the stormy boat ride, Roscoe's threats, the nearby explosion, and the gossipers' barbs. Maybe it was the duke's solid presence or his deep voice, or the pressure of his calloused thumb on her hand, but all of those worries melted away and she simply existed in the moment. The evening air kissed her skin, a light breeze tickled the curls at her nape, and the fireworks lent everything around her a magical glow.

"Nothing." She let out the breath she'd been holding and smiled. "For once, I'm not worried about anything."

She closed her eyes and breathed, feeling light and free.

The *boom* and *crack* of several rockets fired in quick succession startled her; the spectators applauded and cheered.

"The show is over," the duke murmured.

He released her hand, and the crowd around them grew restless. The malicious whispers behind her grew louder. A group of revelers near the hedge grew rowdy. Uncle Alistair looked confused and began to wander.

Beth sighed. The magic, it seemed, had fled.

Chapter ELEVEN

A few hours later—long after she should have been asleep—Beth lay in her bed, pondering all that had occurred at Vauxhall Gardens.

At the conclusion of the fireworks show, Uncle Alistair and Julie had left together in his coach, and for a brief instant, Beth had a fierce longing to join them—to return to her uncle's cozy parlor, cluttered with unfinished paintings, sewing projects, and pages of sheet music strewn across every surface. To be back where she belonged, in the company of those who truly knew and loved her.

But she could not shirk her duty to the duchess who, in the coming weeks, would need her more than ever. Beth didn't pretend to understand the duke's reasons for wanting his grandmother out of his house, but she'd made a deal with him and would honor it.

Their coach ride from the gardens to the duke's May-fair house had been quiet. The duchess's head bobbed against the plush squabs of the coach as she dozed peacefully. The duke had looked out the window, his expression brooding—so much so that Beth wondered whether she'd imagined the connection she'd felt to him earlier.

Now, as sleep proved elusive, she scolded herself for behaving like an ingénue whom the duke could manipulate—for surely that's what he'd been doing. He needed her to convince his grandmother to move to his country estate. Once that deed was accomplished, he'd have no use for her.

She would do well to remember that.

After all, he was a powerful man accustomed to having his way. A rake of the highest order, renowned for his skill in seducing women.

Blast. Too restless to remain in bed, she threw off the sheets and plucked her dressing gown off of the back of a chair. She thrust her arms through the sleeves and tightened the sash before cracking open the door to her bedchamber and peeking down the dark corridor.

Surely, the duke's servants had long since turned in for the night. The house was utterly quiet. No harm could come from a quick trip to the library. She'd select the most boring book on the shelves, take it to her bedchamber, and hope that after reading a few pages her eyelids would grow heavy.

Not bothering with slippers, she picked up the small lantern at her bedside, skulked into the corridor, and padded toward the grand staircase. Feeling deliciously rebellious, she glided down the stairs, rounded the corner, and headed toward the duke's library. She'd never actually been in it, but she'd caught a glimpse of the im-

pressive collection and had longed to explore it at lei-
sure. Tonight presented the perfect opportunity.

She was in the hallway near the library when she
heard a sound. A moan—low and haunting.

Good heavens. What was it the duke had said about
locking her bedchamber door at night? What if he *hadn't*
simply been trying to intimidate her but had legitimate
reasons for issuing the warning?

She swallowed, wondering if her ears were playing
tricks on her. Old houses made noises sometimes.

Then again, so did ghosts. Not that she'd ever encountered one, but she remained open to the possibility—no
matter how much her sisters mocked her.

They loved to tease her about her fascination with
spirits and unearthly creatures. Maybe her slight obses-
sion came from the scary tales their father had spun
while they sat around the fireplace in their parlor. Beth
had shivered in delight each time he told the most chilling bits. Or perhaps she merely wished to believe that
there was more to the world than what one could see.
Something beyond the ordinary and mundane. Something truly exhilarating.

Pure foolishness. She chided herself—but she walked
a bit faster down the hall, just the same.

The library—which would have been an excellent
hideout for spirits, with all its old books and reading
nooks—was blessedly quiet. Beth found a volume on
monsters featured in Greek myths, which had not been
her plan, precisely, but she'd been unable to resist. Besides, who knew? Perhaps tales of the Hydra, Minotaur,
and Cyclops—complete with their detailed, colored
illustrations—would be just the thing to lull her to sleep.

She tucked the book under her arm and headed back to her bedchamber. But once she was in the corridor, she heard the moaning again. This time it was unmistakable—and it seemed to emanate from the duke's dark study.

The sound grew louder as she approached the doorway. Deep and otherworldly, it reverberated through her, sending a shiver down her spine.

She should definitely walk right past the study, go directly to her room, bar the door, and hide beneath her covers. It was the only prudent thing to do. Indeed, every nerve in her body screamed for her to flee.

Instead, she paused in front of the study door and slowly nudged it open. The moaning stopped, which made perfect sense. It wasn't as though any self-respecting ghost would float over and introduce himself.

The lantern she held lit a small section of the room, and all looked as it should. No objects floated in midair. No desk drawers opened and closed of their own accord.

Vaguely disappointed, she listened intently. There was a scraping sort of sound, like boots on the floor. Then a tortured groan, the likes of which she'd never heard before, echoed off the walls.

Dear Jesus. The lantern's handle slipped from her fingertips, the flame extinguished, and darkness enveloped her. She jumped back and knocked her elbow into the doorjamb. Hard. The book fell to the floor with a *thud*, and she slapped a hand over her mouth to muffle the scream building in the back of her throat.

Panic rose in her chest. What kind of creature lurked in the duke's study? She had to return to her room. *Now*.

But she couldn't leave the lantern and book in the middle of the hallway. She dropped to her knees and felt around, frantically searching for both objects.

But then she heard footsteps—felt them vibrate the floor beneath her palms—and she froze.

A large hand grasped her upper arm and forcefully hauled her to her feet. "Who are you?" The voice was gravelly but unquestionably human . . . and she knew exactly whom it belonged to. Oh no.

"Forgive me, your grace," Beth squeaked.

"What in the bloody hell—"

"I didn't mean to disturb you." The moment she spoke the words, heat flooded her cheeks. Though she was hardly an expert on romantic assignations, she felt certain she'd interrupted the duke in the act of . . . that is, while he was enjoying . . . hang it all, she'd caught him making love to a woman. The duke's reputation, combined with the moaning, provided overwhelming evidence of such.

Which meant that there was another person—almost certainly a beautiful young lady—occupying the study and that Beth's level of humiliation was about to double.

"Why are you roaming the halls in the middle of the godforsaken night?"

"I wasn't attempting to spy on you, if that's what you're implying." To be fair, he hadn't implied anything of the sort, but this was all new territory for her.

"Come," he ordered. Still grasping her arm, he pulled her into his pitch-black study and firmly shut the door behind her. "Don't move."

She didn't have much choice in the matter. As he

fumbled around his desk, presumably searching for a candle to light, she wrapped her robe tightly about her, bracing herself for the moment when the room would be illuminated and she'd come face to face with the duke's mistress.

But when the soft glow of the candle banished the darkness, the only people in the study were she and the duke. His jacket was nowhere to be found. His waist-coat and cravat had also apparently gone missing. His shirt was open at the neck, and the sleeves were rolled up, revealing strong, sinewy forearms. The whole effect was rather captivating.

He sat on the edge of the desk and crossed his arms as his gaze lingered first on her unbound hair, then on the collar of her robe, and finally on her bare toes. "Good evening, Beth."

Blast. What on earth had possessed her to permit him to use her name?

She inclined her head in as haughty a manner as she could manage, given her state of utter dishabille. "Your grace."

A muscle in his jaw ticked. "Why are you out of your bed?"

She did not like having to explain herself to him, but she supposed it was a valid question. "I could not sleep."

"So you thought you'd snoop about my study?"

"No." She glanced around the imminently masculine room and shrugged. "I don't find it nearly as fascinating as you seem to think I do."

He arched a sardonic brow. "And yet, here you are."

Touché. "I took the liberty of availing myself of your library. I didn't think you would mind."

"I don't. But you still haven't explained why you were crawling on the floor outside my study."

"If you must know, I heard a sound coming from inside."

He rubbed the light stubble on his chin as though intrigued. "And you took it upon yourself to investigate? What did you think you were going to find?"

Either a ghost or a seduction-in-progress. But she couldn't very well admit to either. One made her sound addle-brained and the other . . . well, lustful. "I don't know, but the sound . . . I thought someone was in pain." As she looked into his glassy, bloodshot eyes, realization dawned. "*Are* you—in pain?"

Beth was far too perceptive for Alex's liking. He'd kept the nightmares secret. From everyone. And with good reason.

Sometimes he awoke drenched in sweat. Other times, his face was wet, like he'd been . . . well, like he'd been . . . *crying*. Not the sort of news he wanted bandied about his club. And he sure as hell didn't want Beth to pity him.

Armed with his most charming smile, he leaned forward and spread his arms wide, palms out. "Do I *look* like I'm in pain?"

She swallowed as her gaze drifted over him. "I don't see any blood. That's a good sign."

"It is indeed."

Her forehead creased in concern. "But perhaps you are ill. Do you have a fever?"

"Are you trying to play nurse with me, Miss Lacey?" An intriguing idea, to be sure. With her flushed cheeks, loose hair, and bare feet, she looked as though she'd stepped directly out of a Botticelli masterpiece. Beautiful enough to make a man forget about horrific nightmares and the recent attempts on his life. Hell, as he stared at the silky robe caressing her curves, he could barely remember his own name.

"No, I am satisfied with my role as a companion," she said dryly. "In any event, you seem to be hale and hearty—a perfect physical specimen."

"If you feel the need to conduct a more rigorous examination"—he flashed a suggestive smile—"I am willing . . ."

"That won't be necessary," she said quickly.

"So you see, there's nothing amiss. All is as it should be." He waved an arm around his study, hoping he sounded convincing.

"All *seems* well," she said with a frown. "But I know what I heard—moans. Tortured moans."

Christ, she wouldn't give up. "You *think* you know what you heard. It's late." He shrugged. "Perhaps your mind was playing tricks."

"No," she countered. "I *know* what I heard."

"Do you?" He pushed himself off his desk and walked all the way around her in a slow, deliberate circle. "There are all sorts of moans, Miss Lacey. Moans of pain . . . moans of pleasure. They sound remarkably similar."

Her eyes went wide. "I do not pretend to be a connoisseur of moans, your grace, but I shall take your word for it."

"It's Alex. And maybe you shouldn't."

"I beg your pardon?" She tossed her head, tousling

her wavy tresses and exposing the delicate column of her neck.

"You shouldn't take my word for anything. A moan of pleasure is something you should experience *for yourself.*"

Chapter TWELVE

Beth could imagine the duke whispering those wicked words to countless women, in ballrooms and bedchambers, parlors and pubs: a *moan of pleasure is something you should experience for yourself.*

Indeed, the line was so ridiculous that she might have laughed out loud—if she'd been able to breathe.

It was difficult to scoff at his words when the delivery was smooth as silk, and full of promise.

Crossing her arms over her breasts, she pretended to consider his proposal—if it could be called such. "Do you want to know what I think?"

He walked up behind her and leaned in close. Though he didn't physically touch her, she felt the warmth of his breath on her neck. "Tell me," he whispered.

Willing her pulse to slow, she turned to face him. "I think that you are attempting to distract me."

His gaze fell to her mouth. "From what?"

"You're hiding something. You don't want to tell me

the truth about what was occurring in here when I happened to walk by."

"I can assure you it was nothing sinister or particularly interesting," he said. "That's the truth."

"You are permitted to have secrets, your grace. You're certainly under no obligation to reveal to me—your grandmother's companion—whatever clandestine activities you may have been engaged in."

He chuckled—a rich, deep sound that heated her blood. "That is a relief."

For the space of several heartbeats, neither of them spoke. Then she said, "I do, however, admit to being curious."

The duke reached for a long curl that rested on her shoulder and gently wound it around his finger. "There's nothing wrong with being curious, you know." If his innuendo wasn't obvious from the words, the smoldering look he leveled at her made his meaning crystal clear.

Beth's breath hitched in her throat. Beneath the thin lawn of her robe and night rail, her nipples hardened and her toes curled. He stood so close that she could see the thick lashes framing his eyes, the light stubble on his chin, and the sprinkling of hair above the open collar of his shirt.

If she was honest with herself, she *was* curious. About him. The man who pushed his grandmother out of his life one moment and doted on her the next. The man who scolded Beth for leaving their party at the gardens but held her hand beneath the fireworks. The rogue who had a reputation for pleasuring London's most beautiful women but seemed to be flirting with a renowned wallflower—*her*.

And if she was very, very honest with herself, she was curious about something else—namely, what lay beneath his shirt.

Lord help her, she was about to do something foolish, but she was too dizzy with desire to care. Keeping her gaze locked with his, she placed a palm against the hard, flat planes of his chest. Beneath her hand, his muscles tensed and his heart galloped—evidence that she affected him too.

"You said you were having difficulty sleeping," he said in a gravelly voice. "I know of two particularly effective remedies."

"Let me guess," she replied, amazed that her tongue was capable of functioning while her fingertips were pressed to the thin, fine fabric covering his chest. "The first would be brandy."

"Very good." He slipped a hand beneath her loose hair and caressed the back of her neck. "Care to guess the second?"

"Er. Willow bark tea?" Heavens, her legs were going to give out any moment.

"Not even close," he murmured. "Let me show you."

Wrapping an arm around her waist, he hauled the length of her body against his—and brushed his lips over hers.

Her skin tingled everywhere he touched her—and even where he didn't. Of their own accord, her fingers curled against his chest, clutching a fistful of his shirt like she was hanging on for dear life.

This was the kiss she'd been waiting for forever. And she hadn't even known it till that very moment.

Everything in the room seemed to be spinning or tilt-ing or sliding—everything except him. Solid and strong, he held her like he desired her. Like he wanted *her*.

His lips, warm and firm, teased the corner of her mouth. The stubble on his face lightly abraded her skin—in the most delicious way. When she parted her lips, he deepened the kiss, exploring her mouth with his tongue as though he wanted to devour her.

It was a heady feeling, being in the arms of London's most notorious lover. Before this kiss, she'd never un-derstood why otherwise perfectly intelligent young women would sully their reputations for a night with him. But as he speared his fingers through her hair and trailed kisses down the side of her neck, she understood all too well.

It would be easy to ignore her good sense and sur-render completely to him.

Not that she had any intention of allowing things to go that far. She would be content with a kiss. And a few caresses. Perhaps even a peek at his chest.

With a large hand on her hip, the duke slowly walked her backward till her shoulder blades bumped against the closed door of his study. She thought it odd—until he leaned into her, pressing his body to hers.

His weight anchored her to the door, but her hands were free to explore. She clung to his shoulders, then dared to touch the bare skin above his shirt collar. All the while, he kissed her like she was the center of his world.

And though she knew very well that she was not, the mere illusion was rather intoxicating.

"Beth," he murmured against her mouth. "Tell me to stop."

She should have. She most *definitely* should have. But she wasn't ready for the dream to end.

Besides, her curiosity *always* got the better of her. She slipped her hand inside his shirt and swept her fingers over the light sprinkling of hair covering the chiseled contours of his chest—and kissed him harder.

He returned the favor, escalating the fever between them to an entirely different level. He plundered her mouth and pressed his hips to hers, letting her feel his arousal. With undisguised hunger, he tugged open her robe and slid his hand inside, taking the weight of her breast and teasing the nipple through the silky fabric of her night rail.

Sweet Jesus. A delicious ache spiraled through her and settled in her core. Never before had she allowed a man to kiss her, much less tenderly caress her breast. Perhaps the witching hour was to blame for her dream-like trance—the one that made her forget little things like rules of propriety and a lifetime of cautionary tales.

Or perhaps the blame lay entirely with the duke and his wickedly skilled mouth.

Grateful for the support of the door behind her, she arched her back and gave herself up to the moment— the improbable moment when this powerful, beautiful, ruthless man belonged to *her*.

Reaching behind her, he cupped her bottom with one hand and lifted her against the door. He wedged a thigh between hers and rocked until she was desperate for something more.

Lord help her, she wanted more.

As though he'd heard her silent plea, he raised the hem of her nightgown and caressed her bare leg.

She moaned.

Pausing mid-kiss, the duke touched his forehead to hers. Breathing like he'd been running hard, he looked into her eyes. "*Now* you've experienced a moan of pleasure," he said, more than a little triumphant.

Of course this was a game to him. A challenge. Mere child's play.

But to her . . . it had been the knee-melting introduction to a whole new world.

With an unexpected hint of vulnerability, he asked, "Did you like it?"

She wished she had a clever response, but all she could say was the truth. "Yes."

"I did too." His lopsided grin melted her last remaining bone.

But this taste of him . . . it still wasn't enough. With more daring than she'd known she possessed, she pulled the bottom of his shirt out of his trousers and slipped her hands underneath. As her palms skimmed the taut muscles of his abdomen and torso, her mouth went dry. "I want to take this off," she said, inching his shirt hem up his chest.

"No." He pushed her hands away, and she gasped.

Feeling like she'd been slapped, she wriggled out of his embrace and took two steps toward the center of the room. Hurt sliced through her. Shame too. She was a novice in these sorts of affairs, but given the circumstances, she'd thought the request reasonable.

"Forgive me," he said. "You did nothing wrong. It's

just that . . ." He muttered a curse as he rubbed the back of his neck and straightened his shirt collar.

And then she remembered—the scars. He didn't want her to see.

Some of the hurt abated, but not all. After all, he'd almost certainly shed his shirt for the women he'd made love to—and yet, he wasn't willing to reveal that much of himself to *her*.

"I understand," she said curtly. "Actually, I think you were quite right to put an end to things. I should be thanking you."

"Beth." He reached for her hand. "Don't do this."

She pulled away. "I'm not *doing* anything." Except perhaps gathering her wits about her.

"You're angry. I wish you'd allow me to explain."

"The only person I'm angry with is myself. I should never have gotten so carried away." Damn the witching hour. Damn her improper desires.

"We *both* got carried away," he said.

"I don't suppose we could forget this happened?" She was trying to imagine sitting with him and his grandmother at breakfast tomorrow morning without bursting into flames from sheer embarrassment.

"Why would we want to forget this?" he breathed. "I don't."

Her body tingled at his admission. No wonder half of London's women would gladly trade their favorite strand of pearls for a night in his bed.

She pulled her robe tightly around her and cinched the sash. "Given our respective roles—as duke and companion to your grandmother—I think it best for us to remain acquaintances."

"Acquaintances," he repeated, with no shortage of skepticism.

"Yes. We should remain cordial with each other. Like we were before."

"I see." Like a hunter tracking a deer, he took a step toward her. "So, I should politely inquire about your family and make insipid conversation about the weather? I should pretend that I never pressed my lips to yours or held your—"

"No." There was no point in allowing their relationship to become more personal. Nothing lasting or genuine could come from it. And it was cruel of him to make her believe otherwise. If she hadn't almost literally landed in his lap tonight, he never would have . . . that is, she never would have . . . Blast.

"It's late," she said, glancing at the clock on the mantel. The duchess was an early riser, and dawn was only three hours away. "I must go."

"I won't stop you," he said. "But I hope that once you've had a chance to sleep, we can revisit the issue."

Oh no, there would be no revisiting of anything. But she did not reply as he escorted her to the door, opened it a crack, and checked the hallway. Frowning, he swung the door open wide, stooped, and picked up the lantern and book she'd dropped.

"I believe these are yours," he said in a tone so perfectly cordial that it almost broke her heart. As he handed both items to her, his gaze flicked to the cover of the book. "*Mythological Creatures*," he mused. "Of all the books in my library, you chose one depicting a nine-headed serpent and a one-eyed giant."

She tucked the book under her arm, and, feeling the

need to defend her choice of reading material, said, "I have always felt a bit sympathetic toward the beasts. I'm sure they didn't *choose* to be trapped in a labyrinth or to turn people to stone. And yet, every mortal and demi-god made it their aim to slay the poor creatures."

The duke leaned against the doorframe and looked at her with an odd combination of respect and amusement. "Well, siren, if you can show compassion for the Minotaur, I have to believe there's hope for me."

"Good night, your grace," she said briskly, fleeing the study like a sacrificial maiden desperate to escape her fate.

His deep, warm chuckle chased her down the corridor. "Good night, Beth. Sleep well."

Chapter THIRTEEN

"Are you certain you want to fight Newton?" Darby asked, incredulous. "It doesn't seem the wisest choice since we've already established that he might be trying to kill you. You could spar with me instead."

Using his teeth, Alex tightened the strips of cloth wound around his hands. "I need a worthy opponent."

Darby shoved him in the chest. "You're a bastard—do you know that?"

"Yes, you're fond of reminding me."

Across the sweltering room at Jackson's Saloon, Newton tilted his head from side to side and jabbed at the air like he couldn't wait to take his swings at Alex.

"It will serve you right if you lose a couple of teeth." Darby propped his hands on his hips. "Newton has a wicked upper cut, so protect that ugly face of yours."

"Will do." Alex shook out his arms and stepped onto the floor. Newton did the same, and they circled around, each taking the other's measure. A few years older than

Alex, the marquess prided himself on his boxing ability and trained three times a week. Barrel chested but lean, he had at least two inches on Alex.

But if Newton had one real advantage in the fight, it was pure anger. His wife had spread the rumor that she'd had a torrid affair with Alex, and the whole ton accepted it as truth. Even if he denied it, no one would believe him. The gossip was too titillating to be dismissed as a lie.

Today's fight was Newton's shot to save face. If he could break Alex's nose or crack a few ribs, his manhood would be restored, and, in the blind eyes of society's elite, justice would be served.

Alex rolled his shoulders backward and smacked his fists together. He had his own reasons for fighting. First, the image of Roscoe's hand on Beth's arm last night was etched into his memory, and throwing the cretin to the ground hadn't been nearly as satisfying as punching his smug little face would have been. If Alex couldn't punch Roscoe, he might as well punch *someone*.

Second, he was angry with himself—for letting his bloody pride spoil his passionate encounter with Beth. But even now, in a room full of shirtless men, he refused to remove his. He didn't mind the scars half as much as what they stood for—the loss of his parents, his home, and his childhood. Exposing the discolored, puckered flesh was like exposing everything he'd lost. And he certainly didn't need anyone's pity.

But the third—and perhaps, most important—reason he was sparring with Newton was to figure out if he was the person who wanted him dead. Alex didn't expect the marquess to confess to poisoning him or to tampering with his coach, but in the heat of battle, raw emotion could make a man reveal more than he intended. Alex was counting on a brutal fight, the bloodier the better.

As the referee reviewed the rules—thirty seconds between rounds, no hitting below the belt—Alex looked into Newton's eyes and saw hate simmering there. In spite of the suffocating heat, a chill made the hairs on the back of Alex's neck stand on end.

The moment the referee gave the signal, fists started flying. Alex's right hand connected with Newton's cheek just as Newton slammed his knuckles into Alex's abdomen, knocking the breath out of him.

Alex doubled over and backed away, gasping. Damn it. If he wanted to keep his head attached to his body, he had to focus.

He dodged the next two blows and landed a punch to Newton's chin. Blood trickled out of the side of his mouth, and he spat on the floor. "You crossed a line, Blackshire," he said, breathing heavy. "I intend to make you pay."

"I have no idea what *line* you're talking about," Alex countered.

"Like hell, you don't." Newton's left hook glanced off Alex's ear and left it ringing. Shit.

Shaking his head to clear it, Alex feinted right and ducked, feeling the breeze from Newton's powerful hook.

Alex straightened and launched a fist directly at Newton's jaw, sending him sprawling onto the floor and sliding a couple of feet.

"That's the end of the round," the referee called. Newton's friend dragged him back to a corner of the room and poured water over his head. He looked dazed, but his face was still contorted with rage.

On his side of the room, Alex gulped water from a ladle and mopped his brow with the towel that Darby tossed him.

"He's out for blood now," Alex's friend warned him. "Avoid his punches for as long as possible, tire him out. If one of his swings connects with your face, it's lights out for you."

"Not if it's lights out for him first." But Darby was right. Alex had to pace himself and wait for the right moment.

"Round two!" the referee shouted, and both fighters approached the center of the room, wary. Newton's chin was already starting to swell. Alex's ear felt like it was on fire, but the pain only helped sharpen his focus.

"In the future," Newton said, "keep your hands off of what's not yours."

Alex shifted his weight quickly from foot to foot, ready to dodge whatever blows Newton launched at him. "Is this about me borrowing your newspaper at the club?"

Cursing, his opponent swung for Alex's head—and missed by a hair. Literally.

"Aren't you the jester?" The cut on Newton's chin oozed blood. "You think you can bed whomever you want," he gasped. "Without recrimination."

"Not true." Alex raised his gloves to deflect the punch that was surely coming. "I would never bed a woman . . . unless she wanted me to."

"You . . . bloody . . . bastard!" Newton didn't swing at Alex's head, like he'd expected. Instead, Newton raised the heel of his boot and kicked Alex squarely in the kneecap.

Holy hell. He hit the ground. Pain exploded in his knee and radiated up and down his leg. Darby charged at Newton, cursing him for hitting below the belt. Newton's cronies crowded around him and pushed back. Above the din, the referee shouted for everyone to clear the floor.

Alex's vision grew fuzzy at the edges as he writhed on the ground, clutching his godforsaken knee. Then Newton leaned forward, his disfigured face looming above Alex's head.

"There's more where that came from, Blackshire," he spat. "You're lucky you're not already dead."

Alex groaned. He had no doubt that Newton wanted him dead.

But he still didn't know if the marquess was the one who'd been trying to kill him.

Alex couldn't unravel it while his knee throbbed. All he wanted at the moment was his bed—and a strong drink.

Beth spent the first half of the day thanking her lucky stars that she didn't encounter the duke. After only three hours of sleep, her nerves were frayed and her emotions were raw. If she'd seen him in the morning—so soon after their romantic tryst—she would have blushed to the roots of her hair, and the duchess would have surely known that something improper had transpired.

And oh, had it been improper. Beth absently pressed a fingertip to her lips, still swollen from the duke's kisses. She must have been mad to allow them—and even madder to kiss him back. When she considered that she was only the latest in a long line of women who'd fallen prey to his charms, she wanted to kick herself. It didn't matter that, by all accounts, his conquests were happy to count themselves among his lovers. Because Beth was not like those women.

Or was she? She'd thought herself stronger. Smarter. More principled. Perhaps, when it came down to it, though, she was as weak as any. She'd certainly melted in his arms.

Which may have explained why she spent the second half of her day wondering where on earth the duke could be and whether he was trying to avoid her. She'd looked for his charming grin around every corner and waited for his broad shoulders to fill the doorway of the drawing room, where she and the dowager now sat.

The duchess, still basking in the glow of her adventurous trip to Vauxhall, sipped her afternoon tea as light rain pattered against the tall paned windows. The weather, combined with the warm tea and cinnamon scones in her belly, made Beth long for a nap, but the dowager was full of vim and vigor. "I would like to do something special for Alexander," she said excitedly. "Something to repay him for doting on an old woman like me."

"He seems happy to indulge you when he can," Beth said. Of course, she was *forcing* him to spoil his grandmother, but she didn't need to know that. It would only break her heart.

"I have an idea," the duchess whispered—even though they were the only two people in the room. "Would you like to hear it?"

"Of course." Beth was betting the duchess wanted to order his favorite dessert. Or embroider him a handkerchief.

She adjusted her spectacles and leaned forward. "I thought I would redecorate his *study*. Wouldn't that be grand?"

Beth blinked. "He certainly wouldn't expect a gesture like that." And she couldn't imagine he'd be pleased at the prospect.

"Alexander spends so much time working in there, and it hasn't been updated for generations. He deserves elegant furnishings and fresh décor."

Oh dear. The duke was rather territorial about his study, and Beth was fairly certain that even if he did wish to update it, his tastes would be vastly different from his grandmother's. "It's a lovely idea, but I'm not certain—"

"You really must observe the shabbiness of the room yourself in order to understand my desire to spruce it up." The duchess set her teacup on the tray and stood. "Follow me, Elizabeth."

Beth didn't think it prudent to mention that she'd seen the duke's study before. Multiple times. In fairness, however, the dim light during last night's encounter had made it rather difficult to assess the quality of the furnishings. Besides, she'd been a little distracted.

The duchess marched down the corridor like she was on a mission for the king. When she reached the study, she didn't hesitate to enter the duke's realm but, rather, pushed open the door and walked to the middle of the worn Aubusson carpet. Sweeping her gaze around the room, she clucked her tongue.

Beth followed, valiantly trying to shake the memory of the kiss against the door. And hoping that her cheeks didn't look as red as they felt. She endeavored to look at the room with an objective eye. It may have had a lived-in appearance, but she suspected that was the way the duke preferred it. "I don't think it's so terrible," she ventured.

The duchess pressed a hand to her chest, aghast. "The desk has water stains. The leather on the chairs is faded and cracked. The wallpaper hasn't been in fashion since the reign of William III. It's a disgrace."

"What's a disgrace?" The duke's booming voice echoed through the room.

Blast. Beth took a deep breath, hoping to regain her composure before facing him.

"Alexander!" the duchess cried. "What's happened to you? You look like you've returned from the battlefield!"

Her heart pounding, Beth spun around to find the duke with his arm slung over Lord Darberville's shoulders. The side of his face was scratched, and he favored his left leg, which was missing its boot. She had to resist the urge to run to him and inspect his injuries up close.

"Good afternoon, grandmother, Miss Lacey." He inclined his head politely. "Would someone mind telling me why everyone has gathered in my study? It seems to be a pattern." He shot Beth a smug look, which she ignored.

"Do not think to avoid my question," the duchess said, raising her nose in the air. "I demand an explanation."

The duke shoved off of Lord Darberville, hobbled to the closest chair, and sank into it. "I sparred at Jackson's today. But no need to worry—I'm not on my deathbed. Yet." He stretched out his bandaged leg and winced. "Darby, a drink."

As Lord Darberville made his way to the sideboard, the duchess propped her hands on her hips. "I thought boxing was supposed to maintain one's health," she said. "In truth, it's naught but an excuse for men to behave like barbarians."

"You have the right of it," Lord Darberville confirmed, handing the duke a glass of brandy. Addressing the duchess and Beth, he said, "Lord Newton neglected to follow the rules of the match."

"My grandmother isn't interested in the sordid details," the duke snapped.

Perhaps not, but Beth was.

The duchess cast a critical glance at the bandages. "Who wrapped your knee?"

"A doctor happened to be training at the saloon. He insisted on bandaging it."

"And what did he *say*?" the duchess inquired, her frustration mirroring Beth's own.

The duke took a long draw of his brandy and shrugged. "I shall live."

For several seconds, the older woman said nothing. Then she smiled broadly, the corners of her eyes crinkling behind her spectacles. "Well, if you are going to live, you shall require new furnishings for your study."

Chapter FOURTEEN

The duke's eyebrows shot up. "I beg your pardon?"

"I was just telling Elizabeth of my plans to redecorate this room. With your permission, of course." The duchess smiled sweetly.

"It's very generous of you to offer," he said cautiously, "however, I like this room. As it is."

"But . . . but"—the older woman's face crumpled—"it's not befitting a man of your status."

"I can assure you, my study suits me just fine. There's no sense in expending effort and money on an unnecessary project."

The duchess's disappointment was palpable. "I wanted to do it," she said meekly, "for you. But if you are dead set against it, I will respect your wishes."

Beth hated to see the duchess so defeated but couldn't blame the duke for refusing. His study was his fortress, a bastion of masculinity and power. Heaven forfend his grandmother should invade with florals and delicate baubles.

Unless—

Perhaps he'd allow the duchess to redecorate his study if it counted as her second wish. Beth might as well suggest it.

"Your grace," she said smoothly, "shall I bring you the ottoman so you may prop your injured leg on it?"

He glanced around his study, wary. "There's no ottoman in here."

"The stool then?" she asked innocently.

"I haven't a stool either, Miss Lacey." He spoke through his teeth, as though he suspected what she was about.

"No ottoman or stool? What a pity. But the situation could be easily remedied if you granted your grandmother her *wish* and allowed her to redecorate."

Understanding registered in his eyes, and he nodded thoughtfully. "An ottoman would be useful, and I suppose that a few items could use updating. Give me a day or two to think it over."

"Oh, thank you, Alexander!" the duchess cried, as if he'd already given her carte blanche. "You won't be sorry—I promise you."

The duke started to protest, then gave his grandmother a weary smile. Beth's chest squeezed at the sight.

"You know," she said, "I believe there's a small stool in the drawing room. I'll fetch it and return in just a moment."

"That's not necessary," the duke replied, but pain was

etched in the fine lines around his mouth, and Beth wanted to do *something* to help.

"It's no trouble," she said.

"Allow me to retrieve it, Miss Lacey," Lord Darberville offered gallantly.

But Beth was already headed for the door. "I'll return in a trice!" she called over her shoulder.

Once she'd escaped to the solitude of the corridor, she closed her eyes and leaned against the wall. She needed a few minutes to herself, enough time to allow her heartbeat to return to normal. Last night's encounter was too fresh in her mind. Even now, she recalled the duke's unyielding body pressed against hers. She could still taste his kisses and feel the heat of his heavy-lidded gaze.

Shaking off the memories, she made her way to the drawing room and selected a small footstool topped with a thickly padded cushion.

Balancing the stool against her hip, she headed slowly back to the study, which she now secretly thought of as *The Scene of the Ravishing*. She wasn't quite sure if she'd been the ravisher or the ravished. Maybe she'd been both. One thing was certain—she was no longer the same girl she'd been yesterday.

God forbid the duke realized the effect he had on her. He already had a lofty opinion of himself. If he discovered that a mere look from him could make her skin tingle . . . well, he'd be impossible to live with. More than he already was.

Taking a bracing breath and pasting on a demure smile, Beth angled the footstool through the doorway and breezed into the study. "Here we are," she announced—but something was amiss.

Frowning, she looked around the room, which was unoccupied, except for the duke. "Where is everyone?"

"Darby went home."

"And your grandmother?"

"She claimed she wanted a nap," the duke said dryly. "But I imagine she's poring over *Lady's Magazine* looking for frippery she can use to trim my study."

Oh dear. If Beth had learned one lesson from the previous night, it was that she really should not be alone with the duke. Moving briskly, she placed the stool in front of the duke's leather chair and dusted off her hands. "Well then, I shall leave you in peace so that you may . . . ah . . . convalesce."

"Sit," he commanded.

Beth crossed her arms. "I don't take orders from you, your grace."

"Why are you behaving like a coward?" he challenged, more thoughtful than irate.

"I don't know what you're talking about. I retrieved a footstool for you, and you respond by calling me a coward. What a unique display of gratitude."

"I do appreciate your thoughtfulness." He used the foot of his good leg to drag the stool closer, then gripped the arms of the chair as he raised his injured leg.

Oh, for the love of—"Allow me to help you." Before she knew what she was doing, she had one hand wrapped around his very muscular, very hard thigh, and the other on his calf. The temperature in the study rose ten degrees. Heaven help her.

Without looking him in the eye, she stood and asked, "How's that?"

"Thank you." He didn't bother to hide his amusement. "Now sit."

Tossing her head, she said, "You are extraordinarily rude."

He shrugged. "If you'd prefer to stand for the duration of our conversation, suit yourself."

Heaving a sigh, Beth looked for a chair, but none faced the duke. "I suppose I shall have to move yet another piece of furniture. Two in one afternoon," she said pointedly.

"You are welcome to sit in my lap." His wicked grin caused her belly to flutter, blast it all.

"And to think I believed you were wholly incapacitated," she said curtly. "It is a relief to see that your injury does not interfere with your usual rakish activities."

"Not at all. But if you'd like to see for yourself—"

"What was it that you wished to discuss, your grace?"

He rested his laced fingers across a taut abdomen. "My study, for one thing. I can't give my grandmother free rein in here."

Beth raised her chin. "Then you should not have raised her hopes."

"If she has her way, my study will resemble a ladies' sitting room."

"How horrifying," she quipped. "Do not tell me that you fear a little lace or a few decorative feathers. I had thought you more secure in your manliness."

"Oh, I'm secure." He arched a dark brow. "Shall I demonstrate?"

"I think not," she answered quickly. "But honestly,

what harm can come of your grandmother undertaking your study as a project?"

He blinked, incredulous. "The harm? She could trade in my desk. Or remove my prized painting."

"Would that be so awful? Your grandmother has impeccable taste—she'd no doubt replace it with something that suits you."

"You don't understand," said the duke. "This is the desk where I played hide-and-seek with my father. He let me carve my initials underneath."

Oh. Beth clung to sentimental objects from her parents too. "We can make certain the desk stays."

"And the painting"—he waved an arm at a hideous landscape featuring a winding green river and a misshapen horse—"may not be removed under *any* circumstances."

Her heart melted a little more. "Did it belong to your parents as well? Or perhaps you painted it when you were younger?"

"That abomination?" he croaked. "I'm no artist, but I could paint a better picture while blindfolded."

Beth sighed. "Then why do you wish to keep it?"

"It's the subject of a running bet. Darby said that if I hung it on my wall for a decade, he'd give me ten pounds. I'm already four years in."

She blinked, wondering if she'd heard him correctly. "You'd stare at a painting you detest for ten years in order to gain a mere ten pounds?"

"No," he said, as if she were the simplest person on the face of the earth. "I'd stare at a painting I detest for ten years *in order to win a bet with Darby.*"

She tilted her head and stared at the landscape to see

if it improved upon a second examination. It didn't. "That's a very odd-looking horse."

"She has a name. It's Phyllis."

"I see. Well, Phyllis may stay too, if you like."

He seemed to relax, ever so slightly. "And if I allow my grandmother to make a few changes in here, you will consider her second wish fulfilled?"

"Yes—as long as you give her wide berth. She was so excited at the prospect of improving this place."

The duke dragged a hand down his face. "I have a bad feeling about this. Couldn't I just take her to the opera instead?"

"No! She already thinks you've agreed. She'll be crushed if you go back on your word."

"Fine. She may undertake her redecorating project—under one condition."

Beth rolled her eyes. "I know. Phyllis stays."

"We've already established that Phyllis is not negotiable. My condition is this: *you* must personally ensure that my grandmother's choices will be tolerable for me."

An unladylike snort escaped her. "I do not know your tastes in furniture, art, or décor. How am I to ascertain what you find acceptable?"

"That's easy," he said smoothly. "Ask me."

Alarms sounded in Beth's head. A project such as this would involve scores of decisions. And if she was to consult him on each one, they'd be spending a considerable amount of time together—alone. The idea wasn't abhorrent to her. And therein lay the danger.

"Why don't you simply tell your grandmother that you'd like to be involved in selecting the key pieces?" she suggested.

"Because I don't," he said curtly. "I don't want to be involved in *anything*. And I *certainly* don't want to be in the position of telling my dear grandmother that the wallpaper or paint or knick-knacks or whatever she has her heart set on would be better suited for a bordello than for my study."

"You're being unreasonable. She would never choose something garish."

He raised a skeptical brow. "Did you see the bonnet she wore yesterday? At least two exotic birds were sacrificed to create it."

"Your concern for feathered creatures is commendable," Beth said dryly. "But you needn't worry that your study will suffer from an overabundance of plumes."

He rubbed the stubble on his chin, thoughtful. "If my grandmother's taste is as refined as you claim, then your job should be simple. All you must do is steer her in the right direction."

Beth let out a long, slow breath. "And in order to determine the *right direction,* I am to secretly consult you?"

"No need for cloak and dagger, but out of respect for my grandmother's feelings . . ."

It was all Beth could do to keep from rolling her eyes. The same man who wanted to send his grandmother away was now concerned about her feelings. But he was correct—it would be better if the duchess were under the impression that her grandson trusted her. Even if he did not.

"Very well," she said. "I will do my best to ensure that your study retains the appearance of an insolvent gentleman's club, untouched by feminine hands."

"Excellent," he said smugly.

"Now that that's resolved, I shall take my leave. Unless you'd like me to move another piece of furniture or save you from a scrap of lace?" She stood and batted her eyes sweetly.

"Don't run off yet, siren," he commanded. "We still need to talk about last night."

Chapter FIFTEEN

"What about last night?" Beth's eyes instantly grew wary, and a blush crept up her neck. "There's nothing to discuss."

"I can think of a few things," Alex said, but she stood in front of him looking like she wanted to be anywhere but there. Jesus. Talking wasn't exactly his forte, either. But he had to make her understand that she wasn't just another conquest for him. "Will you let me pour you a drink at least?"

She exhaled slowly. "Very well."

Alex shoved himself out of his chair and headed to the sideboard, stifling a curse each time he put weight on his knee. By the time he lifted the decanter and poured a glass of wine, he was sweating from the effort to mask his pain. He gripped the edge of the cabinet and took a couple of deep breaths through his nose.

Beth glided to his side and placed a hand on his arm. "Let me help."

"What if I told you I'm beyond help?" He managed a grin so she'd think it was a quip . . . even though it was the God's honest truth.

"I wouldn't believe you." Biting her lip in concern, she wrapped an arm around his waist and steered him back toward his chair.

She took some of his weight as they shuffled across the room, but even better, she provided an effective distraction from the pain. A wayward curl tickled the side of his face, and he had an excellent view of her cleavage.

"Here we are," she said, breathless from her exertions. "Can you manage to sit without bumping your leg?"

"Of course," he said, with more confidence than he felt. Grasping one arm of his chair, he collapsed onto the seat cushion.

Only, his sudden drop must have caught Beth off guard, or perhaps her arm was tangled with his. He yanked her down with him, and she landed crosswise on his lap—her soft bottom pressed against his thighs.

Her eyes as wide as saucers, she froze. "Have I hurt your knee?"

He thought about it. "No." Arousal was winning the battle with pain. Handily.

"I'm going to attempt to remove myself from your lap without jarring your leg," she said.

"Perhaps you should remain just as you are," he said. "I'm quite comfortable."

Her eyes narrowed. "When the doctor examined you

earlier, did he, by any chance, order you to remain in your bed?"

The citrusy scent of Beth's hair and pressure of her bottom and nearness of her lips all made it difficult for him to focus, but he picked up the thread of the conversation. "In my head, all I heard you say just now was the word *bed*. Listen, I appreciate your concern for me. The truth is my knee's a little sore, but nothing's broken. I'll be fine in a few days." He rested a hand on the curve of her hip, barely resisting the urge to pull her close and pick up where they'd left off the night before.

"I'm glad to hear it," she said. "But you didn't answer my question. Should you be in bed right now?"

Hell, yes. He should be in bed, and she should be there with him. Beneath him, on top of him, he didn't really care. But definitely naked. "The doctor may have suggested it."

"I don't know why I should feel sympathy for a man who hits other men for sport and blatantly disregards doctor's orders."

"But you do."

She sighed and rested her cheek on his shoulder. "Do you really think you'll be all right in a few days?"

"I'm feeling better by the moment." Tentatively, he smoothed a hand down her back and brushed his lips across her forehead.

Rain pattered on the windows, and a gust shook the branches outside. Last night, kissing her in the dark, had felt like a fantasy, but this—this felt very real. She hadn't landed on his lap on purpose, but she hadn't scrambled off him either. Beth was here, embracing him, even in the light of day.

She turned her face up to his, expectant, and he crushed his mouth to hers. God, she tasted good. When she kissed him back, curling her fingers into the hair at his nape and pulling him closer, he stifled a moan. She probably had no idea what she was doing to him. His heart pounded out of control, and he was as hard as a rock. He wanted her to straddle him. Better yet, he wanted to drag her up to his bedchamber and make love to her a dozen different ways, his knee be damned.

But from the corner of his mind, reason intruded. She was an innocent and deserved better. Much better. Any hint of a relationship with him would tarnish her reputation forever. Besides, he couldn't let her get too close to him. He was all wrong for her . . . and a man could only endure so much loss.

Reluctantly, he slowed the kiss and ended it.

Dazed, she looked at him, her pretty blue eyes questioning. "Alex?"

Hearing her say his name just about killed him. "I would happily kiss you forever," he admitted, "but I don't think it's wise. We risk being seen."

"Of course." She shook her head like she was waking from a dream. "I don't know what came over me."

"Desire," he said with a grin. And if there had been another force working to push them together . . . well, he'd be a fool to dwell on it. Nothing lasting could develop between them. Even if someone wasn't trying to kill him.

Beth deserved someone as generous and thoughtful as she was. She needed someone to take care of her the way she took care of everyone else. But that someone couldn't be him.

His heart had turned to ash years ago.

Smiling sheepishly, she said, "Help me stand—without hurting you."

"Wait, there's something I want to tell you." He *should* confess that it was he who'd carelessly labeled her with the cruel Wilting Wallflower name that had, unfortunately, stuck. Even though anyone with eyes could see she was far too lovely to be a wallflower. It would be best to admit the truth now, before things between them progressed any further.

"What is it?" She tilted her head and gazed at him, her eyes shining with affection and her lips swollen from their kiss. The tenderness in her expression leveled him like a punch to the gut. Damn it, he *couldn't* tell her. He'd hurt her last night . . . and he couldn't hurt her again. At least not so soon.

"I overreacted last night. Look, my scars aren't pretty, and I didn't want you to see. But I should have explained."

"And what would you have said?" she challenged. "That a girl like me shouldn't have to witness something so revolting?"

"You shouldn't." It was true.

She laced her fingers through his and laid her head on his shoulder again. "You think that I haven't seen truly ugly things? Because I have. I've seen grown men jeer at my uncle. I've seen a debutante spit on my younger sister. I've seen a mother abandon her twin daughters—who now happen to be my nieces. Scars don't bother me, Alex."

"You say that now." He rubbed the back of his neck, feeling the puckered, twisted skin there.

She sat up and arched a brow. "I never would have guessed you to be so vain."

It wasn't about vanity so much as privacy—there was no need for everyone to know what he'd endured, how he'd almost been broken. No one had a right to see that—except, perhaps, his grandmother. But he shrugged nonchalantly. "I am also notoriously shallow."

"That is good to know," she said smoothly. "Now help me up."

Alex lifted her over the arm of his chair, and she landed lightly on her feet.

"Your wine is over there"—he nodded at the sideboard—"if you'd still like it."

"I think I should refrain," she said primly. "But I am glad we made some progress today."

"I agree." Something like hope blossomed in his chest. They *were* making progress. Who knew? Maybe soon they'd be able to converse for more than a few minutes without arguing.

"Your grandmother is pleased with her second wish," she said, "and I will do my best to make sure that your study retains its uniquely manly, messy charm."

Damn. She'd meant that they'd made progress on the duchess's wishes—not with each other. "Maybe we should meet after dinner this evening," he ventured, "to discuss the particulars of this project." It was a transparent attempt to spend more time alone with her, but he couldn't resist.

"As you may recall, I have plans with your grandmother this evening—Lady Claville's ball."

Bloody hell, he'd forgotten. "Of course I remember." He'd have to send word to Darby to keep a watchful, protective eye on both his grandmother and Beth. So far, Alex had been the only target, but if his assailant grew frustrated, there was no telling who else he might attack.

Beth paced slowly, the sway of her hips entrancing him. "The duchess had hoped you'd escort her," she said, "but you now have an excuse not to attend. I must say, your injury was a clever—if extreme—way to avoid accompanying us. I am amazed at the lengths you'll go to in order to shun your duties." The twinkle in her eyes said she was jesting. Mostly.

"I daresay, my grandmother will enjoy recounting the tale of how I bravely limped into the house despite wounds that would have finished off a lesser man."

"Your humility abounds," she countered. Then, turning sincere, she said, "Is there anything you need before I go? A drink or perhaps a pillow beneath your leg?"

He needed all sorts of things. Most of them too wicked to name. "No, thank you. But please take care tonight."

"What do you mean?"

"Keep your distance from anyone who looks suspicious," he said soberly.

The corners of her eyes crinkled in amusement. "I don't anticipate many shady characters will be on the Clavilles's guest list."

"You never know. They invited me."

"Your point is well taken," she said, tossing a smile over her shoulder as she left.

Chapter SIXTEEN

"Well, here we are once again," Beth mused. "The Wilting Wallflowers, reunited."

She had fetched champagne for the duchess and Uncle Alistair and found them comfortable chairs where they could converse with their friends. Now, she and her sisters stood adjacent to the refreshment table, watching a sea of couples surge and swirl in time to the music on the crowded dance floor.

"It reminds me of old times," Meg said wistfully—almost as though she'd forgotten how humiliating it was to be mocked, overlooked, and dismissed. But then, being married to a handsome earl could change one's perspective. Beth's circumstances hadn't changed nearly as much, and yet, there *had* been a shift in her thinking of late.

All because of Alex.

During the past few days, she'd gone toe to toe with him on several occasions. They'd argued, bargained, and *kissed* . . . and somehow, she'd emerged relatively unscathed. If she could survive sparring with a duke—and not just any duke, but the notorious Duke of Blackshire—she could face anyone in this ballroom with confidence.

Which was not to say that she had a slew of dance partners or admirers. But Meg's handsome husband, Will, had gallantly asked her for a dance, as had Lord Darberville. True, both of them likely asked her out of a sense of obligation, but at least she wasn't standing about the potted palms all evening. She wondered whether her night would have been different had Alex been there. Would he have asked her to dance in front of London's elite? Or was she simply an amusing diversion—someone to entertain him on the rare evening he spent at home?

As though she'd read Beth's mind, Meg asked, "Why didn't the duke accompany the dowager and you tonight?"

Julie wagged her eyebrows suggestively. "Perhaps he is with his paramour."

Meg narrowed her eyes. "What do you know of paramours?"

"Not nearly enough." Julie sighed.

"He's not with a lover," Beth said curtly. And maybe a bit too loudly. At Meg's questioning expression, she lowered her voice, adding, "I only meant that the reason for his absence is not nearly as scandalous as our younger sister would like to believe. He injured his leg while sparring today."

"Maybe he and his opponent were fighting over a woman?" Julie asked hopefully.

"Or maybe they were merely engaged in a friendly boxing match," Beth corrected.

"*Friendly boxing match* sounds like an oxymoron to me," Meg said. "I shall never understand men."

"The duke seemed pleasant enough at Vauxhall," Julie said. "But I've since lowered my opinion of him. I cannot condone his decision to move his grandmother to the country."

"Shh!" Beth glanced around. "The dowager doesn't know yet, and when the time comes to inform her, I'll need to do so gently." Goodness, if her sisters guessed that the duke had kissed her, they'd hold him in even lower esteem. Actually, they'd call for the guillotine.

"He said that the move was for her own sake," Beth said in his defense. Because while she didn't pretend to understand his logic, she *wanted* to believe him.

"Hmm," Meg said, skeptical. Beth couldn't blame her.

"Don't look now, but Lord Darberville is heading toward us." Julie jabbed Beth with a pointy elbow. "He must want to ask you to dance again."

Beth rubbed her arm. "Maybe he intends to ask *you*."

"Good evening, Lady Castleton, Miss Lacey, and Miss Juliette." Lord Darberville bowed politely and stepped aside to make room for his companion. "Please permit me to introduce Mr. Richard Coulsen. He's the steward of Lord Claville's Kent estate, and we met at the marquess's house party last year, where he *almost* beat me at fencing."

"I *did* beat him." Mr. Coulsen winked as he bowed over Meg's hand, then Beth's and Julie's.

"Wonderful," Meg murmured under her breath. "Another devotee of blood sports."

Ignoring her sister, Beth smiled at the gentleman. "It's a pleasure." In a room brimming with titled lords and ladies, it *was* nice to meet someone who was on approximately the same rung of the social ladder as she. Not that anyone would guess Mr. Coulsen was of lower social status than most. Tall and fair-haired, he moved and spoke with the confidence of a man who was accustomed to being in charge.

"I have a confession." He lowered his voice and leaned in, as though he really were about to share something intimate. "I asked Lord Darberville for an introduction so that I might properly ask you to dance. Would you do me the honor, Miss Lacey?"

Beth glanced at her younger sister, standing on her right. Surely, Mr. Coulsen wanted to dance with Julie . . . and yet, he seemed to be looking directly at Beth.

Julie's elbow jabbed her again. "He's asking you."

Beth blinked, attempting to hide her surprise. She supposed there was no harm in dancing with Mr. Coulsen, even if she'd only just met him. Besides, Meg and Julie would be watching the dance floor like hawks. "Certainly," she said.

Before she knew it, he was leading her away from her familiar, out-of-the-way spot by the refreshment table and twirling her into the center of the action.

"Forgive me if I'm not as polished as your usual dance partners," he said. "I don't attend many balls—at least not ones like this." He gestured at the massive crystal chandelier sparkling overhead.

"From the way you dance, I would have guessed that you'd been born in a ballroom," Beth teased.

"Hardly." He flashed a self-deprecating smile and maneuvered her expertly around another swirling couple. "Not that I'm complaining. It was most generous of my employer, Lord Claville, to invite me this evening."

"I'm acting as companion to the Dowager Duchess of Blackshire," Beth said.

He raised a dark blond brow. "I knew we'd have something in common."

"Why did you ask me to dance?" Her question bordered on impolite, but she was too curious not to ask.

Shrugging, he said, "You were standing with your sisters—I knew they had to be your sisters—and you were in the middle."

"You asked me to dance because I was standing between my sisters?"

"The middle is sometimes a difficult place to be."

She looked at his face to see if he was jesting, but he seemed most sincere. "Spoken like a middle child," she guessed.

"I have no siblings," he said. "But I do know what it's like to be caught between two worlds."

Beth's heart squeezed in her chest—it was the pang she routinely experienced when she learned of an injustice or slight. And it made her want to right matters, even though she barely knew Mr. Coulsen.

"It seems we have another thing in common," she said.

They danced the rest of the set in companionable silence, but Beth did feel a connection to the gentleman.

Nothing like the headiness she felt with Alex, but rather, a sense of ease.

Her dance partner smiled as they circled one another, and Beth realized she must take care not to mislead him.

At the conclusion of the dance, Mr. Coulsen escorted Beth back to her sisters, conversing along the way. "Thank you for indulging me," he said, "even though I'm certain your feet must be sore from dancing all evening."

"Oh, I haven't danced much," Beth said. "In fact, my sisters and I are known as the Wilting Wallflowers."

Blast. She couldn't imagine what had possessed her to admit that. He was, perhaps, the sole person in all of London who *hadn't* been aware of her humiliating reputation, and she managed to work it into the conversation only minutes after they'd been introduced. Perfect.

He frowned, confused. "The Wilting Wallflowers?"

"My uncle, our guardian, is Lord Wiltmore. I suppose the name was a natural extension."

Scratching his head, Mr. Coulsen opened his mouth as though he'd say something . . . and then he laughed.

Beth's shields went up. She'd thought he'd be a friend—someone who understood her. She should have known better than to trust someone she'd just met.

"Forgive me," he said. "I'm not laughing at you. The name is beyond ridiculous—it's absurd. No one who's ever seen you or your sisters could refer to you as wallflowers. Not while keeping a straight face."

Beth relaxed slightly. "Only a year ago, we were poor as church mice and wearing gowns several seasons out of fashion. We may have new clothes, but the name has stuck with us—not unlike the stench from a skunk."

Mr. Coulsen stopped walking and turned to face her. "I don't care what you were wearing or how poor you were—you're no wallflower."

With that, he bowed and left her.

Chapter SEVENTEEN

When he'd awoken the next morning, Alex discovered his knee had swollen to the size of a cantaloupe and turned several nasty shades of black and green. It was stiff and hurt like the devil when he moved, but damned if he'd spend the day lying around. He'd wrapped the knee, gritted his teeth, and stuffed his foot into his boot. Remaining in bed all day wasn't an option—not while someone plotted to kill him.

And while he still limped, he found that at least he could put some weight on his leg. Unfortunately for Darby, Alex's dining partner, the pain in his leg made him crankier than normal.

"Why in God's name would you introduce Richard Coulsen to Miss Lacey?" Alex demanded, loud enough that several members of his club put down their newspapers and ceased their conversations. Alex glared in response. He sat across a table from Darby in the darkly paneled dining room, questioning his own judgment in having allowed his grandmother and Beth to attend the Claville ball without him.

Darby swiped his napkin across his mouth, attempting to hide a wry grin. "You said yourself he's a decent sort. I only introduced them. It's not as though I ushered them out onto a moonlit terrace and left them alone."

Alex's hackles rose even more. "I asked you to keep a watchful eye on her—not fill her bloody dance card."

"If you want to know the truth, the dance floor was the safest place for her." Darby speared a chunk of roast beef with his fork and popped it in his mouth. "There were too many people around for anyone to attempt criminal activity."

"How comforting." His appetite gone, Alex threw his napkin on the table.

"No harm came to either Miss Lacey or your grandmother. They seemed to have an enjoyable evening."

Darby's patronizing tone grated on Alex's last nerve. He gripped the arms of his chair. "*How* enjoyable?"

Darby's fork froze halfway to his mouth, and his eyes flashed with amusement. "Don't tell me you've fallen for the wallflower."

Bloody hell. His head pounding, Alex lunged across the table and grabbed a fistful of Darby's jacket. A glass tipped and china clattered. Heads turned. "*Don't* call her that."

Darby looked down at his jacket like he couldn't make sense of what was happening.

Alex cursed. What the hell was he doing, picking a fight with his best friend? He unclenched his fist and sat back, ashamed but still steaming.

Darby's nostrils flared as he spoke through gritted teeth. "Have you lost your mind?"

Maybe he had. "I don't care for the way you talked about Miss Lacey."

"The way *I* talked about her?" Darby snorted. "That's rich—pretending to defend her honor when *you* gave her the name in the first place. Bloody hypocrite." His chair legs screeched against the floor as he pushed away from the table. "Find someone else to play guard next time."

Shit. Alex dragged a hand down his face. "Look, I'm an ass and I know it."

Darby called over his shoulder. "The whole world knows it."

"Would it make you feel better if I told you that I banged the hell out of my knee when I went to grab you?"

"It does, actually."

"Good, then sit down and let me buy you another drink."

"That's a pathetic excuse for an apology." Darby stalked back to the table and slumped into his chair. "You're buying dinner too."

"Fair enough." Alex took a deep breath. "I regret giving Miss Lacey and her sisters the name. It was a stupid, offhand comment that should have been forgotten the moment I said it. But for some godforsaken reason, it spread like bloody dandelion seeds in a windstorm. No matter how much I might wish to retract the words, I can't."

"I see. So instead, you've decided you'll throttle anyone who utters the word *wallflower*? An excellent plan," Darby said drolly.

"What would you do?" Alex countered.

Darby shrugged. "You might start by apologizing to them."

He wished to hell he could. It would ease his conscience . . . but now that they'd kissed, the truth would hurt her. "I can't."

Staring into his glass as he swirled his brandy, Darby nodded. "Because you care for her—Miss Lacey?"

Alex shot his friend a look that warned he should tread lightly. "I like her."

"You shouldn't have any trouble charming her into your bed." Darby tipped his glass back to drink, as though he had no idea that Alex was alarmingly close to knocking his teeth out.

"I didn't say I wanted her in my bed. I said *I like her.*"

Darby raised a brow. "So you don't want her in your bed?"

Damn it, of course he did. Ever since they'd kissed, he'd thought of little else. But if he tried to seduce her, he'd be just the sort of scoundrel she thought he was—and that wasn't truly him.

On the other hand, maybe she preferred his rakish charade to the real person beneath. After all, he definitely hadn't been acting like a gentleman when they kissed, and she'd seemed to like kissing. What he'd give to introduce her to passion. To watch her come apart in his arms.

But deep down, he knew she deserved more than a few nights of pleasure—and he was too heartless, too damaged to give her anything more.

"My relationship with Miss Lacey is none of your

concern," Alex said evenly. "But I would appreciate your help in keeping her—and my grandmother—safe."

"I'll do what I can," Darby agreed, "but we're fighting an invisible, unknown enemy. I wish the coward would just come forward and do the honorable thing— challenge you to a duel."

"Believe me, so do I."

Beth tried not to stare at the clock. Alex was out. He had not joined her and his grandmother for dinner, nor had he made an appearance in the drawing room afterward. Of course, he was permitted to spend his evenings however he liked, and he was certainly under no obligation to inform her of his whereabouts. He'd made no promises—either spoken or unspoken—about their budding relationship, and he owed her nothing.

But she did wonder where he was—and who he was with.

She told herself that her impatience stemmed from the need to consult him regarding an important element of the dowager's redecorating plans. It had naught to do with the desire to see him—or to test whether the spark between them would ignite once again.

The duchess had retired two hours ago, but Beth still wore her dinner gown, thinking it would be more appropriate for a meeting with the duke than her night rail. But she'd passed the time reading the book on mythological creatures while sprawled on her bed, and now her slippers were off, her skirt was wrinkled, and her hair was coming undone.

Midnight was her deadline, she decided. If he wasn't

home by then, she would lock her door, undress, and climb into bed.

And in the morning, she'd advise the duchess to pick the wallpaper adorned with pink roses and turtledoves—the duke's masculinity be damned.

Two minutes left. Sighing, she sprang off her bed, loosened the laces of her gown, and threw open the doors of her armoire with considerably more force than was necessary.

And then she heard the duke come in the front door.

Blast. She wanted to intercept him before he secluded himself in his study so she could avoid returning to *The Scene of the Ravishment*. Or ravishment*s*, as the case may be.

With no time to tighten her laces, she plucked a shawl off of her chair, grabbed the dowager's wallpaper samples, and dashed out of her bedchamber. As she glided down the staircase, she spotted the duke in the foyer limping toward his study—a lion retreating to his den.

But she would not feel sorry for him. Wounded or no, he was *still* a lion.

"Your grace," she called.

His head snapped up, and he looked around, making sure they were alone. "Beth. Why are you awake?" At the sight of his disheveled hair, broad shoulders, and lean hips, her traitorous heart beat faster.

"I require a moment of your time. I've a question regarding your study."

"So late?" His words felt like a slap to the face. Naively, she'd thought he might be happy to see her. Or that he might want to pick things up where they'd left off the day before. Pure foolishness.

"Yes," she said matter-of-factly. "You forget, I am all that stands between you and a study fit for a nine-year-old princess."

He shot her a weary smile. "Fine. We'll discuss the decorating crisis in my study."

"I thought that perhaps we could meet in the drawing room," she said.

He glanced down the corridor like it was a five-mile stretch of highway. "If we must." Stoically, he began walking, dragging his left leg with each step.

"Very well." Beth heaved a sigh. "The study will suffice."

She followed him there and waited impatiently as he lit the lamp.

"Here we are," he said, facing her and leaning a hip on the edge of his desk. "I am at your disposal, ready to deal with the emergency at hand."

Scowling at his sarcasm, she handed him three samples and plopped into his leather chair. "Your grandmother has narrowed the wallpaper choices to these three."

He shuffled through them, holding each at arm's length. "I think we can rule out the roses and doves." Recklessly, he tossed the sample over his shoulder.

Beth huffed in protest. "Have a care! I need to return those to the dowager's escritoire in the morning—before she discovers they're missing."

He arched a dark brow. "I did not realize that this project would involve so much subterfuge."

Pressing her fingertips to a temple, she asked, "I already knew that the floral wouldn't pass muster. Which of the other two choices do you like?"

He shrugged. "Either is fine with me. You decide."

Oh no. She'd waited for hours in order to solicit his opinion—and she *would* have it. "Surely you have a preference."

Shaking his head, he tried handing them back to her. "They look the same to me."

"Look again." She shoved herself out of the chair, incredulous. "One of these will cover your walls from chair rail to cornice. It will determine the palette and set the mood for the entire room for at least a decade to come."

He scratched his head as though thoroughly perplexed. "You really want me to choose one?"

"Why do I feel like I'm speaking in a foreign tongue? Yes, you must choose. The whole point of this foolish exercise is for you to maintain a modicum of control over your surroundings. You may not abdicate the decision."

"But I trust you. And I confess that I don't really care about the wallpaper . . . as long as you're near." He laid the samples on his desk, as if to signal the conversation was over.

Well, it wasn't.

She snatched up one of the papers and waved it in front of his face. "The blue-gray scrollwork on a cream background is elegant and understated."

He crossed his arms and smiled, clearly enjoying himself. "If you like it, it's fine."

"We're aiming for something better than *fine*." She waved the other paper—a subtle silver and white brocade. "This one would provide more of a blank canvas, allowing your artwork to make more of a statement."

She'd no sooner uttered the words than they both turned their heads to gaze at the painting of Phyllis.

"So," she said, still staring at the freakishly large-headed horse, "the blue-gray scrollwork it is."

"That was shockingly easy. I told you that you didn't need me," he teased.

"Indeed." Exasperated, she gathered the samples and collected her shawl from the chair. "In the future I shall endeavor to refrain from bothering you with such trivial concerns. Good night."

But before she could manage to take two steps toward the door, he tugged on the laces dangling at the side of her gown, halting her in her tracks. "What if I told you that I *like* it when you bother me? That I *live* for the moments when you bother me? That the last quarter of an hour has been the best part of my *entire* day?"

Beth's breath hitched in her throat. "You have an odd way of showing it, your grace."

"Alex," he reminded her, winding her laces around his fist. As he slowly pulled her closer, his brown eyes promised all sorts of wicked delights. Her belly did a cartwheel in response.

"Tell me," he said, "did anything more than wall-paper bring us together this evening?"

This was the flirtation she'd craved—but she'd sooner die than admit it. "The dowager did mention a new carpet. I thought it best not to overwhelm you."

"Thank you for taking pity. The wallpaper almost did me in."

He continued to hold her captive, looking at her mouth very much like he wanted to kiss her. Much to her relief—or was it disappointment?—he didn't.

It would be so easy to lean into him and let desire take over. But as much as she longed to kiss him, she didn't want to be one more conquest. For all she knew, Alex could have spent the entire evening in the arms of a beautiful widow or skilled courtesan. He could have come directly from another woman's bed—and the thought was more than Beth could stomach.

"I should go," she said firmly.

Reluctantly, he released the laces. "I understand." Surprise and hurt flickered across his face. "But before you leave, I have a favor to ask."

Chapter EIGHTEEN

Between his aching knee, his skirmish with Darby, and a would-be murderer on the loose, Alex was having a terrible, horrible, no good, very bad day. Thinking he'd spare Beth his foul mood, he'd spent the evening at his club and returned home late. Like a schoolboy out past his curfew, he'd tried to sneak into the house undetected.

But she'd caught him—and he wasn't half as dismayed as he should have been. Indeed, his pulse raced at the sight of her.

Now, after he'd endured a boring and seemingly endless conversation that he'd engaged in just to keep her near—about *wallpaper*, of all things—she was ready to bolt. The moment that she'd solved her dilemma of scrollwork versus brocade or some such nonsense, she was going to leave—and just when he'd been on the verge of kissing her.

He wasn't ready to let her go.

"A favor?" Instantly on her guard, Beth crossed her arms. "What is it?"

Alex grinned. "Will you pull off my boot?"

"Your boot," she repeated, dumbfounded.

"My valet has no doubt retired for the night, and my knee's too swollen to bend." An understatement—his leg was about as flexible as the trunk of an oak tree.

"I've never removed a man's boot, but I can't imagine it's very difficult." She pointed at the leather armchair. "Sit."

He hobbled to the chair, fell into it, and raised his leg onto the footstool.

Standing with hands propped on her hips, she cast an assessing glance at his leg. "Is it going to hurt when I pull?"

"Don't worry about me," he said, gripping the arms of his chair. "Do your worst."

Tentatively, she reached for his boot heel and raised it. "Ready?"

"Fire away."

She gave a gentle tug, and when it failed to do the trick, leaned back and yanked with all her weight.

His boot shifted, but his leg was like a sausage stuffed in a too-tight casing. The leather squeezed like a vise.

"Am I hurting you?"

He scoffed as though it didn't feel like a thousand pins were stabbing his leg. "Of course not."

Her cheeks turned pink from the effort of pulling, and when the boot didn't budge, she let go of the breath she'd been holding and carefully set his leg on the footstool. "We might need to cut it off."

"I hope you're talking about my boot and not my leg," he quipped, wiping the perspiration from his brow.

"Then you might want to refrain from vexing me in the future." She leaned over and inspected his knee more closely, feeling the area around the top of his boot. "I can't even slide a finger between your leg and the boot."

"Try one more time?" he asked.

She shot him a skeptical look. "Fine. But it this doesn't work, I'm fetching my shears." Lifting his leg again, she said, "On the count of three. One, two, *three*."

Bracing himself with his good leg, he pulled himself backward while she tugged on the heel of his boot. Slowly, the leather inched downward, squeezing the flesh around it. "Almost there," he said through clenched teeth. "Don't give up."

She didn't. Indeed, she tugged so hard that he almost shot out of his chair.

And just when he thought the situation hopeless, the boot popped free like a champagne cork.

He slammed against the chair, and Beth staggered backward, crashing into a small table and landing sprawled on the carpet.

Dear God. He dove to her side. "Are you hurt?" Brushing a stray curl off her cheek, he turned her face to his.

She blinked, shifted her weight, and pulled a book from beneath her back. Setting it aside, she sat up. "Thank goodness it was nothing fragile."

His heart still pounded with worry. "You didn't answer me, Beth. Are you hurt?"

She smiled, as though his concern amused her. "A

little embarrassed, but otherwise fine." With a sigh, she glanced at the toppled table, a candlestick and flint box that had fallen off it, and his boot.

"Thank heaven."

"We did it," she said proudly. Then she looked down at his bootless leg. "You should let the doctor examine that again tomorrow."

"You're sure you're all right?" He stood on his good leg and pulled her to her feet. "I should never have asked you to help me. You're not a valet."

"I didn't mind. I rather like being needed, if you must know. Besides, if I hadn't helped, you would have had to go to bed wearing one boot. Shall I help you with the other one?" she offered. "It's bound to be easier."

"No. Thank you though." He sat on the stool and easily removed it. "*Why* do you like being needed?"

"Doesn't everyone want to feel useful and . . . necessary?" She righted the pie crust table and bent to pick up the items that had fallen.

"Leave them," he said curtly. "You needn't go to any more trouble."

One hand on the book, she froze. "You don't understand—I can't leave things strewn about the floor. The disorder would keep me awake."

"I believe I've already mentioned the cure for sleeplessness. Brandy or—"

"I remember," she said, quickly straightening and dusting off her hands. "Very well. If you don't need me . . ."

He *did* need her. Not for what she could do for him, but for the way she made him feel. With each day that passed, he realized it more.

But he couldn't tell her that—it wouldn't be fair to her.

". . . I shall retire. Good night, your grace—er, Alex."

"Good night, Beth."

Halfway to the door, she hesitated. "Will you be able to manage the staircase?"

Ah, hell no. It might as well have been Mount Olympus. "I'm going to sleep here." He pointed at the ancient leather chair.

Frowning, she said, "Wouldn't you be more comfortable in your bed?"

He shot her a wicked smile. "Are you propositioning me, Miss Lacey?"

Blushing prettily, she crossed her arms. "Merely offering to help you upstairs."

He considered this for approximately two seconds. If she helped him, they'd be walking hip-to-hip, with his arm around her shoulders and her arm around his waist—all while in the vicinity of his bedchamber. Decision made.

"I accept your generous offer."

She approached cautiously. "We'll take it slowly," she said, as if she could be referring to any number of things.

"Any way you like," he agreed. Just as he was about to wrap an arm around her shoulders, she ducked, and dashed behind him.

"One moment," she said, scooping the book and other fallen items off the floor. "I couldn't leave them there." She set them neatly on the table she'd righted, then retrieved his boots and stood them beside the footstool.

He arched a brow. "Feel better?"

"You have no idea." Taking her place beside him once

more, she held him firmly around his waist, the wall-paper samples in her free hand. "Don't be afraid to lean on me."

If only it were that easy. The truth was, he didn't like to lean on anyone, either physically or metaphorically. But he would make an exception tonight—for her.

They walked through the otherwise sleeping house in silence, muffling their laughs when he almost tripped on the skirt of her gown. His progress up the stairs was slow but less awkward and painful than he'd anticipated.

He suspected Beth had everything to do with that.

Even though she thought him unscrupulous, cold-hearted, and morally corrupt, she'd seen his pain and wanted to help. She liked to fix things. And it just so happened he needed a lot of fixing.

Having his arm around her shoulders felt natural and right. Her long, lithe legs occasionally bumped against his, and her shapely hip pressed against his upper thigh. They seemed to fit together perfectly. But Alex knew better.

Even if he could convince her that his reputation as a philandering rake was undeserved, he couldn't reveal who he really was or what he'd done.

Besides, she would eventually learn that he'd coined the name that had caused her, her sisters, and her Uncle untold pain. And when the truth came out—as it was bound to—she would be hurt all over again.

And yet, he craved her company. Without even try-ing, she chased away the shadows of his past and bright-ened his house. He wanted whatever part of her she was willing to give, and if that made him a greedy monster . . . well, he'd been called worse.

They reached the landing at the top of the staircase and made their way down the corridor to his bedchamber. He could have easily limped the rest of the way to his room by leaning against the wall instead of her, but he'd have to be the world's greatest idiot to send her away.

When they reached his door, she sighed in satisfaction. "Here we are. And you shall rest much more comfortably in your room."

His arm still around her slender shoulders, he leaned close to her ear. "Maybe we should ask my grandmother to install a bed in my study."

"Why? I do hope you're not planning on making these types of injuries a habit."

"No. But you never know when a bed might come in handy." Damn it, spouting innuendo came so naturally that he couldn't turn it off, even when he wanted to.

Though the darkness made her face impossible to read, he imagined she rolled her eyes. "If you wish to plop a bed in the middle of your study, it matters not to me. However, that is a conversation you will have to have with your grandmother *yourself.* Now, if you don't require anything else . . ."

He couldn't help himself. "I don't suppose you'd be willing to help me remove my trousers?"

"Good night." She released his waist and nimbly ducked out of his embrace.

"Wait," he said. "May I ask you something?"

"What is it?" She tossed her head—a subtle act of defiance that only made him want to crush her mouth with his.

"I wondered if you enjoyed yourself at the ball last night."

"I did," she answered warily, "and I believe your grandmother did as well."

"I'm sorry I missed it," he said.

She glared at him for a long moment, as though she doubted his sincerity. At last, she said, "Never fear, I predict you shall receive more than your share of ball invitations in the future." Her chilly tone didn't deter him—he knew from experience that beneath her hard shell she was warm and passionate. He only had to crack through her exterior, and if it took a bit of effort . . . she was worth it.

"True," he said earnestly. "But I would have liked to attend last night's ball . . . with you."

She sniffed. "That is exceedingly easy for you to say when your injury made it impossible."

"I would not have said it if I didn't mean it."

She stepped closer, her eyes flashing in the darkness. "And I suppose you would have asked me for the first dance, paraded me around the ballroom, and introduced me to all your important friends—if only your injury didn't prohibit it."

Chuckling, he reached for her hand and smoothed his thumb across the back. "Is that so difficult to believe?"

She pulled away. "I'm not as naïve as I appear, your grace."

"It's Alex. And what does that mean?" he said, all too aware that the conversation was a minefield.

"I am not under the illusion that you were suffering alone all evening. I trust you found a pleasant distraction."

He blinked. "You think I spent last evening with a woman?"

"Maybe. Last evening, this evening, tomorrow evening—it is none of my concern." But her voice cracked, as though she *did* care.

"Beth," he said softly, "I was here last night. Alone. And I was at my club tonight, With Darby."

"My," she sniffled. "Two whole nights without female companionship. That must be a personal record."

"I wasn't without female companionship," he countered. "I was with *you* yesterday, before the ball. And I'm here with you now."

"I'm your grandmother's companion—*not* yours."

Smiling at that, he placed a hand on her hip and drew her closer. "Even you have to admit that there is something between us."

"I don't pretend to understand it," she said breathlessly.

"Nor do I. But I will tell you this." He circled an arm around her waist. "I don't like that you danced with someone else last night."

Chapter NINETEEN

Beth huffed, indignant. "I will dance with whomever I choose."

"That doesn't mean I have to like it," Alex growled.

A shaft of moonlight shone through the window at the end of the hallway. Beth's room and the dowager's were on the opposite end of the house, leaving this entire wing to the duke. At this late hour as they stood in the doorway of his bedchamber, it was easy to imagine that only the two of them existed, and the steady pressure of his hand on her waist was both thrilling and distracting.

"How do you know I danced with someone?" she challenged.

He hesitated a second too long. "A beautiful woman always has dance partners."

Of all the—"Lord Darberville told you."

"We had dinner tonight," he admitted. "Why'd you have to dance with Coulsen?"

"Why wouldn't I? He was well-mannered and kind."

"Damn it, Beth. Most men aren't to be trusted."

Oh, that was rich. "I see. And I suppose *you* are exempt from scoundrel status?"

Ignoring her question, he said, "You don't know anything about Coulsen. You shouldn't be dancing with strangers."

"Let me make sure I understand," she said slowly, attempting to keep her temper in check. "You may consort with whomever you wish at any time of the day or night, but I am not permitted to dance in public with a gentleman to whom I've been properly introduced?"

He winced as though the evidence of his bullheadedness wasn't entirely lost on him. "Something like that."

She clenched her jaw but didn't pull away. "You are insufferable."

"That's hardly news," he grumbled.

And then the realization struck her, warming her insides. "Do you want to know what I think?" she mused.

"Always."

Sliding her palm up his chest, she tipped her face to his. "I think . . . that you are jealous of Mr. Coulsen."

"Not bloody likely." Staring at her hand on his waistcoat, he paused for the space of a heartbeat. "Maybe."

A cold corner of her heart melted a little, but she couldn't resist teasing him. "Say what you will about Mr. Coulsen. What he lacks in social standing and wealth, he makes up for in other ways."

Alex snorted. "Let me guess—he ties his cravat in a fancy knot? Or recites stilted poetry?"

Beth slipped a hand around his neck, pleased that he

didn't flinch when she touched his scarred skin. "If you must know, he is an excellent dancer, and his manners are perfection."

In a blink, he captured her wrists and pinned them to the wall behind her, pressing his hips to hers. "Good manners are highly overrated."

Before she could reply, he slanted his mouth across hers, kissing her like he wanted to claim her. Like he'd die if he couldn't have her.

Desire blossomed in her chest and slid lower. She arched her body, needing to touch more of him.

"Oh God, Beth," he murmured, grazing her neck with his lips. "Tell me I'm not mad. Tell me you feel it too."

He sounded so sincere, so genuine that she had to remind her heart to remain aloof. She was no one special to him. If he was jealous, it wasn't because he harbored tender feelings toward her. He'd said himself that a dog always wanted another dog's bone.

She couldn't let herself be taken in, or worse, fall in love.

On the other hand, she wasn't going to walk away from this—a chance to grow closer to Alex, to connect with him on another level . . . to peek into his wounded soul.

"Yes," she whispered. "I feel it too."

"Come with me." He laced his fingers through hers, pulled her into his bedchamber, and closed the door behind him. "Stay here," he said, "while I light a lamp."

Nodding, she closed her eyes, imagining what the infamous duke's bedchamber must look like. A massive bed heaped with tasseled pillows? Silk bedsheets in decadent red and black? Walls lined with paintings of naked couples engaged in scandalous acts?

She felt his hand on her hip and opened her eyes, fully prepared for the shocking display that awaited her.

Only, the room, now dimly lit, looked rather ordinary. Masculine, yes—but tasteful. "Oh," she said, taking in the muted blues and browns. "It's not what I expected."

"You were thinking something more along the lines of a bordello?"

She shrugged. "Yes, actually."

"Beth," he said, kissing the back of her hand. "There's something you should know."

"I don't need to know everything," she protested. "It's probably better if I don't."

"I've never brought a woman to my room before."

She told her silly heart to hold firm. "You've probably never had an eligible woman living under your roof. If you had . . ."

"That's not fair," he scolded. "Why can't you believe that *this*"—he pulled her body flush with his—"is special?"

She *wanted* to. But the people she trusted invariably let her down. Her own father—a vicar—had gambled and played so deep that he'd secretly wagered her older sister's hand in marriage. And when her parents died suddenly, most of her relatives had turned their backs on her and her sisters. More recently, when they'd become laughingstocks of the ton, Beth's few friends had abandoned her.

But maybe Alex would be the one to prove her wrong. Maybe he would restore her faith.

"Make me believe," she whispered, pressing her forehead to his. "Show me this is real."

"Real?" He caressed her cheek, thoughtful. Then he said, "Do you believe in dragons?"

"What does that have to do with—"

"Like the creatures in your mythology book. Do you believe in serpentlike, fork-tongued dragons?"

Dear God. Maybe he'd been hit in the head as well as the knee. "Of course not," she said slowly. "By definition, mythological creatures are just that—make-believe."

"What would you say if I told you that I could show you a dragon?"

"In a book?" She was doubting the wisdom of entering his bedchamber. With every twist of the conversation, she realized she was in way over her head.

"Not in a book. Right here, with me."

"I wouldn't believe you." Unless *dragon* was some sort of euphemism for his . . . that is, perhaps he used it to refer to his—

Good heavens.

He smiled, his white teeth gleaming in the dark. "Come." Pulling her by the hand, he limped around the end of his four-poster bed and swept aside thick curtains to reveal French doors leading to a small balcony. He opened the doors and led her through, guiding her to the wrought-iron railing that overlooked a lush garden. A warm breeze rustled the tree leaves and kissed her skin.

"You have a pet dragon living among your rose bushes?" she asked.

"No, not down there." He pointed to the northern sky.

"Up there." Pinpricks of light shone through a velvety black backdrop.

"Is it an invisible dragon?" she asked, skeptical. "Or perhaps it's flown away? Because I'm still not seeing it."

"It's there," he said confidently. "If you know where to look." Shifting her in front of him, he lowered his head so his eyes were level with hers and pointed to a spot on the horizon. "Do you see that steeple in the distance?"

"I think so." Her hands braced on the railing, she was very aware of his hard body behind hers and his breath near her ear.

"Follow a straight line directly above it to the brightest star. That's the ear of the dragon—one point of the triangle that forms his head."

"Oh," she whispered, oddly touched. "A dragon made of stars."

"A real dragon. He's Ladon, charged with guarding the golden apples."

"I remember the story," she said. "Hercules had to steal the apples as one of his twelve labors."

Alex moved his outstretched arm, outlining the serpent. "The creature's body winds up and slightly to the left, then way over to the right, and curls up again."

She leaned into the solid wall of his chest as she squinted at the stars, not really seeing a dragon—but not really caring.

"Sometimes," he said softly, "things that seem fantastical can be real. *Now* do you believe?"

"I think I might be starting to," she admitted.

"Only *starting*? Then I have a little more convincing to do."

Slowly, as if they had all the time in the world, he swept aside her hair and kissed the back of her neck, kneaded her shoulders, and stroked the tops of her arms.

He was so sweet and attentive that it was easy to forget the image of him as a rake who'd pleasured at least a dozen different beautiful women in the past year. At the moment, Alex was focused on *her*. His hands on her body, his lips on her skin.

Nothing could have been more real.

Around them, the city slept, the silence punctuated only by the whisper of a breeze or the distant howl of a dog. She and Alex were queen and king of all they surveyed, and the moonlit balcony was their lofty throne.

When her knees wobbled, he turned her to face him and plundered her mouth with his. She kissed him with equal fervor, and restraint gave way to abandon. The iron railing was at the small of her back, but he held her tightly, wedging a hard thigh between her legs and letting her feel his arousal.

He *desired* her. Three cruel years of being called a wallflower had taken its toll on her confidence. No girl could hear the label day after day, and live it ball after ball, without being affected. But tonight, at least while she was in his arms, she could shrug off the name like a dowdy dress.

And be the woman she truly was, underneath.

Growling, he slid a hand up her side, cupped her breast and tweaked its tight bud with his thumb. She let her hands slide down from his waist, over his taut backside.

"Beth," he breathed, "I'll never have enough of you."

The laces of her gown already loose, her neckline

dipped shockingly low, exposing her breasts to the cool evening air. Wantonly, she gripped the rail and arched her back, eliciting an appreciative curse from him. He dipped his head, taking one of the taut peaks in his mouth. A lovely ache began there, then spiraled downward, settling in her core. "Alex," she murmured, "I need . . . you."

She knew he was going slowly for her sake, but she didn't *want* slow. Slow was tentative and ethereal and magical. She wanted powerful and primitive and *real*.

As though he understood, he wrapped an arm around her waist, lifted the hem of her gown, and rocked against her. His trousers pressed to her naked flesh, he moved in a rhythm that entranced her—and set her blood on fire.

In a million years, she'd never have guessed that she'd lose her virginity to the most infamous rake in London in the middle of the night on an open balcony.

But she was about to, and—Lord help her—she wanted him with all her heart.

"Can I touch you, Beth?" He sounded as desperate as she felt. "I want to please you."

Unable to speak, she nodded, her cheeks flaming in a mix of embarrassment and desire.

"Jesus." His hand traced a tantalizing path up the inside of her thigh, and his fingers found her entrance, teasing the warm, wet folds there and driving her mad. "Tell me what feels good," he said.

"You would know better than I." Her head lolled, and she grasped his shoulders for support as his fingers grazed the most sensitive spot.

"There," he said, his voice brimming with satisfaction.

"Yes." A beautiful tempest gathered inside her, fierce and itching to burst from the clouds.

Utterly intent on pleasing her, he bent his head to her breast once more, circling his tongue around the tip as his wicked fingers stoked the storm, bringing it closer. She could almost hear the thunder, could almost feel the ground shake—

He lifted his head abruptly and frowned. "Did you feel that?"

Dizzy with wanting, she swallowed. "What?"

Suddenly curt, almost cold, he dropped the hem of her gown and inspected the ground near their feet. "The balcony shook." Narrowing his eyes, he focused on a small crack between them and the door to his room. "Damn it. It's not safe—*go!*"

Chapter TWENTY

Alex yanked Beth away from the railing and shoved her in front of him, toward the doorway leading from the balcony to his room. Beneath her feet, the crack turned into a fissure, and the balcony tilted precariously. "Jump!"

She leaped just as the floor beneath them lurched. Alex fell backward and slammed into the iron railing, unable to see her. The balcony was still attached to the house—for now—but hung at a forty-five-degree angle.

Dear God. He couldn't bear it if anything happened to her because of him. "Beth!"

She peered over the base of the doorway, on all fours.

At the sight of her, unharmed, the vise around his chest loosened.

"Don't move," she ordered. "I'm going to get help."

"There's no time." He'd no sooner said it than the balcony shifted again. Besides, anyone who came to rescue him would know that Beth had been in his room. "Stand back—I'm going to jump."

"But your leg!"

"I'm too worried about falling to my death to feel pain."

"That's not funny," she said.

"Move out of the way." He positioned himself so he could use the railing as a springboard. "This balcony is about to fall off the side of the house."

"Be careful!" She crawled backward, and he gathered his strength, mentally counting to three.

One . . . two . . . three.

He leaped toward the house just as the balcony collapsed entirely. His body slammed against the crumbled brick and mortar, knocking the breath out of him and almost making him lose his grip. Somehow, he hung on to the bottom of the doorway by his fingertips, his legs swaying.

Through a cloud of pain, he heard Beth's voice. "Hold on, Alex. I'm going to help you up."

"Move away from the edge," he gasped. "It's not safe."

"I'll return in a moment." She disappeared from view but returned three seconds later—with his bed sheet. "When I tell you to, you're going to use this to haul yourself into the house."

She left one end next to his white knuckled hands and disappeared again. After a bit of shuffling and grunting, she called out. "Now!"

Good God. There was no way he would risk pulling her down with him. He'd use what strength he had left to try to haul himself up by his fingertips, and if he fell, maybe he'd be lucky and land in a bush. He hazarded a glance below him to check—and damn if he didn't hang directly above a pile of jagged stone and bent iron. Shit. Falling wasn't an option.

Ignoring the sheet hanging next to him, he strained to bend his elbows and lift himself. If he could place one elbow on the bottom of the doorframe, he'd have the leverage he needed to drag the rest of his body into the house.

"Alex!" Beth called to him from inside. "Grab the sheet. I've wound it around the leg of your bed and am holding onto the other end. Trust me."

He couldn't reply. Every ounce of strength he possessed was devoted to lifting himself. His arms quivered from the effort, but his elbows were bent and his head was almost level with his hands.

"Please," she urged.

Sweat trickled down the side of his face. The muscles in his forearms screamed in pain. His right hand was slipping. In two seconds, he'd lose his grip entirely. The sheet brushed against his shoulder. He had to trust Beth— with both their lives.

The sheet dangled to his right, and he lunged for it. He clutched it with one hand, then the other, relieved to discover it was secure. He closed his eyes and hung there for one second, starting to believe he might not die. On that night, at least.

Gasping for breath, he walked himself up the side of his house and spilled through the doorway into his bedchamber, somehow managing to pull the drapery rod out of the wall and on top of him.

His chest heaved as he wrestled to free himself from the curtains. His knee hurt like hell. "How was that for an entrance?" he gasped.

She knelt beside him, still frantic. "Dear Jesus. Alex, are you all right?"

"I'm fine, siren. You saved my godforsaken life. But if the noise of the balcony breaking didn't wake the whole house, the sound of the curtain rod crashing surely did. You need to go quickly," he urged, "before anyone sees you here."

Her expression one part relieved and one part dumbfounded, she made no move to go. "Why didn't you grab the sheet sooner?" she asked.

"I was afraid I'd pull you down and we'd both break our necks."

"You should have had faith in me," she said, her eyes wounded.

"I did. I do. I didn't want to risk hurting you. Look, when the sun comes up, I can thank you properly. And we can discuss all the things I did wrong tonight. But now, you need to leave."

She stood with a sigh, looking weary and, somehow, more beautiful than ever.

"If you see anyone in the corridor," he said, "pretend you were on your way here to investigate the noise."

Nodding, she looked at his bedroom, which appeared to have been ransacked. "When I came to ask you about wallpaper samples, I never imagined the night would end like this."

"It wasn't all bad," he said casually—while desperately hoping she agreed.

"No, it wasn't." Hesitating, she gave him a weak smile. "Good night, Alex."

The next morning, Alex and Darby stood in the garden, examining the rubble beneath Alex's bedchamber.

Eyeing the impressive heap of stone and metal, Darby let out a long, low whistle. "You'd never noticed a crack in the balcony floor before? No wear and tear?"

"No. It seemed solid. As structurally sound as the rest of the house."

Darby propped his hands on his hips, perplexed, then thought out loud. "Maybe someone snuck into the garden and weakened the supports underneath. They could have sawed partially through the braces, so that the balcony would give way when you walked onto it."

"That's my theory," Alex agreed. "But there's not enough of the balcony left to prove it. Even if I could find the braces in this pile, there's no way to discern whether they were intentionally compromised or merely damaged during the collapse."

"But given the totality of circumstances . . ." Darby mused.

"It seems safe to conclude this was another attempt to kill me—and it almost succeeded."

"What in the hell were you doing out on the balcony in the middle of the night?" Before the question was even out of Darby's mouth, a knowing gleam lit his eyes. "Entertaining a beautiful woman, perhaps?"

"No," Alex said—maybe a bit too sharply.

"Easy, old chap. Your secret's safe with me."

"I don't know what the hell you're talking about." But

Alex's heart pounded. Darby couldn't know about Beth. No one could.

"It all makes sense now. Even the sturdiest of balconies is no match for London's most legendary lover."

For the love of—*This* was how rumors started. "Is something wrong with your hearing? No one was with me."

Darby rocked from his toes to heels and back again, amused. "If you say so." More soberly, he asked, "What next?"

"I'm going to track down Newton and Haversham to find out what they know about this latest accident."

"Assuming one of them was behind it, do you honestly think they'd admit it?" Darby looked skeptical.

"No, but at the very least I can figure out if they had the time and opportunity to tamper with the braces."

Nodding, Darby said, "A sound plan. Shall we split up? I'll take one suspect, you take the other."

Only a true friend would offer to insert himself in a mess like this, and Alex couldn't ask for a better ally than Darby—even if he *had* been on the verge of punching him twice in the past two days. "Good idea. You talk to Newton. You're likely to get more out of him than I—especially if he's still fuming over our boxing match. I heard his jaw's so sore he can barely chew."

Darby looked at Alex's leg. "And your knee's so sore you can barely walk."

"My knee is fine." Er, not exactly true, but it *was* feeling better.

"Well, you look like hell."

"Thanks," Alex said dryly. "I didn't get much sleep last night." Haunted by *what if*s, he hadn't slept a wink.

What if Beth had fallen off the balcony? What if she'd been discovered in his room in the middle of the night? The possibilities had played out over and over in his head. "I'll talk to Haversham. He's been avoiding me of late."

"I'd avoid you too, if I owed you five thousand pounds," Darby said. "Incidentally, the best place to look for him is the gaming tables. Shall we meet at the club later tonight to compare notes?"

Alex hesitated. "I don't want to be away from the house any longer than necessary. My adversary—whoever he is—grows bolder by the day. I'm afraid my grandmother or another innocent party will be caught in the crossfire." Just like Beth almost had been last night. "Why don't you join us for dinner here?"

Darby nodded affably. "As long as you taste the food first."

Chapter TWENTY-ONE

"The transformation shall be spectacular!" the dowager declared. She referred to Alex's study, of course. Collapsed balcony notwithstanding, she'd talked of little else all day, leaving Beth's head swirling with scores of combinations of carpets, furniture, and ornamental pieces.

From his end of the dinner table, Alex shot Beth a pointed look that said the transformation had better not be *too* spectacular. She turned to the duchess. "While the end result will most definitely be different, I feel certain your choices will suit the duke perfectly."

He grunted, only slightly mollified. The dark circles beneath his eyes suggested he'd had even less sleep than Beth, and her brain was so fuzzy that she was having trouble forming coherent sentences. If she didn't catch up on her sleep, she'd soon sound like Uncle Alistair.

Lord Darberville had joined them for dinner, much to the duchess's delight. She even solicited the marquess's opinion on velvet drapes during the dessert course. He'd good-naturedly confirmed that solid midnight blue was an impeccable choice, sure to complement the duke's eyes. The marquess's tongue-in-cheek comment was lost on the dowager but elicited a surly growl from Alex.

Beth had barely swallowed her last bite of pastry when he announced, "Darby and I have a few matters to discuss but will join you ladies in the drawing room shortly."

"Excellent, my dear," the dowager said. "I was just thinking that I'd like to see how the chair fabric will look next to the walls. For the life of me, I can't figure out what I did with those wallpaper samples. They must be buried in the mess atop my escritoire."

Oh dear. Alex coughed, and Beth made a mental note to locate the samples after the duchess went to bed—provided they weren't at the bottom of the balcony rubble in the garden. "I'm sure they'll turn up somewhere," she said, offering her elbow to the dowager and escorting her from the dining room.

Beth wished she could stay and hear the men's conversation. If she hadn't known the duchess would frown upon it, she'd have been tempted to press her ear to the door. She suspected the discussion had something to do with the balcony, and she prayed that no one but Alex knew she'd been there last night when the ground had literally crumbled beneath their feet.

An hour later, the men still hadn't joined them, and the dowager began to doze off while sitting at her escritoire, gazing at sketches. Yawning, she rubbed her eyes beneath her spectacles, then straightened her desktop.

"My eyes are crossed from looking at these books all day. I'm for bed."

"Let me see you to your room," Beth offered.

"No, you stay and make my apologies to Alexander and Lord Darberville," the duchess replied wearily. "Then see that you retire early as well—you look as exhausted as I. I'm sure it's the result of our decorating efforts, and I'm most grateful for your help."

Beth blushed. If the duchess knew the extent to which Beth had helped, she'd be shocked and dismayed. "We'll resume tomorrow, immediately after breakfast, if you wish."

"Indeed. No rest for the wicked, you know." The dowager winked and squeezed Beth's hand before gliding from the room.

Beth walked around the perimeter of the drawing room, lingering at the spot nearest the dining room and straining to hear a snippet of the men's conversation, but the walls proved vexingly thick.

She was contemplating eavesdropping in earnest when Alex suddenly strode into the room, making her heart beat faster. "Where is Lord Darberville?" she asked.

"He had to leave. We didn't intend to talk for so long. Where is my grandmother?"

"In her room. She could barely keep her eyes open."

"So we are alone." His eyes crinkled and his mouth curved into a knee-melting smile.

"Relatively speaking," she whispered. "There are still some servants about."

Taking her hand and pulling her toward the settee, he said. "I wasn't planning on ravishing you. But if you'd like me to . . ."

She wasn't about to let him avoid a real conversation. "Alex, is something going on that I should know about?" She sat beside him—close, but not distractingly so.

"What do you mean?" he said, wincing as he stretched out his injured leg.

"I sensed some tension between you and Lord Darberville at dinner. Does it have anything to do with the balcony? Does he know I was there when it happened?"

"No," he replied quickly. "No one knows, and I intend to keep it that way."

Relieved, she said, "I keep thinking how fortunate we were. You could have died. I could have been discovered. Instead, the only casualty was your balcony."

"Fortunate, indeed," he said drolly. Squeezing her hand, he gazed into her eyes. "I had hoped the night would end differently."

Beth had too. But perhaps it was for the best. If she wasn't the innocent she once was, at least she hadn't been thoroughly compromised. "I know."

"I'm glad we have the opportunity to talk."

There was a catch in his voice that made her sit up straight. "Talk about what?" she asked warily.

"The deal we made."

Good heavens. "Is this about the wallpaper?" she asked. "Because if you've changed your mind about the blue-gray scrollwork, I can inform your grandmother."

Regret washed over his face. "It's not about my study. Honestly, at this point she can paint it pink for all I care. Circumstances have changed. I need you and my grandmother to move out—as soon as possible."

His words were a slap in the face. "But . . . you've only delivered one wish. True, you've started the second,

but it's far from fulfilled, and . . . and . . . you promised."
Blast. She was rambling on about their deal when she
really didn't give a fig about it, apart from what it meant
to the duchess.

Beth thought that perhaps she'd seen a change in him.
That he'd softened in his stance regarding his grandmother. That he'd enjoyed spending more time with her
of late. And that, in the process, he might have let down
some of his walls—and developed feelings for Beth.

How foolish she'd been. While she'd been secretly
dreaming of reforming the world's greatest rake, he'd
been counting the days till she and his grandmother
were gone. And now, apparently tired of waiting, he
wanted to speed up their departure.

"I know we had a bargain," he said, "and I wish I
could honor it. But for reasons I can't explain, I must insist that you and my grandmother leave."

She twisted her hand free of his and scooted back.
"You can't explain your reasons?"

Stone-faced, he wouldn't meet her eyes. "No."

"Well, allow me to try. You thought you would play
a game with me—because you imagined a wallflower
would be an easy conquest."

His jaw dropped. "Beth—it's nothing like that."

"Don't deny it," she said, willing herself not to cry.
"You relished the challenge of seducing an innocent.
But things didn't go exactly as planned, and now you've
reversed course, deciding that an argumentative, awkward virgin isn't worth your effort."

"That's not true." Leaning forward, he swallowed. "I
care for you. And that's precisely why I need you to
leave."

"You're spouting nonsense." Too hurt and proud to share the settee with him, she stood and paced the carpet. "Why even bother with lies? Have some integrity and admit that you've grown tired of me. It certainly didn't take long," she said dryly. "What has it been—a week?"

"Stop." He stood, squarely blocking her path. "Don't do this," he begged. As if it had been *her* choice to end their budding relationship.

She jabbed a finger at his chest. "Does my honesty offend you? What would you have me say?"

Placing a warm, steadying hand on her hip, he said, "Tell me I'm an idiot. Or a scoundrel or degenerate. But *don't* call me a liar—not when I say that I care for you."

Her eyes burned and her throat swelled, blast him. "You have a very odd way of showing it."

Jesus, he'd botched this horribly. Raking a hand through his hair, Alex took a turn pacing the length of the room.

He'd considered telling Beth about the attempts on his life, but when he'd discussed the idea with Darby after dinner, his friend had counseled against it, reasoning that the less she knew, the safer she'd be. Alex was inclined to agree—except that his relationship with Beth complicated everything. And Darby knew nothing of what had transpired between them.

Seeing her now, hurting—and worse, doubting his feelings for her—made him think twice.

Facing her, he took a deep breath. "When the balcony fell off the side of the house last night, you could have died."

"I suppose we both could have," she said. "What does that have to do with anything?"

"The balcony collapse wasn't an accident." Damn it, he'd opened Pandora's Box. There would be no going back now.

She eyed him warily. "Someone knew we were together on your balcony?"

"Not necessarily. I suspect someone weakened the supporting beams days before, betting that I would walk out of my bedroom one night for a breath of air—and that it would be my last."

Beth pressed her fingertips to a temple. "Why would anyone do that?"

"An excellent question. I'm working on finding the answer."

"Are you certain? About the balcony, that is? Buildings age . . . accidents happen."

"It's not the first accident. I was poisoned recently. And not long after, my coach rolled over."

She seemed to digest this for a moment. "Your knee injury—did it truly happen during a boxing match?"

He nodded. "No one to blame but myself for that one."

Sinking onto the settee as though her bones had turned to jelly, she gazed up at him. "Someone tried to poison you," she repeated.

"Yes. And a few days later, a mysterious broken axle caused a serious coach accident. And then the balcony."

She blinked. "Someone really is trying to kill you?"

"I'm afraid so. *Now* do you see why I don't want you and my grandmother staying here one more day than is necessary?" He *needed* her to understand he wasn't the cold, heartless bastard he appeared to be.

Holding his breath, he waited for her answer—and a shot at redemption in her eyes.

Her chin trembled. "Yes."

He sat beside her and took her hand in his. "I don't *want* you to leave, but I couldn't bear it if something happened to you. The mere possibility keeps me awake at night."

"I believe you, Alex."

A huge weight lifted off his chest, and he leaned forward, pressing his forehead to hers. "Thank you."

She sniffled, her blue eyes shining with emotion. "But there's no reason to believe I'm in danger. *You're* the target, unfortunately, and you should have told me before now. I can help you."

Good God. This was exactly what he'd been afraid of. He sat up and shook his head firmly. "I don't need your help, and I don't want you involved."

"Like it or not, I already am. You said yourself that there's something between us." She looked down at their entwined hands. "Don't push me away. I harbor no false illusions about the future. I know our respective roles. I'm the prickly wallflower destined for spinsterhood; you're the brooding duke destined for a life of philandering. But right now, you *need* me, and I . . . well, I need to be needed."

Chapter TWENTY-TWO

Lord help her, Beth believed him. Alex wasn't trying to rid himself of his grandmother and her meddling companion, after all. He was trying to *protect* them.

When, in truth, *he* was the one who required protection.

"You have that all wrong. Worse, you don't understand," he said, frustration oozing from each word. "I cannot fully devote myself to finding the would-be killer if I'm sick with worry over you and my grandmother."

She understood wanting to protect family and the people one cared about all too well. It was why she couldn't leave Alex.

"I need to know that both of you are safe," he said. "Once I discover who the culprit is and deal with him, you may return."

It was a sweet sentiment, but Beth knew better than to imagine a long-term arrangement, wherein she lived under the same roof with Alex and his grandmother. Beth's relationship with the duke was like the fireworks at Vauxhall, lighting up the sky for an all-too-brief moment before fizzling out.

When he tired of her—as he most surely would—he'd revert to his rakish ways, spending night after night in the arms of London's most beautiful women.

And while she knew it to be inevitable, she didn't wish to witness it with her own two eyes. When she moved out of the duke's house, she wouldn't be coming back.

But she wasn't at all ready to say good-bye to him yet.

"I need some time to come to terms with this news," she said. However, what she really needed was time to devise a plan—a way she could help Alex before gracefully exiting his life with her dignity intact. She wasn't foolish enough to imagine her *heart* would remain intact, but she'd have a lifetime to lick her wounds.

For now, she'd focus all her energy on convincing Alex to allow her to stay. She could be quite persuasive when she put her mind to something, and lately she'd acquired a new weapon in her arsenal: seduction. She hadn't yet become a master at wielding it, but she was a quick study.

And she was learning from the best.

"Time is in short supply," Alex said. "Every day you remain here places you at greater risk of injury—or worse."

"I'm not asking for days. Come to me later tonight, when we can talk freely about our options."

"There are no options, Beth. You must—"

The sound of servants talking in the corridor cut him short, and he stood quickly, putting distance between them.

"I think I shall check on the dowager before retiring for the night," Beth said loudly. In a whisper, she added, "I'll wait for you."

It was after midnight when Alex hesitated outside Beth's bedchamber. He probably shouldn't have come, but he couldn't forego the chance to hold her one last time. And before she left, he needed to convince her that she was no more a wallflower than he was a rake. Making a clean breast of it wasn't going to be easy, but she deserved to know the truth.

He reached for the handle, found the door slightly ajar, and quickly entered, turning the key in the lock behind him.

Bathed in the soft glow of a bedside lamp, Beth sat in a chair with her feet tucked under her, wearing nothing but a diaphanous night rail. The long, loose waves of her hair begged to be touched; her luminous, dewy skin begged to be kissed.

Christ. She was the antithesis of a wallflower. Most definitely a siren. And in that moment, he knew that no matter how noble his intentions had been, he was powerless to resist her.

Upon seeing him, she smiled serenely, set down her book and glided toward him, her breasts bouncing with each step. Twining lithe arms around his neck, she pressed her body against his. "I was worried you wouldn't come."

"You should have worried that I *would*," he growled, running his hands over the silky fabric of her nightgown.

"No. I'm glad you told me about the attempts on your life. Now I understand why you want your grandmother to move to the country. I shouldn't have assumed the worst about you."

"I'm no angel." It was an admittedly half-hearted attempt to warn her off. "If I were, I wouldn't have come to your room."

"I'm no angel either." She brushed soft lips above his shirt collar. "If I were, I wouldn't have invited you."

Already painfully aroused, he moaned. "We should talk. About how to effect the move as quickly as possible. I know my grandmother will be disappointed about not having time to finish redecora—"

"Shh." She pressed a cool fingertip to his lips. "We can discuss those details later. You haven't slept in two days. Come, lie down."

Beth was right. He was dead tired and probably not in the best frame of mind to make decisions. The bed looked incredibly inviting. So did she.

Taking his hand, she turned and pulled him toward the four-poster, her deliciously curved bottom swaying as she walked. "I'm glad I don't have to remove your boots," she teased, patting a pillow near the upholstered headboard.

"I'll rest for a bit if you will too," he said, laying his head on the feather pillow and sinking into the thick mattress.

"I napped earlier today, while you were out." Nimble

as a cat, she climbed onto the bed and leaned over him, running her fingers lightly through his hair and over his face. "While I was lying here, I thought about last night. I was remembering the stars in the sky and the breeze on my skin and your hands on my body. But mostly I dreamed of how lovely you made me feel . . . when you touched me."

Jesus. "Beth, there's something you should—"

"And then I thought that I would like to touch you. To make you feel the same way."

He swallowed, momentarily speechless—and hard as a rock.

"You don't have to do anything except tell me what you like," she said, shrugging adorably. "I'm quite new at this."

"You could have fooled me." He took one of her hands, turned it over, and pressed a kiss to the palm. "I like everything about you, Beth. Everything."

Seemingly pleased, she opened his shirt at the front, pushed it to his sides, and stared at his naked torso. As her fingers traced the contours and planes, lingering on the fuzz above the waistband of his trousers, his heart pounded. Hell, it was all he could do not to haul her down and crush her mouth with his.

"I want to taste you." She didn't wait for him to grant permission, but rather, bent her head and trailed kisses over his neck, chest, and abdomen. As she leaned over him, her silky hair tickled his chest and her night rail gaped open, revealing the pink tips of her full breasts. That did it.

Growling, he flipped her over and pressed a leg between hers. "I can't lie still while you touch me."

She smiled seductively. "You could touch me back."

Before the words were out of her mouth, he slid a hand up the inside of her leg and kneaded the supple flesh of her thigh. "Out on the balcony last night . . . is this what you liked?" he asked.

"Not quite," she said breathlessly.

He cupped her bottom, caressing the sweet curve just above her leg. "How about this?" he teased.

"You're getting closer."

At last, he stroked the spot that would give her pleasure. "And now?"

A moan escaped her as she opened to him. "Yes."

Thank God—and the widow who'd pulled him into a pantry during a ball two years ago and showed him, quite explicitly, how to pleasure a woman in this way. With the widow, it had been a lesson—a perfunctory act in which he felt more like a detached observer than a participant.

But being with Beth was all-consuming. Her pleasure was his, and he wanted nothing more than to feel her come apart . . . for him.

He pulled down the collar of her nightgown and took the peak of her breast in his mouth, sucking lightly.

"Alex." She gripped his shoulder and whimpered with need. God, he hoped it was with need. He wanted this, her introduction to passion, to be amazing for her.

If his sexual prowess was half as impressive as the ton believed, she'd be crying out in ecstasy by now. The truth was that he hadn't bedded a woman in over two years . . . and would have to make up for what he lacked in skill with pure determination and effort.

He brushed his lips over her skin, loving the taste of

her, and skimmed his palms over her curves, reveling in the perfection of her body.

He speared his fingers through her hair and poured everything into the kiss that he could not say. *I'm not the man you think I am. You are more than I deserve. And I want you more than anything.*

He touched her, listening intently for every hitch of her breath, every sigh and every moan, seeking to discover precisely what brought her the most pleasure. Humbled by her trust in him and awed by her beauty, he committed it all to memory. The birthmark to the right of her navel, the ticklish spot behind her knee, the sensitive skin at the curve of her neck.

Though he was far from a legendary lover, Beth seemed to appreciate his efforts.

Flushed with arousal, she clutched fistfuls of his loose shirt. "Alex," she panted. "This feels . . . oh, God."

As her body tensed and the wave overtook her, he held her, reveling in the glorious power of her release.

A minute later, she smiled sleepily at him, looking both sated and stunned. "I never knew."

The hell of it was, neither had he. Brushing a curl away from her face, he asked, "How do you feel?"

"Hmm," she said, rolling her eyes mischievously. "I feel like that was extremely enlightening."

"Enlightening is good," he said, both pleased and relieved with her verdict.

She propped herself on an elbow and gazed down at him while trailing her fingertips over his chest and abdomen. "But I think that I'd like another lesson."

He closed his eyes, trying valiantly to maintain control. "Beth, I'd love nothing more. But I think we should—"

Her hand slid lower, over the front of his trousers, which barely contained his erection.

And just like that, any semblance of coherent thought was obliterated.

Chapter TWENTY-THREE

Beth could hardly believe her own daring. But she trusted Alex and was immensely grateful that at least *one* of them knew what to do.

Letting instinct guide her, she stroked the hard length of him through his trousers. Encouraged by his moans, she slipped her hand beneath his waistband and reached for—

"No," he said, pulling away and rolling off the bed onto his feet.

Good heavens. It seemed she couldn't do anything correctly.

As though privy to her thoughts, he said, "It's nothing you did. Believe me, I would love nothing more than to spend the whole night in your bed. But it wouldn't be fair to you."

She shook her head, disbelieving. She'd been under the impression that someone like him had no scruples. That he cared about nothing except taking pleasure where he could find it. Perhaps his protest was merely part of the rake's repertoire—some heartfelt words meant to seduce innocents who were reluctant to surrender their virtue.

Didn't he realize that she was *willing*? There was no need to ply her with pretty—if empty—words.

"I fail to see how spending the night in my bed would be unfair to me. Do you snore excessively or steal the sheets?"

"No." He shot her a weak smile. "It would be unfair because you can't stay. If I were to lie with you and send you on your way, I'd be the worst kind of scoundrel."

Beth had to bite her tongue. After all, he was rather *known* for being the worst kind of scoundrel, and the label had never seemed to bother him before.

Why did he hold a piece of himself back? She wanted him to trust her, to invite her in to the darkest corners of his heart. Let her chase away the demons.

When she trusted herself to speak, she said, "Very well. I've been thinking about your request that your grandmother and I leave."

"It's not a request," he interrupted. "It's a necessity. For your safety and my sanity, you need to move out of this house."

"Then I suppose you will have to tell your grandmother over breakfast. It will break her heart, of course. At this very moment, she's probably dreaming of wainscoting, draperies, and sconces."

"Beth," he pleaded. "I need your help with this. She wouldn't understand. She'd think I was simply trying to rid myself of her. And I can't hurt her like that. I'm not adept at showing it, but she's the center of my world."

She shrugged as though the admission didn't touch and cut her at the same time. It must feel lovely to be at the center of his world. Not that she wanted to encroach on his grandmother's place in his heart. "I feel certain you'll find the words to make her understand."

Dragging a hand down his impossibly handsome face, he sank onto the mattress beside her. "She cared for me after the fire. Day and night for weeks. My pain was hers, and she refused to leave my side. Not even to attend my parents' funeral."

Tamping down a wave of empathy, Beth held firm. "She's a strong woman, and she loves you."

"Indeed. If I were to tell her about the attempts on my life, she'd be beside herself—hysterical, even. I'm afraid she'd make herself sick with worry."

"I quite agree." Feigning nonchalance, she hopped off of the bed, plucked her robe from the chair, and slipped it on. "Once your grandmother recovered from the shock, I'm sure she'd go to the authorities. She might even write a letter to the king informing him of the situation." His jaw twitched at that. "Then she'd likely spend her days sitting by a window, fearing the day a messenger brings news of your demise."

"We can't tell her about the murder attempts," he said emphatically.

"I don't plan on telling her *anything*."

More stunned than angry, he approached her, imploring. "You could persuade her to move to the country without telling her the truth."

With his naked torso glistening in the lamplight, and his heated gaze focused on her, it was difficult to deny him anything, but she resolved to remain strong. "You give me too much credit," she said. "Besides, we had a deal. I'll abide by the terms we set forth earlier."

"The *deal*?" he asked, incredulous. "I inform you that someone's trying to kill me and that you and my grandmother are almost certainly in danger, and you demand that I uphold my end of an inane deal?"

"Aren't you trying to hold me to my end?" she countered.

"Well . . . yes," he stammered. "But now you know the reason *why*. It could be a matter of life and death."

"The reasons are irrelevant," she said with feigned callousness. "A deal's a deal."

"Beth." When he gazed into her eyes, she wanted to melt. He looked so sincere, so vulnerable. "Please help me."

She'd never been able to resist an earnest plea for help, and from him it was doubly hard. But she wouldn't capitulate. "Regardless of what you may believe, I do want to help—just not in the manner you'd prefer."

"What does that mean?"

"I may have a way for you to grant your grandmother's third wish *and* catch the killer."

He leveled a look at her, skeptical. "I'm listening."

Beth took Alex's hand and led him to the chair she'd been reading in earlier. She perched on a footstool opposite him and leaned in. "I presume you have a list of suspects?"

"Just two, as of now." His and Darby's inquiries earlier in the day hadn't ruled out either Newton or Haversham. Both had plenty of time and opportunity to damage Alex's balcony. "Darby and I have been keeping an eye on them, waiting for one of them to make a mistake."

"Instead of spending so much effort trying to track them down," she said slyly, "why not make them come to you?"

"I see. I should throw open the front door and invite them to dinner?"

She bit her lip. "I thought perhaps a ball."

"A ball?" He repeated, incredulous.

"Er, not just any ball . . . a masquerade."

Over his dead body—which, unfortunately, was not a stretch. "Absolutely not."

Beth stood, circled behind his chair, and trailed her fingertips up one of his arms and across his shoulders, making it damnably hard to think straight.

"Your grandmother admitted to me this morning that it's her fondest wish." She sighed. "My first inclination was to agree with you—that a masquerade would be ill-advised."

"Scores of people wearing disguises and mingling in a room with two potential murderers is a *horrible* idea—a recipe for mayhem."

She leaned close to his ear. "Unless we had a carefully orchestrated plan to unveil and capture the scoundrel."

"Beth, this isn't a serial novel featuring a bumbling, guileless villain. We're not playing a game here. I won't willingly put you, my grandmother, and a couple hundred guests at risk."

"I know that," she said soberly. "Neither would I. But with each day that passes, our enemy grows bolder. You don't know where he's lying in wait or when he will strike. If we control the setting, we have the advantage."

Though her use of the pronoun *we* warmed him, it also scared the hell out of him. She shouldn't be inserting herself into this mess. "What makes you think the real villain would come to a ball?"

"He will not want to raise eyebrows by refusing. It's the best way for him to avoid suspicion," she reasoned.

Alex pondered this. "Assuming the would-be killer *does* attend, how would we go about exposing him?"

"I haven't quite figured out that aspect of the plan," she admitted. "But I'm sure that between you, Lord Darberville, and me, we will think of something rather ingenious."

"Your confidence is impressive," he said dryly . . . but perhaps the plan had some merit.

"Do you resist because you don't wish to wear a costume?" she teased, kneading his shoulders with a sorceress's fingers.

"That's not funny." He paused for a heartbeat. "But I *do* detest costumes. Why does it have to be a masquerade ball?"

She shrugged. "Mostly, because your grandmother requested it. However, there are some benefits. If the villain believes his disguise will hide his true identity, he might be more reckless—and more inclined to make a mistake."

She had a point. "We would need to know where both suspects are at all times. Disguises would complicate things, but if we stationed someone at their houses to follow them here, we could be certain we know who is behind the masks."

"Precisely," she said, pleased as a cat. Rounding the chair, she perched on the arm, her legs tantalizingly close to his. "Shall I inform the duchess at breakfast tomorrow that her dearest wish is about to come true?"

"I still don't like it." But the citrusy scent of her hair and the sultry look in her eyes clouded his thoughts. "How quickly could you arrange the ball?"

She gazed at the ceiling as though she was making a few mental calculations. "A week." She blew out a long breath. "It won't be easy, and I'll need to fabricate a plausible reason for our haste when I tell your grand-mother of the plans . . . but I think I can make the nec-essary preparations in a week."

"No longer. Every day that you remain under my roof, we are tempting fate." He pulled her off the arm of the chair so that she plopped onto his lap. She shot him an amused smile and rested her head on his shoulder.

"Then it's settled." She yawned and cuddled closer to him.

Not quite. "There's one more thing."

She gazed sleepily up at him. "Hmm?"

"If we're not able to catch our man at the masquer-ade, you and my grandmother will need to leave the next day." He hesitated. "I'll need your word."

Beth swallowed. She'd already pushed Alex to his lim-its, and she knew it. But how would she ever accomplish everything that needed to be done in a week? Invitations, costumes, musicians, menus, decorations . . . all while assisting the duchess with her redecorating project. And at the end of that week, she would also need to say good-bye to Alex—even if his life were still in danger.

Her prolonged silence provoked him. "I won't nego-tiate any further, Beth. There can be no more excuses, no more delays. After one week, you and my grand-mother will relocate to the country. Do I have your word . . . or not?"

She had no choice. If she didn't agree, he'd be packing their bags tomorrow. "You have it."

"Thank you." She heard the relief in his voice and wished she felt a smidgen of it.

Their time together was limited—she could almost hear the clock ticking. But at least he was here now, his strong arms wrapped around her, keeping her worries at bay. "Do you think we could stay like this . . . and rest for a while?"

"I don't see why not." His husky voice caressed her skin, warming her like a quilt. She nuzzled her cheek against his bare chest, breathing in his scent and leaning into his solidness.

Sighing contentedly, she savored the feeling of closeness . . . and wondered if it could possibly last.

Maybe it didn't always have to be her against the world.

Maybe she had an ally.

She'd always had her sisters, of course, and she always would. But wouldn't it be lovely to have someone else on her side who was solely *hers*? Someone like Alex.

With their legs entwined and her hand over the steady beat of his heart, she drifted off. For tonight, at least, he was hers.

When she woke some time later, he was carrying her. She blinked in the darkness. "Alex?"

"Everything's fine," he said softly. "I'm taking you to your bed."

She snuggled into his neck. "Good." Bed was even better than the chair. They could lie on the soft mattress, his body curled around hers, until the birds began to chirp outside her window.

Tenderly, he laid her down and tucked the coverlet around her. Confused, she reached for him. "It's not dawn yet. Don't you want to stay?"

"I can't," he said curtly, and she let her arms fall. He pressed a quick kiss to her forehead. "Go back to sleep. Tomorrow will be a busy day."

Hastily, he stuffed his shirttail into his trousers. "Good night, siren."

Chapter TWENTY-FOUR

The next night, Alex squinted as he entered the windowless, smoke-filled gambling hell, giving his eyes a moment to adjust to relative darkness. Periodic shouts sounded from the far corner, where peers, tradesmen, and soldiers alike crowded around the hazard table, their fortunes hanging on a roll of the dice. With a glance at each face, Alex could discern whom fortune had favored—and whom she'd frowned upon.

He took a seat across from Haversham at a sparsely populated card table. Foxed, as usual, the viscount reclined with one arm slung over the back of his chair, his belly straining the buttons of his waistcoat. "Come now, Blackshire—give me the chance to win back my money."

"Your request presupposes that you've *paid* your debt. I think you mean to say that you'd like the chance to reduce the substantial amount you owe me."

Haversham waved a dismissive hand. "You know full

well what I mean. What do you say to a game of vingt-et-un? If I win, my debt is erased."

Alex snorted. "Those stakes are too high for one of us, and I'll give you a hint—it's not me."

The viscount lit a cigar. "That's not sporting, duke. You can't quit playing just because you happen to be up at the moment."

Rubbing the stubble on his jaw, Alex pretended to consider this. He'd come to Pall Mall looking for Haversham. Not just to escape his town house and the questions in Beth's eyes, but also because he believed in the adage *keep your enemies close*.

He had no proof that Haversham was responsible for the attempts on his life, but the man certainly had motive. If he was to blame, maybe he was inebriated enough that he'd say something to incriminate himself. "Very well. But only five hundred pounds on the game."

The viscount rubbed his hands together. "Excellent."

Alex played recklessly, taking cards when he would normally stand—and still managed to make twenty-one on two separate deals, winning easily.

Haversham's jovial mood evaporated. "What's your trick, Blackshire?" he sneered.

"I don't employ tricks," Alex drawled. "I rely on the most basic of math skills and an ounce of good sense." Both of which the viscount sorely lacked.

"It's uncanny." Haversham snorted and narrowed his bloodshot eyes. "If I didn't know better, I'd think you could predict each card before it's dealt."

"Tread lightly," Alex warned. "The last time you

accused me of cheating, I blackened your eye. Next time, I'll aim for your nose."

"I don't need to listen to this." The viscount scrawled a note, then pushed himself up from the table, indignant. "Here is my IOU. You'll have your payment shortly."

"By the end of the month, Haversham," Alex said. He was being far too generous. "A gentleman honors his debts."

"A gentleman doesn't attempt to seduce another man's wife," he spat.

"Agreed." Alex stood and smoothed the front of his jacket. "Fortunately for me, I find the wives are all too willing."

"Bastard!" The viscount shouted, eyes full of venom.

"The end of the month," Alex reminded him as he walked away. The old codger had plenty of money. It wasn't as though he'd have to sell his house or pledge the family silver. He'd simply have to pay a visit to his safe.

Though he'd had his fill of cards, Alex meandered through the tables, greeting acquaintances and enjoying a glass of brandy. He didn't want to give the appearance that he was running away from a greasy-haired man well into his fifth decade.

And he wasn't quite ready to return home—to Beth.

If he bided his time, she'd retire for the evening and he wouldn't have to see the hurt on her face. He wouldn't have to explain to her why he'd sneaked away in the middle of the night, or admit that he was plagued by nightmares that made him wake up drenched in his own sweat and shaking like a frightened boy.

He didn't like having secrets from her. But the nightmares were worse than his scars. They showed how damaged he *truly* was.

"Would a Persian carpet pair well with a gothic bookcase?" the duchess asked. She held two drawings side by side and tilted her head, considering her own question.

Beth set down the invitation list for the masquerade, padded across the drawing room, and peeked over the older woman's shoulder. "I like the geometric pattern of the carpet . . . but I suspect the bookcase is too ornate for the duke's taste."

The duchess sighed. "You're quite right, of course. I should have recognized it myself. How are the invitations coming along?"

"I've only half a dozen more to finish." Including two that she'd address to the men suspected of attempting to kill Alex. But he'd never mentioned their names last night, and she needed to know who they were.

"Why don't you let me help you?" the dowager offered.

"Thank you, but it's not necessary. I'm almost done, and you should prepare for bed. Tomorrow we will have the invitations delivered and begin contemplating our costumes."

"Normally, I'd be too excited to sleep, but I confess that redecorating the study has exhausted me. It is far more involved than I'd imagined. I'm determined to please Alexander . . . and he's rather particular."

"Yes," Beth mused. "He is."

"And his particular tastes are not limited to furnishings. Consider women."

Beth gulped. "I beg your pardon?"

"I daresay, he could have his choice of the misses on the marriage mart. Between his title, wealth, and dashing good looks, I can't imagine any young lady would refuse him. And yet—none of them has captured his heart."

Beth glanced sideways at the duchess, wondering if she suspected they'd kissed—and much more. "Maybe he doesn't wish to be captured."

"Right you are, dear. But when he finds the right woman, he won't feel as though he's being captured at all." The duchess patted Beth's shoulder. "Do not stay up too late yourself. We have much to do tomorrow— including the opera in the evening."

Blast. She'd forgotten, and she had the entire week scheduled, almost to the hour. Oh well, she'd have to make some adjustments. "I'm looking forward to it. Sleep well."

She tidied the duchess's desk, completed the remaining ball invitations, save the two for the men Alex had yet to identify, and rifled through the stack, comparing the names on the envelopes to the ones on her list. Satisfied that she'd left no one out, she reached for a blank piece of paper, intending to begin a proper list of potential costumes for Alex, the dowager, and herself. But after taxing her brain for a quarter of an hour and imagining Alex's reaction to the suggestion that he disguise himself as a Turkish sultan or a harlequin, she stuffed the paper in a drawer, cursing Alex and his particular tastes.

She wandered down to the library and plopped herself onto the sofa, reasoning that she'd accomplished more than enough for one day.

Now, she had naught to do but wait for Alex.

She supposed she could seek him out tomorrow morning and ask him for the suspects' names, but he was a slippery one, and she didn't want to risk him getting away from her again. Besides, she missed him.

So she sank into the sofa's plush cushions, tucked her feet beneath her, and rested her eyes. Sometime after she'd slipped into the twilight between waking and sleep, a creak echoed through the otherwise silent house.

She sat up and listened intently. A faint shuffling, boot heels on the marble floor, a muffled curse.

Alex was home.

Gathering her wits, she reminded herself of the ostensible reason she'd waited—the suspects' names.

She glided out of the library and found him with one foot on the bottom stair, looking heartbreakingly handsome and, unless she was mistaken . . . guilty.

His hair stood on end, like a woman had run her hands through it—repeatedly. His rumpled jacket and trousers appeared to have spent a significant portion of the night on the floor. And half of his shirttail hung loose at his side, as though he'd left *somewhere* in a rush.

Beth swallowed, telling herself not to jump to conclusions. "Good evening, your grace."

He jerked his head around and closed his eyes, clearly dismayed to have been caught creeping into the house.

"Beth," he said with forced cheer, "what a pleasant surprise."

She flicked her eyes over the bare skin at his neck. "You seem to have lost your cravat."

"What?" He looked around him, as though he expected to find it on the floor at his feet. "How odd."

"It is indeed. You must have had quite an eventful evening."

"No, no," he said quickly. "It was an ordinary night."

"I'm sure it was—for you." Hang it all, she couldn't help herself.

"Wait—you're under the impression that I—"

"It's none of my concern," she interrupted. "I only waited for you because I need the names of the suspects for the ball invitations."

"No." He crossed his arms over his vexingly muscled chest.

"What do you mean, *no*?"

"I'm not telling you who my suspects are. The less you know, the better."

"I see. You think I'm a frail hothouse flower, too sensitive to handle the truth—that I'll swoon at the sight of the villains."

"Actually, I fear the opposite—that you'll take it upon yourself to interrogate and apprehend one or both of them before I've had a chance to gather all the facts."

She sniffed. "If you take much longer to *gather all the facts,* you'll be dead."

"Allow *me* to worry about the suspects, Beth. I already regret involving you."

"That's not fair," she protested, pointing a finger at his chest. "You haven't even given me a chance. How am I supposed to invite the suspects to the masquerade if I don't know—"

She leaned forward and examined his chiseled cheek. Beneath the stubble was a distinct red smear. "Is that . . . vermilion lip rouge on your cheek?"

Frowning, he swiped at his cheek, checked his palm, and wiped it on his waistcoat. "It's nothing."

"If you say so," she said breezily—as if the evidence of another woman's lips on his face barely affected her.

As if she wasn't going to have a good cry into her pillow at the very first opportunity.

"It's not what you think." He let out a long, weary sigh. "Why don't you show me the invitation list for the ball? It's possible the suspects' names are already there."

Goodness. She hadn't even considered the possibility, and the idea that a villain could be hiding among the gentlemen on her list was rather terrifying. Somehow, she'd imagined there would be a telltale physical sign of guilt—beady eyes or a seedy mustache or the like.

"Very well," she said coolly. "My list is in the drawing room."

"After you." As he made an exaggerated wave and a slight bow, a flap of fabric near his left knee caught her eye.

"What is that on your trousers?" She was almost afraid to hear his answer.

He looked down, confused, then reached for the flap. "It's just a tear. Must have caught on something." As if that were the end of that, he stood up. "Now, let's have a look at that invitation list, shall we?"

"Wait just a moment. Why, exactly, do you look as though you've been dragged through the streets of London?" The skin at the back of her neck tingled. "Good heavens. *Have* you?"

"Of course not!" He balked, as if the suggestion were the most absurd thing he'd ever heard.

"Then I'm sure you won't mind if I have a look at that." She inclined her head toward his ripped trousers.

"Why? So you can alert my tailor? File a report with my valet?" He shrugged and turned back toward the stairs. "If you've changed your mind about having me look at the invitation list, I'll just—"

She hooked a hand around his impossibly hard arm. "Stop."

Like a thief who'd been caught red-handed, he froze and resigned himself to his fate.

She stooped to examine the rip in his trousers and found his knee bloodied beneath. Slowly, she stood and circled him, observing all the clues. His mussed hair, missing cravat, and hopelessly disheveled appearance weren't the result of a lover's tryst.

No, the truth was much worse than that.

Chapter TWENTY-FIVE

"That wasn't lip rouge on your face, was it?" Beth challenged.

Alex should have let her believe it was. "I told you it wasn't."

"Blood?"

Shrugging, he said, "Not mine." But it could have been.

Her pretty blue eyes clouded with fear. "Alex, what happened?"

There would be no wriggling his way out of this confession. He sat on the second stair and tugged on her hand, pulling her down beside him. "I was at a gambling club in Pall Mall and decided to walk the few blocks home."

She arched a brow. "By yourself?"

In an effort to lighten the mood, he said, "You may have noticed I'm not a debutante who requires a chaperone."

"Please, just tell me what happened."

"It's barely worth mentioning," he said, waving a hand. "A pair of ruffians jumped out of the shadows and attacked me—or, they tried to. But I made short work of them. Both will have the devil of a headache when they wake."

"Were you hurt?" Without waiting for his answer, she took his face in her hands, turning his head from side to side, looking for signs of injury. It was nice having her fret over him. Unnecessary, but nice.

"Nary a scratch. Although, I'll admit this *was* my favorite pair of trousers," he quipped.

"You could have been killed," she said soberly. "I don't know how you can make light of such a serious matter."

Her concern warmed him, but he didn't want her worrying. "I'm fine. Trust me, I'm perfectly capable of handling a pair of two-bit thugs." The knives they wielded *had* made things interesting—but he saw no need to mention that.

"This makes at least four attempts on your life in . . . what? Three weeks?"

"Yes, but who's counting?" He grinned.

Unamused, she bent to look at his knee once more. "I don't like the look of this wound, Alex. It's red and jagged, almost like a—" Eyes wide as saucers, she glared at him.

"I'll make sure I clean it before I go to bed. I barely feel it."

"This gash is from a knife."

"Gash? No. More like a scratch—it's not deep. See? It's not even bleeding anymore."

"You don't have to protect me, you know." She was still poking around his knee like a nursemaid—of the beautiful, sensual variety. "You think that you're sparing me, but without all the facts, my imagination conjures the worst scenarios."

What was he going to tell her? That he'd grabbed one attacker's head and bashed his face against his raised knee? Or that the other one had his blade pressed to Alex's throat before he'd flipped him over his shoulder? That he'd jogged the last two blocks home, in case the thugs had reinforcements lying in wait, ready to come after him?

"There's nothing else to tell," he lied, lacing his fingers through hers.

"Of course there isn't," she said skeptically. She stared at him for the space of several heartbeats, giving him a chance to change his story. When he didn't, she sighed. "Very well. We're going up to your room to clean this *gash*. Right now."

He knew better than to object. And at least she'd given up on learning the suspects' names—for now.

Besides, if she wished to accompany him to his bedroom for *any* reason, he wasn't about to complain.

Silently, they climbed the stairs, hand in hand, and made their way to his room. He closed the door and lit a lamp, while she poured fresh water into his wash basin and dampened a towel. Placing a hand on her hip, she pointed at a chair. "Sit."

"As you wish, siren." He did and placed his left leg on an ottoman.

"Your other knee has barely healed," she said with a *tsk*, "and now this."

She knelt beside his leg and dabbed gently at the cut, brushing away the pebbles and road dust. She rinsed the cloth and repeated the procedure twice before she was satisfied. "There. You should bandage it before you dress tomorrow, but I think it shall be fine for tonight."

"Thank you."

Tentatively, she sat on the ottoman opposite him and bit her bottom lip, as though she were suddenly nervous.

"What is it?" He put his leg on the floor and leaned forward. "Please don't worry about me, Beth. I promise I was never in any real danger."

She took a deep breath and continued. "I beg to differ, but it's not that. It's about downstairs, earlier. I shouldn't have assumed that you had been with a woman. I'm afraid I have the tendency to be rather quick to judge. But it wasn't fair of me . . . and I'm sorry."

He chuckled. "Given my reputation, I can hardly blame you."

"No, it wasn't right, and of all people, I should know better. After all, I've spent the last few years trying to shrug off my own reputation as a wallflower. Without much success, mind you, but I *do* know that we are all much more than the sum of our reputations."

"Indeed." She was much, much more.

"So you forgive me?" She looked so vulnerable. And beautiful.

"There's nothing to forgive," he said, taking her hand in his. "If anything, I'm flattered."

She balked. "You're flattered that I assumed you'd been . . ."

"Bedding a woman?" he provided smoothly. "No. I'm flattered that you were jealous."

"I never said I was jealous," she said, tossing her head.

"You didn't have to. I could tell by the fine lines on your forehead and the way you crossed your arms and your chilly tone of voice."

She made a sour face but smiled grudgingly. "I might have been a *little* jealous."

He traced small circles on her palm with his thumb. "Would it help if I told you that there's only one woman I want to bed? And that it's you?"

"How very charming," she said dryly. But he could see her melting a little. "Most gentlemen try to woo ladies with poetry."

"I'm no gentleman." He pressed a kiss to the inside of her wrist. "And I can do better than poetry."

He heard her sigh as he kissed the soft spot inside her elbow. "I don't know," she said breathily, "a romantic sonnet can be quite moving."

"I've no use for sonnets." He peeled the tiny puff of her sleeve down her arm and playfully nipped at her smooth shoulder.

"Song lyrics then?" Her eyes fluttered shut. "Perhaps a stirring ballad?"

"Why would I need words or music to express how I feel about you," he growled, "when I can do this?" Spearing his fingers into her thick hair, he kissed the column of her neck.

"That's very nice," she said huskily, even as he trailed kisses along her jaw. "But sometimes a girl likes to hear the words too."

Reluctantly, he sat back. "What do you wish for me to say, Beth? That I think about you when I brush my teeth and when I lay down at night? That I look for you every time I walk into a room?"

She swallowed soberly. "You do?"

"You don't know the half of it," he admitted. "I like many, many things about you."

Arching a brow, she asked, "Such as?"

He raked a hand through his hair. How in the hell was he supposed to tell her that she made every day better and brighter just by being there with him?

He thought for a moment. "Well, you always find a way to make my grandmother smile. And I like how you take it upon yourself to fix everything, even when it doesn't need fixing."

"I'm not sure that's a compliment," she said, wrapping her arms around his neck. "Tell me more."

More? He touched his forehead to hers and searched for the words. "I like how you scoff at dragons, spirits, and monsters when, secretly, you find them fascinating. Maybe you even hope they are real."

Sniffing, she said, "I should like to meet a unicorn or a griffin, but I hope I never encounter a werewolf or vampire."

"Coward," he teased, placing his hands on her hips, which reminded him. "I like how perfectly we fit together and how you feel in my arms."

"I like that too," she purred.

But if he was being honest, his feelings for her transcended the physical. That was why this was so complicated and why he was so damned tongue-tied. That was why he was terrified that she'd discover the type of man he really was.

"Mostly," he said earnestly, "I like the way I feel

when I'm with you. Even when we're bickering with each other, I know we're really on the same side . . . and that we can depend on each other." He shrugged. "When I'm with you, I'm more than a scarred, ornery duke. I'm the one who can make you sigh and smile. And I like that job."

"Do you want to know what I think?"

"Always."

"I think that you're a better poet than you know."

He snorted but was secretly relieved that he might have managed to say something right.

Brushing her lips along the edge of his jaw, she whispered, "Do you recall a few moments ago, when you said that I was the only woman you wanted to bed?"

He barked a laugh. "Beth, I'm likely to forget many things—Latin conjugations, my grandmother's birthday, your favorite flower—but I can promise you that I would never, *will* never, forget the way I desire you."

"Good. Because I'd like you to take me to your bed . . . right now."

Chapter TWENTY-SIX

Alex gaped at her, apparently at a loss for words.

Beth kissed the spot just beneath his ear. "Unless you've changed your mind . . ."

"No," he said quickly. "No. I just . . . are you certain?"

The decision wasn't nearly as hard as it should have been. He wanted her, and she wanted this night with him. "I am sure."

The words were barely out of her mouth before he swept her into his arms, carried her across his bedchamber, and laid her on the soft mattress. Moonlight streamed through the French doors that had once led to the balcony. It hadn't yet been repaired, and the temporary boards behind the door were a stark reminder that life could be snatched away at any moment. She and Alex could have perished that night on his balcony. Or he could have been stabbed as he walked home tonight.

But even if they managed to escape death for the next few days, their time together was limited. He would send her away the day after the masquerade ball—in less than a week.

So she knew better than to take his words to heart. Once she moved to the country with his grandmother, as she'd promised he would, Alex *would* forget her—no matter what he'd said.

Oh, she believed that he'd truly meant the things he said to her—she could see the sincerity in his eyes and hear the candor in his voice. But men like him were fickle creatures. The string of broken hearts he'd left behind was proof enough of that.

But for tonight, at least, he was *hers*.

His dark eyes shining with desire, he tugged off his boots, laid beside her, and pulled her into his arms. "I don't deserve you," he said.

She smiled at the silly, if sweet, sentiment. "How can you say that? You're a duke, and I'm a wallfl—"

"Don't, Beth. Please." He looked directly into her eyes and spoke with an intensity that she felt in her bones. "You're the most beautiful woman I've ever known, and anyone who's ever called you a wallflower is daft-headed. Trust me on this."

"You never noticed me until I moved into your house—even though we attended some of the same balls before then. You certainly didn't think I was beautiful when I was wearing dowdy dresses."

He shook his head ruefully. "I must have been blind. Or stupid. Probably both. *Definitely* both." Pushing a lock of hair away from her cheek, he said, "Promise me something. The next time someone calls you a wallflower, see yourself the way I'm seeing you right now—a siren with your hair gleaming in the moonlight and your eyes shining like diamonds. Don't give that word an ounce of power over you. Don't let it define you."

Touched and surprised by his impassioned speech, she said, "I won't. I promise." With that, she dragged his head toward hers and kissed him with everything she felt inside. Desire, hope, longing, and . . . love.

Alex tugged down her bodice and pushed up her hem, touching her everywhere and claiming her for himself. "You should also know," he said breathlessly, "that you are much too skilled at kissing to be wallflower material."

Chuckling, she pulled his shirt over his head and tossed it onto the floor. And though he tensed at first, his shoulders slowly relaxed. "I don't show my scars to anyone," he admitted.

"Except me," she said.

He blew out a long breath. "Except you."

"Thank you," she said sincerely. "No secrets, no holding back. I want all of you, Alex."

"Careful what you wish for." He traced her collarbone with the tip of his finger. "Some things you shouldn't have to see."

A shiver stole over her skin, and somehow she knew he wasn't referring to the scars on his neck and back—but rather, something deeper.

"I meant what I said. I want the good and the bad. Everything. Otherwise, it's not real." And she desperately needed this night with him to be real—even if it was only as real as a dragon made of stars.

"You want real."

"Yes. Always."

He hesitated for a long moment, causing her to shiver. Swallowing, he said, "Then you shall have it."

Alex sat up and turned his back to Beth. He couldn't bear to see disappointment and disgust cloud her eyes when she learned the truth about him. But he had to tell her before he made love to her—so that she would have all the facts. So she could change her mind if she wished.

She knelt behind him, slipped her arms around his waist, and brushed her lips over the scarred skin on his shoulder. Cloaked in warmth and intimacy, he closed his eyes. This must be what it felt like to be loved and accepted. He committed the sensation to memory in case he never felt it again.

He took a deep breath and prepared to tell the story. The scene had played out in his nightmares for the last twenty years, and he'd never given voice to it—till now.

"The winter I turned six, we traveled to my uncle's house for Christmastide. That's where the fire happened. It started when the entire household was asleep. Maybe a spark from the Yule log landed on a rug; maybe a candle was left burning too close to the curtains. However it started, it blazed through the house like a tornado. Especially in the wing where my parents and I slept."

Beth hugged him tighter. "Go on."

"I woke up coughing, crying, screaming for my parents. It was so smoky and dark that I couldn't find the way to my door. But my father rushed into the room, grabbed me off the floor where I'd collapsed and ran through the flames back into his room. He shook my mother as she lay in bed, but . . . her eyes wouldn't open." His voice cracked. "The smoke."

"Oh, Alex. I'm sorry," she murmured into his neck.

He continued his tale in a hoarse whisper. "She wasn't dead, just unconscious. My father didn't want to leave her. He asked me if I could run out of the house. He pleaded with me to try. He needed to carry my mother out. But he couldn't carry both of us."

Alex felt Beth's warm tears on his shoulder. "You were a little boy. You couldn't have—"

"I clung to him," he said, cutting her off. "I begged him not to put me down. I told him I couldn't do it. That I couldn't breathe."

"You were frightened," she said. "As anyone—but especially a child—would have been."

"I gave my father no choice. We left her. He pulled a blanket off the bed, wrapped me in it, and carried me out of the house. Flames seared my neck and back. I smelled burnt flesh and hair. The fire roared and popped—so loudly that I couldn't hear my own screams. When at last we burst through the front door, my uncle, aunt, and most of their staff were outside, some standing barefoot in the snow. They ran over, tackled us, and rolled us over the icy ground until the flames were out . . . and steam rose off our burnt skin."

Beth sniffled. "Dear God."

"Well-meaning people restrained my father and told him not to go back in. They warned him that he'd never make it out again. But he twisted free, shouting that he couldn't leave my mother inside. She needed him. So he ran toward the inferno, through the front door. He yelled over his shoulder for someone to tend to me. And I never saw him again."

Beth sighed and held him tight. "It wasn't your fault."

He snorted. "I sat in the snow, sobbing and writhing in pain. And I watched that front door for the longest time. To me, it looked like a demon's mouth. My aunt wanted to put me in the back of a wagon and take me somewhere. Out of the cold, to a doctor. But I wouldn't go. I just watched the door, praying that my father would walk out with my mother in his arms. I don't know how long I waited. It seemed an eternity, and even then, my uncle had to drag me away."

"And your grandmother took care of you."

Alex nodded. "She was heartbroken—utterly devastated by the loss of her only son and daughter-in-law. She said she refused to lose me too and never left my side. Not in the excruciating days and weeks afterward, when I wanted to die. Not when I had a raging fever that made me delirious. She was always there, humming softly and telling me that everything would be all right. Someday."

Beth pressed a kiss to his temple. "I've always admired your grandmother greatly. Now she is my hero. The love she has for you transcends . . . everything."

"You don't know the half of it," he said dryly. "It took months for me to heal. And all that time, I barely spoke to her. Every time I looked at her, I saw my father's face, and worse, her grief. It was too much, so I avoided her. Shut her out."

"I'm sure she understood," Beth whispered. "Sometimes grandmothers know us better than we know ourselves."

"I behaved like a surly, ungrateful brat." He shot her a sardonic grin. "Sometimes I still do."

"You lived through a terrible ordeal," she said. "Allowances must be made for that."

"Not this many years later." He turned and took her in his arms. "I can't repay my grandmother for all she's done and sacrificed. But I can try to make her happy."

"You've been doing a fine job of late. She's probably dreaming of side tables and window seats to furnish your study as we speak," she teased.

"Well, that's all thanks to you. Earlier, when I said I don't deserve you . . . I was speaking the truth. Now you know what I did and who I am. And I wouldn't blame you if you walked out my door right now, never looking back."

"As it happens, your grace"—she skimmed a hand down his shoulder and over his hard bicep—"I am not going anywhere." With that, she pulled him down beside her on the bed and entwined her legs with his. "Now I understand, more than ever, why you're fiercely protective of your grandmother. And I think it's very sweet."

Awed by his confession, Beth brushed the hair off Alex's forehead. He shifted her beneath him, and she savored the solid weight of his body across her hips. "She's not the only one I'm intent on protecting, Beth. I care about you too. I'm already responsible for the deaths of my parents, and I couldn't bear it if something happened to you or my grandmother."

"First of all, you're *not* responsible for your parents' deaths. It was a horrible, tragic accident." She willed him to look in her eyes and believe her, but he gazed out the window, down at their entwined hands, anywhere but at her.

"And secondly," she continued, "*nothing* will happen to your grandmother or me. Now that I know about the danger, I can take precautions to ensure our safety. And we shall catch the villain soon." At the masquerade ball, if all went according to plan. "The important thing is that you're not alone any more. Neither am I. We have each other."

At least for now. And if they only had six days left together, she intended to make the most of them.

"I never told anyone about that night," he said, "until now."

"And the sky didn't fall, did it?" she teased. "We're still here, together. And I still want you." More than ever.

Heat flared in his eyes. "What I want," he drawled, "is to strip this gown off of you. Is that real enough for you?"

Her breath hitched in her throat. "It's a very good start."

Chapter TWENTY-SEVEN

Alex heaved a sigh of relief. He'd told Beth his darkest secret, and she hadn't run away. Instead, she gazed up at him like he was some sort of god.

"You must tell me what to do," she said softly.

He brushed his lips over the satin-smooth skin of her neck and loosened the laces of her gown. "Follow your instincts," he instructed.

Slowly, he tugged her dress down, over her breasts, hips and legs, leaving a trail of kisses as he went. She removed the pins from her hair, and he ran his fingers through the long, silken tresses. He stripped off her corset and camisole and tossed them over his shoulder, not caring if they ever found them again.

At the sight of her lying naked beside him, his mouth went dry. "Beautiful."

When he ran a hand over the curve of her hip and around her bottom, she moaned and nuzzled against his chest. "When we're together like this," she said, "I forget all my worries. I only think of you ... and me ... and us."

He swallowed as he digested what she'd said. He felt that way too.

"Beth, there's something else you should know."

She blinked at him and propped herself on her elbow, her skin glowing in the moonlight. "I'm listening," she said huskily. "But you're not going to scare me off."

"Let's hope not." He released the curl he'd been twining around his finger and put a little distance between them—just so he wouldn't be distracted. "Earlier we were talking about how sometimes reputations are undeserved."

"I remember." She smiled seductively.

He covered her delectable curves with a blanket so he could follow the thread of the conversation. "I'm afraid that my reputation as a legendary lover ... falls squarely in the undeserved category."

She feigned surprise. "Do you mean to say there's a man somewhere in London who is more skilled than you?" Playfully arching a brow, she said, "If so, I must insist you find him and bring him here at once."

"There are many men more skilled than I," he admitted. "But no one who will work harder to please you. I haven't lain with a woman in quite some time."

She tilted her head, puzzled. "Forgive me for saying so, but your exploits are widely known and ... well documented."

"They're falsely documented—at least for the past few years."

She nodded as though understanding had dawned. "Is this a sweet but misguided attempt to somehow convince me that I'm different or more special than the legions of other women you've bedded? Because, honestly, it's not necessary. In fact, I'd rather not think of them at the mo—"

"There *are* no legions. I'm not entirely without experience, but accounts of my prowess . . . have been greatly exaggerated."

She stared at him, dumbfounded, then sat up, holding the blanket to her chest. "Forgive me. It's not that I don't believe you. It's only that you seem so . . . Well, on the occasions that we've been together, you seemed so knowledgeable . . . that is, you knew exactly how to . . . Blast it all, you knew what you were doing."

"I'm glad you thought so. I suppose I know something of the mechanics." But his previous sexual experiences had been futile attempts to escape the pain of his past and fill the emptiness in his soul. Knowing how to pleasure a woman was not the same as knowing how to love. "You may have noticed that I have a habit of pushing people away. I never met a woman who I truly longed to make love to. Until you."

"I must say"—she shook her head in disbelief—"I never dreamed that so many people could be wrong about you."

"Why not?" he said. "Look at all the people who are wrong about you. As you know all too well, these rumors take on a life of their own."

"Why didn't you refute them?"

"No gentleman likes to call a lady a liar, and I'm not sure anyone would have believed me. Besides, it wasn't exactly a hardship to be known as a legendary lover." Not like being labeled a wallflower. He shot her an apologetic smile. "I never set out to deceive anyone. But I certainly didn't go out of my way to set the record straight."

She nodded thoughtfully. "I'm not certain you could have."

"I suppose I could have placed an advertisement in the paper."

Scrunching her nose adorably, she smiled. "I'm glad you didn't."

"I wanted to tell you before now, but it's difficult to work into conversation."

She looked up at him with clear blue eyes. "So many women have claimed to have been with you . . . and most of them lied. Why? Why would they do that?"

"I suspect some craved the notoriety, others wished to make their husbands jealous. Some just didn't want to be the odd woman out."

"So they were using you." Her cheeks flushed as though she were outraged on his behalf. "And I am no better, because I accepted their false claims as truth. Even before I knew you personally, I took the rumors at face value . . . and now I feel awful."

"Please, don't." He clasped her hand and pressed a kiss to the back of it as he tried to read her face. Did she still want him? After all, she had assumed that this—her first sexual experience—would be with a man who knew a hundred different ways to pleasure a woman. Instead, she was getting a man who'd learned a few tricks behind hedges, in dark closets, and on remote corners of terraces.

He knew the basics—in other words, just enough to know what he didn't know.

And he knew even less about love . . . but he was starting to understand a few things.

"I told you the truth because you said that you wanted everything between us to be real. I do too."

"You know . . . I think I'm relieved. If I bumble something, the error won't be as glaring."

He chuckled softly and brushed his thumb across her cheek. "There is no way you could bumble anything. Believe me."

"We shall see." She let the blanket drop and leaned in for a kiss. Her soft hair tickled his shoulders, and the peaks of her breasts brushed against his bare chest, instantly reigniting his desire.

"I'll try to make it good for you, Beth," he murmured. God help him, he would. And he'd take care not to spill his seed inside her.

"I already know it will be heavenly," she said. "You seem to have a strange power over me."

"The feeling is mutual."

Growling, he stood, stripped off his trousers, and rejoined her on the bed. He explored every inch of her satin skin with his mouth, lingering on the places she liked—the hollow at the base of her throat, the soft underside of her breasts, and the flat planes of her belly.

"Do you ever wish," she breathed, "that you could bottle up a feeling and save it?"

He wedged a leg between her thighs and rocked against her. "You don't need to bottle it up. There's plenty more."

Doubt flickered in her eyes. "Perhaps. But I shall savor the moment nonetheless."

For his part, he savored everything about her. Her

candor, her fearlessness, her kindness . . . and the seductive way she arched her body toward his. The scent of her skin drove him wild, even as the earnestness of her expression touched something deep inside him.

His pulse galloped out of control. He wanted her—now. But he knew the act would be more pleasurable for her if she was ready. So he kissed a path around her navel and lower . . . and lower.

"Alex?" Her fingers were splayed through his hair, and her leg muscles tensed.

Damn. He wished he knew what the hell he was doing. "I've never done this before . . . but I think it will make you feel very good."

She frowned slightly. "What about you?"

He shot her a wicked grin. "I think I'll like it too."

With her tangled hair and flushed cheeks, she had never looked more vulnerable—or more desirable. "Well . . . then . . . I'm willing to try."

More determined than ever to please her, he took his cues from her soft moans and sighs. God, he loved the taste of her and the way she quivered with need.

"Oh." She opened her thighs wider, and he knew he'd found the right spot. The right amount of pressure. The right rhythm.

Her head fell back and she whimpered softly. As though she were on the brink.

Her arousal mirrored his own. He needed to bring her bliss. To make her his. To make this a night she'd remember always.

He could feel the crescendo starting inside her. It was in the arch of her back and the flush of her skin; the tremor of her muscles and the pitch of her cries. As release took her, he stayed with her, seeing it through.

And when it was over, he laid beside her and hauled her into his arms, feeling stunned.

Like he'd just been a part of a small miracle.

Chapter TWENTY-EIGHT

Beth's legs felt like jelly—but in the best possible way. "For a novice," she said to Alex, "you're very good."

He snorted and playfully nibbled her neck. "I knew I shouldn't have told you."

She sighed, loving the way the stubble on his jaw lightly abraded her skin. "No secrets," she chided. "You once promised that you'd always be truthful with me."

His eyes clouded momentarily. "To the extent that I can."

"I am not entirely certain what that means," she said. "But at the moment I am not sure I care. Our time together is limited—I would not waste it parsing words."

"How would you like to spend it?" He caressed her breast and bent his head to take the tip in his mouth.

"More of that would be nice," she managed to say as desire pooled in her belly once more.

He slipped a hand between her legs. "And how about this?"

"Mmm. More of that too," she breathed. "But mostly I want *you*. All of you."

At last, he moved over her, his arms braced on either side of her head. With his dark hair hanging across one eye and his biceps flexed, he exuded power. The hunger in his eyes made her shiver deliciously.

"You're sure?" he asked.

In answer, she wound her hands around his neck and pulled his head down for a kiss.

He pressed his hips to hers, and the hard length of his arousal nudged at her entrance.

"Tell me if I'm hurting you," he said, swallowing— and she could see what his restraint cost him.

"You're not," she assured him, "and you won't." On the contrary, the delicious pulsing had started again, making her long to rub against him.

He positioned himself and slowly eased in, filling her. It was an odd sensation . . . but when Alex started moving again, she moaned and wrapped her legs around his.

A sheen of perspiration shone on his forehead, and concern lined his face. "You're all right?" he asked hopefully.

"Yes," she said, touched. She swept his hair off his forehead.

"I don't want this to end."

She warmed at his admission. "This is only our first time. It's already better than I'd dared to hope."

"You should . . . raise your expectations," he said breathlessly, as he began to move inside her. As though struggling to maintain control, he closed his eyes tightly and rocked against her in the rhythm that made her blood pump faster.

This was not the ethereal stuff of poems—but better. Much better. Hot, sticky, and raw. Slick skin, fevered panting, pure desire. Real.

The pulsing in her core began to build, and she grasped his shoulders, her fingers digging into his flesh. She arched closer, taking him deeper, urging him on.

Cursing, he opened his eyes and looked into hers. He thrust harder and faster, and when she could tell he was about to lose control, he pleaded, "Come with me, Beth."

Those four whispered words pushed her over the edge. Alex went still.

She cried out as the first wave crashed through her body, starting at her center and rolling through her limbs.

But before the ripples had subsided, he suddenly left her. He pulled out, turned on his side, and caught his seed in his hand.

They laid there for several moments, catching their breath and gazing at the ceiling.

Making love to Alex had been beyond exhilarating, but now that their passion had been spent, she felt suddenly nervous and awkward.

He looked at her guiltily. "I didn't want to risk . . ."

"Of course not," she answered quickly. She was grateful that he'd thought to avoid getting her with child. "Shall I fetch a towel?"

"No, stay." He rolled off the bed, padded across the room to the washstand, and cleaned himself with a damp towel. When he was done, he brought her a fresh cloth. "Would you like me to . . ."

She shook her head and plucked the cloth from his fingers. "Thank you, but I can manage."

As though he sensed her self-consciousness, he turned to look out the French doors. Naked as the day he was born, he seemed to have no qualms parading before her. As she washed away the evidence of their lovemaking, she admired his broad shoulders, lean hips, and muscled thighs.

The burns were in plain sight too, and now that she knew the full story behind them, they seemed even more terrible.

She slipped out of bed, hung her cloth on the edge of the washbasin, and went to his side. Leaning her head against his shoulder, she gazed through the glass panes at the night sky. "Is the dragon out tonight?"

He wrapped an arm around her waist. "It's too cloudy to see him, but he's there."

She wanted to ask him what this night that they'd spent together meant to him and whether it changed anything. She wanted to know if she had pleased him and whether his mind was spinning as fast as hers. But there was every chance that she wouldn't like his answers. And she didn't want to risk putting a damper on the cozy, intimate mood.

So, like a coward, she avoided questions. For now. "Let's go back to bed and rest a while before dawn breaks," she suggested.

"You sleep." He nudged her toward the bed. "I think I'll remain awake for a while."

Returning to bed was less appealing if he wasn't going to join her. Pouting, she said, "There's no need to stand guard, you know. The doors and windows are locked. No harm will come to us tonight."

"I wouldn't have thought any harm would come to us on the balcony either, but it almost did. I don't know who the enemy is, and I can't anticipate his next move, but I swear I'll do everything in my power to protect you."

"Couldn't you protect me while we're in bed?" she ventured.

"No," he growled. "I'd be tempted to do other things."

Frustrated by his stubbornness, she crossed her arms. "Fine. If you aren't going to lay with me for a while, I may as well return to my own bedchamber." She made a halfhearted attempt to find her chemise and corset, but he clasped her wrist in his hand.

"Go, if that is what you truly wish," he said. "But I would prefer it if you stayed here. With me."

If he hadn't asked so earnestly, and if there hadn't been a slight catch in his voice, she would have been strong enough to resist him, but as it was . . .

"Very well. But you must promise not to laugh at any odd faces I make in my sleep. And do not mention it if I snore."

Chuckling, he gave her one, last knee-melting kiss and squeezed her bottom. Then she slipped between the cool sheets, feeling deliciously scandalous without her nightgown.

"I'll wake you when it's time to return to your room," he assured her.

"You could always wake me earlier if you wanted to . . ." she said suggestively.

"Sleep well."

Blast. But she drifted off quickly, and her dreams were full of all sorts of lovely, naughty things.

At breakfast the next morning, Beth attempted to make polite conversation with the dowager.

Which was difficult to do while the duke sat across from her, looking impossibly handsome in a perfectly tailored, dark blue jacket.

And it was *particularly* difficult to do while remembering him naked and moving above her.

"I declare," the dowager said. "I've never seen Elizabeth eat half as much in one sitting. You must be famished, dear. Have another helping of ham."

Alex shot her a wicked look. "How odd. Coincidentally, I find that my appetite is also larger than usual this morning."

"There's plenty of ham for you too." The duchess clucked, shaking her head. "And while I'm thinking of it, do not forget that the painters will arrive this afternoon."

Alex blinked over the rim of his coffee cup. "Painters? You never mentioned them."

Oh dear. Beth was supposed to have informed him the day before but forgot due to any number of things, including jealousy over his nonexistent mistress, concern about his knife wound, and the bliss of her first sexual experience. She gave the duke a pointed look. "They can work around you. We'll just have them cover all the furniture."

"Not my desk," he muttered. Turning to his grandmother, he said, "I thought you'd settled on wallpaper."

"Of course I did," she exclaimed slowly, as though speaking to a very young child, "but there is trim work, including the fireplace, mantel, and shelves. All of it needs a fresh coat of paint. I've chosen soft ivory."

"Shelves?" he grumbled. "I have to move all my books?"

"Unless you'd like the painters to paint around them," she quipped.

"Fine with me," he bluffed. Or did he?

Exasperated, Beth huffed. "I'll go in and pack them up—temporarily—after breakfast."

"Why, thank you, Miss Lacey." Alex smiled at her suggestively, crinkling his eyes at the corners, and she knew the direction of his thoughts mirrored hers: they had an excuse to steal a few moments together in his study.

Heaven help her. The wicked looks he sent her way, the silent signals solely between them were heady things—more potent than wine. Suddenly warm, she fanned herself with her napkin. Vigorously.

"What are your plans for the day, Grandmother?" he inquired, before chomping on a slice of toast.

The dowager adjusted her spectacles and glanced at a list beside her plate. "Oh, I'm afraid we shan't be able to attend the opera."

Beth could see the relief plain on Alex's face— probably because he worried every time they left the house. Or because he detested the opera. Most likely, both.

"Elizabeth and I have countless things to do in preparation for the masquerade," his grandmother was saying, "not the least of which is procuring your costume."

Grunting, he said, "If finding costumes is a bother, we could always host a normal ball, where guests dress in a civilized manner rather than pretending to be shepherdesses and fortune tellers."

His grandmother *tsk*ed. "Costumes are not a *bother*—they're festive. When did you become so stodgy? You sound as though you're eighty-eight instead of twenty-eight."

Beth hid a smile behind her napkin.

"I am only trying to maintain a shred of dignity. I'll trust you and Miss Lacey to select something appropriate. Not too eccentric. Nothing outlandish."

The dowager pressed a hand to her chest as though affronted. "Why, I wouldn't dream of it." She waited until Alex had picked up his newspaper, then turned to Beth—and winked.

Chapter TWENTY-NINE

Alex's study was under siege. Sometime that morning, an army of workers had invaded and left a pile of ladders, tools, and jars of paint. The carpets had been rolled up and propped against the wall. Old sheets covered most of the furniture—including his desk.

Cursing, he yanked the cloth off his desk and, in the process, knocked over a lamp, toppled an ink jar, and scattered a pile of papers.

Normally, this sort of chaos would have put him in the foulest of moods.

But not today.

Last night with Beth had left him feeling oddly . . . hopeful. Which made no sense at all.

Less than ten hours ago, two scoundrels had flashed knives in the vicinity of his neck. He'd slammed one of them against a wall and demanded that he reveal who'd sent them. But the moment Alex had released his throat so he could talk, the thug squirmed free and ran, leaving him none the wiser.

He still didn't know who was trying to kill him or why, but he thought that *if* he could solve that mystery and effectively deal with the villain, his life would return to normal. And then, he could begin to envision a future with Beth. If he was honest with himself, he already was.

Of course, it wasn't a foregone conclusion that she'd have him, but she seemed to care for him in spite of his scars and his ornery disposition and the undeniable part he'd played in his parents' deaths. And she definitely seemed to like kissing and lying with him.

She trusted him . . . and that's why he had to protect her. At all costs.

As he righted the objects on his desk and retrieved the scattered papers, the object of his thoughts peeked her head through the doorway.

"May we come in?" she asked.

Dismayed that she wasn't alone, Alex peered over her shoulder and saw a footman carrying two large trunks. "If you must." If he was polite, the staff would be suspicious.

"Place them beside the bookshelves, please," she said to the footman.

"Shall I pack the books in the trunks for you, Miss Lacey?" he offered.

"No, thank you. I'll see to it."

The moment the footman left, Alex went to her. In deference to the open door, he refrained from hauling her into his arms. Instead, he whispered, "How are you feeling this morning?"

"I feel wonderful," she said, blushing. "How do you feel?"

He chuckled. "Do you really need to ask?"

"I was referring to the attack. I thought there might be some lingering effects. How is the wound?"

"Forgotten," he said truthfully. "You must have healed me."

"All I did was wash the cut."

"I was referring to what you did *after* that."

Inclining her head toward the door meaningfully, she swatted at his arm. In a voice loud enough to be heard by passersby, she said, "It won't take long for me to remove the books from your shelves, and I shall endeavor not to disturb you, your grace."

"Is that a fact, Miss Lacey?" He dared to caress her shoulder and brush his lips against her temple, eliciting a soft sigh.

"I know how particular you are about your study," she said, as though she were still speaking for the benefit of others. "And would not wish to interrupt the important business you're conducting."

Pretending to consider this, he walked behind her, bent his head, and kissed her nape. Keeping one eye on the door, he whispered, "Understand this: I have no business that's more important than you. And if we had sufficient privacy, I would ravish you—at this very moment, right here on my desk, contracts, deals, and ledgers be damned."

She leaned back against his chest, and he skimmed his hands over her silky gown, around her hips, and up her flat belly, till he was cupping her full breasts in his hands. His fingertips circled the tight peaks, and she arched her back so her soft bottom pressed against him.

Good God. Heart hammering in his chest, he barely resisted the urge to hike up her skirt and—

"Alex," she whispered urgently. "We shouldn't. Not now."

"You're right." Reluctantly, he let his hands fall away. "Forgive me."

"There's nothing to forgive. I love . . . the way you make me feel."

His breath hitched in his throat. For a moment, he'd thought she was going to say that she . . . but that was ridiculous.

"Why don't I help you pack the books? If my hands are busy, they'll be less likely to stray."

"Excellent idea," she said, smiling. "But before we begin, I thought you might want to take a look at this."

Beth withdrew a paper from a pocket in the folds of her gown and handed it to Alex. "It's the invitation list for the masquerade."

"About the ball," he said slowly. "I thought about it for much of the night. And after the attack yesterday, I think it prudent to cancel."

Oh dear. "It's too late."

He shook his head regretfully. "I know my grandmother will be disappointed, and I'll find a way to make it up to her. I almost told her at breakfast earlier, but I wanted you to know first."

Once, Beth would have jumped to the conclusion that he wanted to cancel the ball so he could rid himself of her and his grandmother that much sooner. But now . . . she believed him.

There was only one problem. "The invitations were delivered this morning," she said. "To everyone on the list you're holding."

"Damn." He pressed his lips into a thin line as he unfolded the list and scanned the names. She searched his face for a sign that the suspects were among the invitees, unsure of whether she hoped they were there . . . or not.

After a minute, he wordlessly folded the paper and handed it back to her.

"Well?" she asked expectantly.

He made a sour face. "Did you have to invite Coulsen?"

Shrugging, she said, "Your grandmother suggested it. Apparently, he's staying in town for a couple of weeks, and he was quite cordial at the Clavilles' ball."

He grunted. "I'd rather Coulsen not become too cordial with you."

"You're avoiding the real issue." She waved the guest list in frustration. "Are the suspects on the list?"

"I'd rather not say," he replied.

"Alex!"

"Allow me to finish. I'd rather not say because I want to keep you safe. On the other hand, you're already involved. So we will have to compromise." He reached for her hand and laced his fingers through hers.

Immediately suspicious, she narrowed her eyes. "What sort of compromise?"

"I will admit to you that both suspects are on the list."

"They are?" The hairs on her arms stood on end.

"It's no small wonder," he said. "You've invited half of London."

"Who are the suspects?"

He shook his head slowly. Firmly. "It's better if you don't know. Let Darby and me make arrangements to track them and see that they don't inflict injury on anyone."

"You and Darby?" she asked, incredulous. "You seem to have forgotten that it was *my* plan. You may not exclude me now."

Alex rested his large hands on her shoulders and kneaded them softly, trying to appease her. "I don't wish to exclude you. I wish to *protect* you. There's a difference."

Though his heart may have been in the right place, his masculine attempt to enlighten her sorely grated on her nerves. Crossing her arms, she said, "I'm sure you wish to protect Darby, and yet, you're not excluding him."

"Darby can protect himself."

"As can I," she retorted.

Chuckling, he said, "I once witnessed you attempt to protect yourself with a parasol. You failed spectacularly."

"How gallant of you to remind me. But I was caught off guard that night at Vauxhall. I'd be better able to defend myself if I knew my enemy."

"Don't worry. I would give my life to defend you." He looked at her soberly. "If it makes you feel better to be cross with me, then by all means, be cross. But I'm doing what I think is right. And I'm not going to change my mind about this, Beth."

His declaration touched her, but she also felt hurt. Shut out. Didn't he understand that they were in this situation together? She would never rest easy, knowing he was in danger.

Shoving the list in her pocket, she resolved to study it later. Perhaps she could determine who the suspects were by process of elimination. But it was going to be difficult, as it *was* a rather long list.

"I've no wish to argue with you," she said frostily. "Let's pack your books in these trunks before the workers arrive."

"If you give me the cold shoulder," he said smoothly, "I shall consider it a personal challenge."

She tossed her head, as though she was only mildly interested. "How so?"

"I will make it my mission to thaw you." He removed an armful of books from a top shelf and handed a few to her.

As she knelt and stacked the volumes neatly in a trunk, she breezily asked, "And how, precisely, do you intend to accomplish that?"

"I'm not yet certain. But make no mistake." He leaned close to her ear, the low timbre of his voice promising all manner of wicked delights. "I'll find a way."

Her traitorous heart beat faster . . . but two could play his game. While he attempted to thaw her, she would focus on ascertaining the identity of the suspects.

And if he didn't wish to include her in his plans on the night of the ball, then perhaps she'd devise a few plans of her own.

Chapter THIRTY

"Alexander has been rather churlish of late," the dowager announced. "It would serve him right if we required him to dress as Pan. You would make a lovely wood nymph, and I should rather like to be Minerva."

Oh dear. With the masquerade just one day away, Beth and the dowager could no longer delay the decision about costumes. The women had ventured out to a dressmaker's shop on Bond Street, where a spry gray-haired seamstress with a deft needle had agreed to help them quickly assemble a trio of costumes for the ball.

The challenge was finding a costume acceptable to Alex.

"You would be magnificent as the goddess," Beth said. The seamstress, who held a swath of silver silk beneath the duchess's chin, nodded in agreement.

"However," Beth continued, "I can't think that the duke would be pleased to host a ball dressed as a half-goat, half-man creature carrying a lute. Never mind the horns on his head."

No, Pan would *never* do.

"I could create a Zeus costume for him," the seamstress offered. "Surely, the duke would not object to being king of the gods."

"No, no." The dowager shook her head. "There are sure to be at least three Zeuses in attendance. We need something considerably more original."

As they sat in the back corner of a bustling shop, all three women pondered the possibilities.

"A Turkish sultan?" the seamstress offered.

Beth tried to picture Alex wearing a turban . . . and couldn't.

The dowager held up a finger. "I have it!" Pointing at Beth, she said, "You could be Red Riding Hood."

There were worse costumes . . . and it would be bold and daring to wear a brilliant scarlet cape. "What would you be?"

"The grandmother, of course. I suppose I shall have to wear a nightcap and robe."

"I could fashion both from the silver silk for an elegant effect," the seamstress mused.

"Perfect!" the dowager declared. "And Alexander shall be . . ."

"The wolf," Beth provided. She contemplated the idea for a few seconds. "It could work."

The seamstress laid a finger alongside her cheek. "Perhaps a fur-trimmed, hooded cloak complete with pointy ears . . . with matching fur-trimmed gloves."

"Ooh," the dowager exclaimed. "How delightfully fearsome."

Mentally questioning the wisdom of fur in July, Beth piped up. "I suspect the duke would prefer to keep the costume simple. Perhaps just a half-mask that he could wear with a dark evening jacket would suffice?"

The dowager sighed dramatically. "Elizabeth is correct. My grandson will be infinitely happier with a simple mask. But I trust you to give it a few ferocious details, Adelaide."

"That I can do." The seamstress smiled. "Allow me to take a few measurements for each of you, and I will ensure that Miss Lacey is a lovely Red Riding Hood and you are an eminently stylish Grandmother."

An hour later, Beth and the dowager were in the coach, gazing out the windows as the sunny streets of London rushed by. They were on the way back to Black-shire House, where they would soon review all the final ball preparations with the housekeeper, butler, and cook. Before the guests arrived tomorrow night, each member of the staff would know precisely what was expected of them in order to make the masquerade a smashing success.

How different this ball would be from the one Beth and her sisters had thrown less than a year ago at Uncle Alistair's town house. Then, they'd had to do the bulk of the preparations themselves—including cleaning, cooking, and gardening—and they'd barely had two shillings to rub together. But somehow, it had all worked, and the night had been magical.

In contrast, the preparations for the masquerade had barely required Beth to lift a finger. The duke's staff had already been instructed to hang swags of silk, fill vases of flowers, and trim scores of candlewicks. Every surface

in the expansive, gilded ballroom had been polished.
The menu was set; champagne was already chilling.
No expense had been spared.

And yet, Beth found herself longing for the old days,
when it had been she and her sisters against the world.
At least then she'd known where she stood. Lately, her
status was rather murky.

She'd only seen Alex a handful of times during the
past five days, which had passed in a flurry of list-
making, shopping, and arranging. When she did see
him, they always seemed to be in the company of others.
She searched his handsome face for clues that he missed
her as much as she missed him. And while his eyes held
a delicious hint of wickedness, they also held worry—
for her and his grandmother.

Meanwhile, Beth and the dowager had purchased
most of the new furniture and accessories for the duke's
study and ordered footmen to remove the items that
were no longer needed. Two of the four walls had been
papered, and the workers had been given strict instructions to paper *around* the odd-looking landscape that
hung on the wall without removing it—even briefly. A
bet was a bet, after all.

Somehow, she and Alex had gone the better part of
the week living under the same roof without stealing
any time alone together.

And now they had only two days left, for she had
promised to leave on the day after the ball. She was no
closer to knowing the identities of the men whom Alex
suspected might be trying to kill him.

Even more vexingly, she was no closer to knowing
what their future held.

As the coach rumbled to a stop in front of Blackshire House, Beth roused the duchess, who had dozed off. "Let us go inside," Beth said softly, so as not to startle her. "You have time to rest before our meeting with the staff."

"Yes, I think I will," the older woman said groggily as she alighted the coach. "Be sure to wake me with time to spare."

"Of course," Beth said, offering her arm. Impulsively, she asked, "Will you be glad when this is all over?"

Squinting as though she were still disoriented, the dowager pushed her spectacles onto the bridge of her nose. "Whatever do you mean, dear?"

Beth shrugged. "Soon the study will be finished and the ball will be behind us. Will you be glad when life returns to normal?"

"Both projects are labors of love," the duchess replied with a yawn. "But I suspect I will feel a sense of relief when they're accomplished."

As they shuffled up the sidewalk toward the front steps, Beth considered how best to pose her next question. "I suppose I'm wondering if you've ever wished for a change of pace. A more peaceful existence."

The duchess eyed her curiously. "Why would I wish for my circumstances to change? I live with my dear grandson and have friends nearby. I'm blessed to have a companion who dotes on me. And I could attend a different social event every night if I wished. Soirees, musicales, balls, the opera . . . all of them are just beyond my front door."

Drat. Convincing her to move to the country would be difficult indeed—even if Beth initially couched it as an extended visit. But she wasn't at all comfortable lying to the dowager. Swallowing, she told herself it was for the older woman's own good.

"I don't know." Beth ushered the duchess into the foyer. "The countryside has much to recommend it—fresh air, wildflowers, a sense of freedom."

"I have all the freedom I require," the dowager said, patting Beth's hand affectionately. "I've no desire to run though muddy meadows or dodge pecking hens each time I venture out of doors. More importantly, I'm needed here. You see, Alexander may not admit it—he may not even *know* it—but he needs me."

As Beth contemplated the duchess's words, her lady's maid met them in the foyer, fussed over her mistress a bit, and offered to take her upstairs.

Alex and his grandmother had a bond forged through pain, grief, and love. Maybe the dowager was correct, and Alex really *did* need her nearby. Or maybe she only *wished* to be needed.

Beth knew the feeling all too well.

The dowager gratefully handed her bonnet to the maid. To Beth, she said, "You should rest as well. I shall see you later this afternoon for our meeting."

"Yes, of course." But Beth had no intention of resting. There was far too much to be done. For one thing, she should see how the wallpapering was progressing in the study. And if the workers were not currently there . . . perhaps the duke would be.

When she rounded the corner, she found the door closed. Which meant either that the workers were finished for the day or that Alex had kicked them out.

The thought of seeing him made her belly flip.

Smoothing her hair behind her ears, she approached the door and raised her hand to knock—but froze at the sound of voices coming from within.

Shamelessly, she leaned close, her ear almost touching the door. One of the voices was definitely Alex's, and the other seemed to be Lord Darberville's. It was difficult to make out the entire conversation, but she heard muffled snippets.

". . . I'll wait outside Haversham's house . . ."

". . . don't let him out of your sight . . ."

". . . nowhere near Miss Lacey . . ."

". . . I'll track Newton . . ."

". . . a costume could hide weapons . . ."

Despite the warm weather, a chill ran the length of her spine.

So, the suspects were Lord Haversham and Lord Newton. Beth never would have guessed. Not that she knew either gentleman particularly well, but Lord Haversham seemed too old and portly to be much of a threat to someone as fit and strong as Alex. And Lord Newton had always seemed a decent sort—at least he had never openly ridiculed Beth or her sisters.

But Alex must have his reasons for suspecting them, and, clearly, whoever wanted him dead was enlisting the help of other, equally unscrupulous villains.

Shuffling sounds from within the study roused Beth from her thoughts. Quickly, she backed away from the door and glided down the corridor to the drawing room, where she sat at the duchess's escritoire and pretended to be absorbed with the papers there.

Her pulse had scarcely returned to normal before Alex strode into the room, his broad shoulders and dark hair making him look more swashbuckling pirate than privileged duke. He glanced around the room. "We are alone?"

"Your grandmother is resting after our outing to the dressmaker's," she said breezily, pushing aside a paper as though it were an important piece of business when, for all she knew, it could have been a list of items needed from the market.

His mouth pressed into a thin line, and his brown eyes flashed with something akin to . . . anger. "You shouldn't have left the house without telling me, Beth."

"I might have thought to inform you," she said coolly, "if you had been here—but, alas, you were not." Why did he wish to pick a fight with her when their time together was so limited?

He stalked closer and stopped, his boots stopping only inches from her slippers. "You knew the danger, knew the risk, and yet you still choose to gallivant about London with my grandmother in tow?"

She stood so that he would not tower over her. At least not as much. "The risk is to you, not us. And if *you* don't confine yourself to the house, I don't see why you should expect us to."

He wiped a hand down his face, beyond exasperated. "Because you seem to forget, Beth, that there are very bad people in this world. People who would hurt those I l—"

Without finishing his thought, he turned, stalked across the room, and sank onto a sofa, his head in his hands. But she was almost sure she knew what he'd been about to say, and tears filled her eyes, unbidden.

She took a second to compose herself, then went to

him. "Alex," she said, sitting close, "no harm came to us—not so much as a scratch. We are both fine."

"I shouldn't have raised my voice," he said, "or directed my ire at you. Hell, I don't know *who* to be angry with. Forgive me."

"I understand. You want to protect me and your grandmother." She brushed a lock of hair away from his forehead. "I'm touched by your devotion. But you look exhausted. Have you slept at all these last few days?"

"A little," he admitted. "A killer is out there, and I have no idea when he will strike. I'm constantly trying to anticipate the next move of an unnamed enemy."

She nodded thoughtfully. "But you do have some idea."

"Just a couple of theories. And it's possible neither is right." He snorted as he rubbed a hand along his jaw.

Her heart ached for him. "You've been living under a constant threat. That would take a toll on anyone."

"It's not the threat that has me pulling my hair out. It's the fact that there's nothing I can do. No decisive action I can take. All I can do is minimize the risks. That's why I don't want you or my grandmother to leave the house unescorted. I'm trying to exert a modicum of control . . . even though I know it's futile. Sometimes, I feel as though I'm going mad."

"You're not," she said firmly.

"Maybe not. But I've realized there are more than a handful of people in the world who would dance a jig on my grave. It's rather disheartening."

Boldly, she placed a hand on his thigh—and heard his intake of breath. "So, you have a few detractors. But you also have me. And I . . ."

She wanted to tell him that she would go to the ends of the earth for him.

That no one else had ever made her feel as special or trusted or understood.

That she loved him.

But the timing didn't seem quite right. She took a deep breath and gazed into his wounded brown eyes. ". . . well, I happen to think that you're not so bad." With a shrug and a smile, she added, "For a womanizing duke."

A wicked grin slowly lit his face. "You're not so bad either. For a prudish wallflower."

"Prudish?" she said, blinking. "Have you forgotten?"

"God, no." He slid a hand behind her neck and caressed the curls at her nape. "I've missed you, Beth. More than you could possibly know."

Her throat constricted. "But you've been avoiding me."

He closed his eyes briefly before speaking. "You must have faith. I am not in a position at the moment to make promises," he said carefully. "But I hope that someday soon, I will be. Until then, you must believe that this"—he paused to press his lips to the back of her hand—"is real."

The mere brush of his lips over her skin made her weak with desire. "Give me proof," she demanded, leaning close and kissing his neck. "Make me believe. Again."

Chapter THIRTY-ONE

For five days, Alex had done his damnedest to resist Beth.

Now, as she trailed kisses over his neck and slid her hand over his thigh, he realized the futility of it. Nothing could keep him from claiming her, from showing her just how much she meant to him.

From making her *his*.

And yet, he couldn't ravish her on the drawing room settee at four o'clock in the afternoon while the door was ajar. No, he definitely had to find a more optimal location.

Her bedroom was too close to his grandmother's, and he didn't want to risk one of the staff finding her in the vicinity of his bedchamber either. It was impossible to walk two feet in his study without tripping over a hammer or paintbrush, and one never knew when an army of workers would descend, so that room was out of the question as well.

Good God, there must be close to forty different rooms in his house, and he couldn't think of one suitable for an afternoon tryst. Unless—

"Come with me." He pulled her toward the door. "Most of the staff are working in or around the ballroom, but if we should happen to encounter any of them, allow me to explain our presence below stairs."

Though her eyes were full of questions, she followed him silently into the hall and waited there while he retrieved a key from the desk in his study. Then he led her down the staircase to the ground floor and down a back staircase to the basement.

They were tiptoeing past the stillroom when a servant carrying a tall stack of crates and whistling an unrecognizable tune headed toward them.

Damn it. Alex ducked into a dark storeroom, pulled her in with him, and pressed her back to the wall. Dank and dusty, the closet smelled of Brussels sprouts.

Beth, on the other hand, smelled like citrus and sunshine. He nuzzled her neck while he waited for the servant to pass.

"What happened to *explaining our presence*?" she whispered dryly.

"This option seemed less complicated." Regretfully, he peeled himself off of her and stuck his head into the hallway. "But I think it's clear now. Come."

They glided past the housekeeper's room and stopped in front of a low, arched door.

"The wine cellar?" she mouthed.

Grinning, he pulled out his key. "Precisely." He'd recently had the cellar repaired and renovated, and while it might not be as comfortable as a bedroom, it was intimate and charming.

Quickly, he opened the door, ushered her inside, and lit a candle before locking the door once more.

He stooped to avoid hitting his head on the low, domed ceiling, but Beth was able to stand upright. She made a slow circle, taking in the barrels at the end of the long, narrow room and the neat rows of bottles lining the walls on either side of them.

For a wine cellar, it was clean. Alex's butler fawned over the room like it was his newborn baby. Not a speck of dust was permitted to settle on a bottle. Not a drop of wine was allowed to stain the floor. While there was no furniture, a sturdy basket above the barrels contained a few provisions—a large quilt, extra candles, and a pair of wine glasses. Alex supposed they were there in case of emergency. If someone were trapped in the room for any length of time, at least they'd be drunk and warm.

Swallowing, he tried to view the room through Beth's eyes. He found the brick walls and uneven stone floors appealing, but when paired with the lack of windows, he feared she might find the accommodations rather . . . dungeonlike.

At least she didn't scare easily. It was one of the things he loved about her—and one of the things that drove him mad. If she had a care for her own well-being, she wouldn't be staying in his house or investigating murder attempts. Then again, she wouldn't be here with him now.

"What do you think?" he asked.

"Delightfully cozy." Crossing her arms, she shot him a saucy smile. "However, I'm not particularly thirsty."

"Neither am I, siren." With a low growl, he hauled her against him and captured her mouth in a kiss.

She melted into him. Hair pins hit the floor as he speared his fingers into her hair. His cravat landed on the neck of a wine bottle. Desire thundered through his veins.

"Alex," she whimpered, "I need you."

It was almost his undoing. He loosened the laces of her gown and corset, then tugged both down, baring her breasts. She wriggled her gown over her hips and kicked it aside, so that only her chemise hung loosely from her shoulders.

Her hair, a glorious mass of curls, shone in the candlelight. Her satin skin begged to be touched. Sweet Jesus, if he could stare at her for a hundred years, it wouldn't be long enough.

He kept his gaze fixed on her as he hastily shrugged off his jacket and waistcoat. "At the risk of sounding trite, I've never longed to be a painter—till right now."

"And what would your painting be titled?" she teased, pulling his shirttail free and sliding a hand inside.

Easy. "A Wallflower's Revenge."

"I like that," she murmured. "And I *will* have my revenge."

"I have no doubt." She'd already turned his world upside down—in the best possible way. "Now . . . come here."

Beth's breath hitched in her throat. Alex's heavy-lidded eyes held the promise of pleasure—and more.

She stepped into his arms, and he guided her toward the barrels at the end of the room, where he reached into the basket and pulled out a soft, clean quilt.

"I can spread this on the floor," he said to her. "Or we could try something . . . different."

Dear God. Her knees went weak, but not because the choice was particularly difficult. "Different."

With an approving, feral smile, he laid the folded quilt on top of a barrel that was about as high as her chest. "Turn around," he said.

Trembling with anticipation, she faced the barrel. He swept aside the curtain of her hair and nibbled on her ear, neck, and shoulder. "Tomorrow night at the ball," he murmured against her skin, "when other gentlemen pay you compliments and twirl you around the dance floor and whisper pretty things in your ear"—he hiked up the hem of her chemise and reached in front of her, touching the sensitive flesh between her legs—"remember this."

Dear God. As if she could forget. "I . . . will . . . try."

He took the weight of her breast in his hand and squeezed, lightly pinching the taut peak between his finger and thumb. An exquisite form of torture, his touch sent a razorlike hum of desire through her body.

When she whimpered, he breathed, "I would be by your side for every moment of the night if I could. But even when I am not there, you may be sure that I'm thinking of you."

He found the center of her pleasure, his wicked fingers circling the spot till she was coiled tightly, on the brink of bursting.

"Alex," she gasped, leaning her bottom against the hard length of him, "I need you. Now."

With a muffled curse, he briefly released her and unbuttoned his trousers. His hard, warm flesh pressed against her bare bottom, and she thrilled in the knowledge that he wanted her as much as she wanted him.

Settling a large hand on her hip, he pressed against her entrance and slowly, tentatively eased into her. "I want this to be good for you," he said huskily.

He hesitated, wanting confirmation that she was all right.

But while she appreciated his thoughtfulness and consideration, she was all too aware of how fleeting their time together was. And if this was to be their last time making love together, she didn't want half-measures or lukewarm passion. She craved every part of him—the wounds, the strength, the grief, and the joy.

So rather than answer him in words, she rocked back, taking all of him inside her.

"Jesus, Beth." Breathing hard, he froze—as though he still feared hurting her.

But she knew he wouldn't. At least not physically. She *would* be hurt when she had to say good-bye to him, but she couldn't think about that now. Nay, she could scarcely think of *anything* when she was this close to him. As close as two people could be.

"I love . . . the way you make me feel."

Alex growled in response. He began to move inside her, and she met him thrust for thrust. She felt him all around her—his chest at her back, his mouth near her ear, his hand in her hair. His muscles quivered with restraint.

"Come for me." He slid a hand in front of her and touched her where their bodies joined. Instantly, the delicious pulsing in her core began to crescendo, lifting her until she was floating. Her legs trembled, but Alex held her tightly, whispering in her ear. "God, you feel good, Beth. This is how it should be . . . you . . . and—"

Her release came, fast and long and sweet, drowning out his words and taking over her body. She grasped the quilt and let the waves of pleasure rush over her, savoring each exquisite moment.

Alex held her, patiently waiting for the last blissful ripples to subside, then pulled out. Still in a dreamlike state, she watched as he grabbed his cravat and spilled his seed onto it. She adjusted her chemise and went to him, resting her head on his back and lightly running her fingers over his scarred flesh.

"I didn't mean to take you so hastily," he said. "You must think my surname fitting."

She thought for a moment. "Savage?" she said, smiling. "You may be a bit uncivilized, but if you must know, I rather like your rough edges."

He tossed aside the cravat, reached for the quilt, and laid it on the floor. "Come." He sat with his back against a barrel, his long legs extended and crossed at the ankles. Patting a thigh, he said, "Lie down and rest your head for a while."

She sank onto the quilt, surprised to find it quite comfortable.

But maybe her sense of contentment stemmed more from having recently been duly ravished.

Resting her cheek on his hard, warm thigh, she sighed happily. With heartbreaking tenderness, he ran his fingers through her hair and caressed her shoulder, lulling her into a trancelike state.

"We need to talk, siren."

Chapter THIRTY-TWO

Alex felt her tense, and she sat up abruptly.

"What is it?" Beth asked, her blue eyes full of concern. "Don't tell me there's been another attempt on your life."

"None that I know of," he said, smiling. "But there are some things that I need to say, and since I'm not certain when we'll have a chance to speak privately again . . ."

She nodded soberly, as though bracing herself for the worst. "I'm listening."

Hoping to reassure her, he held her hand. "Please don't take unnecessary risks at the masquerade tomorrow night. I know you are eager to help me discover my assailant, but Darby and I have matters well in hand." It wasn't quite the truth, but she needn't know that.

Bristling a little, she said, "I won't take any risks I deem unnecessary."

"I couldn't bear it if something were to happen to

you," he said firmly. "You demanded more from me than I thought I had to give. I never revealed myself—and I'm not just speaking of my scars—to anyone. Until you."

She pondered this for a few moments, then swallowed. "Why me?"

"Your goodness, your light . . . you made it worth the risk."

Her cheeks turned pink. "You've changed me too," she said, nuzzling the side of his neck. "I've learned that I shouldn't be so quick to judge. Sometimes, everything I think I know about a person is wrong—like I was wrong about you."

She hadn't been entirely wrong. There was the small matter of him dubbing her and her sisters the Wilting Wallflowers. And it was high time he owned up to it. "Actually—"

"And because of you," she interrupted, "I've realized that ugly names and hateful labels only have the power to hurt if we let them. Because of you, I don't *feel* like a wallflower."

"You're not," he said firmly. "Not by any stretch. And you should know—"

Her eyes shone with unshed tears. "I love you, Alex."

His chest squeezed. Her love was more than he'd hoped for—and definitely more than he deserved. He placed a tender kiss on her forehead. "I love you too, siren."

With a happy sigh, she rested her head on his shoulder. "Were you about to say something else?" she asked.

God, he couldn't tell her about the wallflower name right now. She was too vulnerable, her emotions too raw. "Only that you've bewitched me."

Reluctantly, she sat up straight. "I should make my way upstairs soon. I promised I'd wake your grandmother in time to meet with the staff, and fear I may have lost track of the time."

"Wait."

He couldn't let her go without giving her some idea of his intentions. "After the ball tomorrow night, we must part—for a while."

The light fled from her eyes, and she looked away. "You've made that abundantly clear."

"But I hope that our parting is only temporary, Beth. I want you in my life. Hell, I *need* you in my life. And even though I don't deserve you, I want . . . to be with you."

She looked at him expectantly, waiting for him to elaborate. But he couldn't. He couldn't ask her to marry him as long as there was some sort of bounty on his head. An engagement would only place her in greater danger and he would not risk her life—no matter how much he wanted to claim her for his own.

He dragged a hand through his hair, wishing to hell he give her more than a vague promise. His heart hammered as she stood and paced the length of the room. "When this is all over, I would like to properly court you."

Beth could scarcely breathe. Her stomach fluttered as though she'd suddenly taken a fever.

She had given herself to Alex—body, heart, and soul—and he was announcing his intention to *court* her. It all seemed rather backward.

"You're asking if you may court me . . . at an unspecified, future time?"

"I would have done so before now, but the combination of my scandalous reputation and your position as my grandmother's companion made that nigh impossible. And as long as someone's trying to kill me, I won't risk making our association public, endangering you."

"I understand." In her head, she did. But her heart remained stubbornly unconvinced. He'd referred to their relationship as an *association*—but it was more than that. At least, it was to her. And if he truly loved her, nothing should have been impossible. Not even the most unlikely of courtships.

Blowing out a long breath, he placed his warm hands on her shoulders and stroked the tops of her arms. "I'll grant you that it's complicated. But make no mistake, Beth—once this nightmare is finally over, we will be together. If you'll have me."

She closed her eyes and let his words echo in her mind. *We will be together.* It wasn't a proposal, but if that was all Alex could give her right now . . .

"Of course, I'll have you."

He lifted his head, his brown eyes hopeful. "You will?"

"Yes."

Jubilant, he wrapped her in his arms and swung her around, pressing his lips to hers. "You've made me so happy, Beth. Everything will work out. You'll see. If it takes a week, a month . . . even a year, we will be together. And we'll have the rest of our lives to make up for lost time."

"I just want you to catch the person who's been try-ing to kill you." As soon as possible. So that she might stop fretting and searching his person for wounds each time he entered the house.

And because she knew all too well how much could change in the course of a week or a month or a year. He professed to love her, but she'd said it first. And over time, passion faded, promises were forgotten, and hearts were broken.

"Do not worry about me," he said. "Now that I know you'll wait for me, I'm more determined than ever to solve the mystery. You may count on it."

"Good." She gazed at his face, determined to mem-orize the affection, confidence, and tenderness in his ex-pression. "I'm afraid I really must go." Secret promises notwithstanding, she needed to make herself present-able, wake the duchess, and oversee the preparations for a ball with at least two murder suspects on the guest list.

Groaning in protest, Alex released her and dutifully began collecting hairpins from the floor while she hastily donned her corset and gown.

"Remember what I said." He dropped a handful of pins into her palm. "Take no unnecessary risks tomor-row night. Remain in the ballroom at all times, if pos-sible. There is safety in numbers."

"And you?" she asked pointedly. "Will you follow your own advice?"

"I'll do what I must."

Sighing, she wound her hair into a knot and secured it as best she could. "This evening I plan to broach with your grandmother the subject of moving to your country house. I'll tell her that we must leave the morning after the ball so that we may attend the Lammas Eve festival on the following day. Once we're there, I'll convince her to extend our stay indefinitely. I dislike having to be untruthful with her, but . . ."

"Excellent." He buttoned his waistcoat and jammed an arm into his jacket. "And I hope that the separation won't be for long."

Tears sprang to her eyes. It was unlikely they'd have time for a private good-bye before they left for his manor house in Essex. "I'll miss you."

Cursing, he took her face in his hands and kissed her as though he wished to claim her for all eternity. As though he intended the passion contained in that kiss to sustain them both for every second they were apart. When it ended, she was weak-kneed and gasping for breath.

As far as good-byes went, she had to admit it was rather splendid.

With a heart-melting grin, he unlocked the wine-cellar door and peered outside. "No one is about," he said. "Leave now, and I'll follow in a few minutes."

Just as she was about to sneak out, he laid a hand on her arm. "I almost forgot. What will you be at the masquerade?"

"Wouldn't you like to be surprised?"

"No. I need to be able to keep an eye on you—for your protection and my own sanity."

Warmed by the sentiment, she decided to spare him the torture of keeping her disguise a secret. "Red Riding Hood. And you shall be the wolf."

"Fitting." He nodded approvingly. "And my grandmother will be . . . the grandmother?"

She arched a brow. "Well done."

"I have no doubt that scarlet will become you," he said huskily. "Be sure to keep the costume after the ball . . . I may have other uses for it."

Her belly flipped at the delightfully wicked suggestion, but her last words to him were sober. "The last thing you need right now is a distraction. Please focus your efforts on simply . . . surviving tomorrow night."

Chapter THIRTY-THREE

"Where the hell is your costume?" Darby asked. He'd stalked across the ballroom and up a half flight of stairs to stand beside Alex on the mezzanine overlooking the dance floor, opposite the large doors at the entrance.

Alex glanced sideways at his friend. "I could ask the same of you." Darby's only nod to the evening's masquerade theme was a black scarf with eye holes tied around his head.

"Lady Thorndike told me I resembled a raccoon," Darby said with a shrug. "I've decided to embrace the idea."

"You're a better sport than I."

"That's hardly newsworthy. But honestly, how does the host of a masquerade ball manage to avoid wearing a costume?"

Grudgingly, Alex pulled the wolf mask from his jacket pocket and held it in front of his face.

Darby cowered in mock horror. "Never mind. Those

menacing eyes and sharp teeth would frighten all but the sturdiest of maids."

"I would wear it," Alex said, tossing the mask onto a small table next to the mezzanine railing, "if it didn't make seeing so bloody difficult."

"A rather weak excuse for refusing to participate in the evening's festivities. How many pounds did that mask you're not wearing cost you?"

"I don't know," Alex admitted, "and I don't think I want to."

Chuckling, Darby nodded toward the dance floor below. "This is an excellent vantage point."

Alex surveyed the silk-draped walls, the glittering chandeliers, and the colorful, animated crowd. The costumes lent an air of debauchery to the evening—and while he wasn't opposed to a little wickedness, he didn't want it occurring anywhere near Beth.

Unless *he* was the source of said wickedness.

His chest tightened at the sight of her wearing her scarlet, hooded cape. A pale blue gown peeked from beneath the vivid red silk, and her hair hung in long, loose curls down her back. Even now, as she mingled with guests near the entrance of the ballroom, he imagined sliding his hands beneath the folds of her cape and hauling her body against his.

But she'd been correct yesterday in the wine cellar when she'd warned him that he didn't need distractions. Much later tonight, after the last guest had left, he'd go to her. For now, he dragged his mind to the present.

"The view from here does suit our purposes nicely," he said to Darby. "I assume all is going according to plan?"

"Of course. I followed Newton and his wife from their front door to yours."

Alex had spotted them when they entered. "The monk in the brown robe and the nun in the black habit?"

Darby nodded.

"Anything suspicious about Newton's behavior?"

"No." Darby scratched his head. "He and his wife were arguing about something as they alighted their coach, but I couldn't make out the conversation."

"Try to discover what that's about. I recently arrived myself, only a quarter of an hour ago. Haversham is the sorcerer. Or some sort of magician. He's wearing the long, white wig, a fake beard, and a blue cloak."

Through the round holes of his black scarf, Darby quickly directed his shrewd gaze toward the marquess. "He's certainly easy to spot in that brilliant blue," Darby remarked.

"Agreed," said Alex. "Interestingly, he is already foxed, slurring his words, and swaying on his feet. He's had a glass of brandy in his hand since arriving, but he must have started drinking beforehand. I can't decide if his drunkenness will make the task of tracking him easier or considerably harder."

"With any luck, he'll soon pass out under a table and remain there for the better part of the evening," Darby remarked, squinting at the dance floor. "The woman dressed as a gypsy—is she Lady Haversham?"

"No, Lady H. is the peasant on the other side of the dance floor wearing the short skirt." She was raising eyebrows as she twirled and batted her eyes at a sailor. "I'm not certain who the gypsy is." The woman flirtatiously waved a scarf in front of Haversham's face, causing his jowls to shake with mirth.

"At least you should have plenty of entertainment as you track Haversham throughout the evening. I hope Newton proves to be half as amusing," Darby said.

"Nothing would please me more than a boring ball," Alex said soberly. "I'd consider it a great success if tomorrow's gossip papers proclaimed it uneventful, unremarkable, and dull."

"We will adhere to the plan then." Turning business-like, Darby pulled a watch from his pocket, and Alex did the same. "I have half past nine."

"As do I." Alex slipped the watch into his waistcoat. "We'll meet here at half past ten, and every hour after."

"And if either of us doesn't show at the appointed time, the other will go in search," Darby confirmed.

Alex nodded. "Right, because if either of the suspects leaves the ballroom, we follow."

"And if we do exit the room, we leave our scarf or mask behind as a clue to the direction we went." Darby rubbed his chin and grinned. "What could possibly go wrong?"

"*What* is that on your arm?" Beth squinted at the un-tidy mass of feathers strapped to Meg's wrist.

Her older sister, dressed in a flowing Grecian gown, held up the fluffy glob and stared at Beth, incredulous. "Isn't it obvious?"

"It looks like a bird and a squirrel had a terrible row and neither won," their younger sister, Julie, declared.

"I was afraid of that," Meg said with a sigh. "The

twins made it for me. It's supposed to be an owl, and I'm supposed to be Athena, of course."

"The goddess of wisdom," Beth said approvingly. "Very apropos for an ex-governess. You look lovely, as always. Which god did your husband choose? Let me guess. Ares—god of war?"

Meg rolled her eyes good-naturedly. "The twins insisted that he dress as Zeus and made him a lightning bolt to carry. He refused to wear anything approximating a toga, however, claiming that the lightning bolt is all the costume he needs."

"I do hope he's wearing *something* besides the lightning bolt," Julie murmured.

Smiling, Meg shook her head. "You're incorrigible— do you know that?"

"Be careful," Julie teased, brandishing her bow. "I have a quiver of arrows, and I'm eager to use them."

"Whoa, Artemis." Beth arched a brow at her younger sister, who wore a gorgeous silvery tunic and a crown of white and yellow flowers on her head. "Where did you find the bow and arrows?"

"Uncle Alistair's attic. He never gets rid of anything." She smiled at their uncle as he chatted with the dowager duchess a few yards away. "Doesn't he make a wonderful Renaissance man?"

"Indeed," Meg agreed. "He enjoys playing the part. When I greeted him earlier, he told me he couldn't linger as he was off to enjoy a pint with his merry men."

Beth smiled, but her thoughts were elsewhere. Throughout the day, even as she'd been rushing to and fro, overseeing preparations, and arranging flowers, she'd been remembering her time with Alex in the wine cellar.

His words played over and over in her head, so many times that she'd started to believe it wasn't just a lovely dream. Everything she wanted—love, respect, and passion—was hanging in front of her like a golden ring. All she had to do was reach out and grab—

"Red Riding Hood." Amused, Meg waved a graceful hand in front of Beth's face. "You were miles away. Be a good girl, and tell your dear sisters what's going on in that mind of yours."

Beth swallowed. Should she? The happiness that bubbled up inside her was almost impossible to contain, and she longed to tell them about Alex. She, Meg, and Julie had always shared everything, and after all the heartache they'd suffered together—their parents' deaths, their financial struggles, the ridicule of the ton—they deserved to celebrate the good things too.

But a niggling voice inside her said it was best to keep their relationship to herself for now. Her sisters wouldn't understand why he hadn't asked for Uncle Alistair's permission to court her, or why she had to leave for the duke's country house the next day. They would have questions. Questions Beth couldn't quite answer.

"I'm just delighted that we're all together and that everyone is well," she said.

She prayed Alex was well. She hadn't seen him all day and had started to doubt the wisdom of inviting the suspects into his house. But at least she knew who they were, and she had instructed a trusted footman to keep a close watch over both the sorcerer and the monk and to alert her immediately if either gentleman's actions seemed suspicious.

"That answer was vexingly vague," Julie declared. "But I shall spare you further interrogation as it appears that a knight is coming to your rescue."

Thinking that her sister must be referring to Alex, Beth's breath hitched in her throat. But when she looked up, it wasn't him, but an actual knight. Or, rather, a gentleman wearing the white mantle and red cross of a Templar knight.

He strode toward them, made a predictably gallant bow, and flashed a charming smile directly at Beth.

"Good evening, ladies."

Beth extended her hand. "What a pleasure to see you, Mr. Coulsen."

Chapter THIRTY-FOUR

Over the last hour, the size of the crowd had doubled. The orchestra's music floated up to the mezzanine, and dancing had commenced. Alex scanned the throng for a brilliant red cape. "Any developments on your end?" he asked Darby.

"Nothing significant. The discord between Lord and Lady Newton seems to stem from his unwillingness to invite her parents to his house party next month. He said he can't bear her mother's incessant chatter. She replied by saying that at least *her* mother doesn't cheat at charades." Darby shook his head in disgust. "Makes me damned grateful to be a bachelor, you know?"

"Er, I suppose." Alex still couldn't find Beth.

Darby leaned on the mezzanine railing. "Has Haversham fallen down yet? Or better yet, casted up his accounts?"

"No. He's been consorting with the gypsy and another woman, who is wearing man's breeches."

Intrigued, Darby nodded. "My fondness for masquerade balls grows by the minute."

Alex snorted. "Don't let a woman in breeches make you forget the plan." Although, even he was beginning to wonder if their machinations were necessary. The ball had been blessedly uneventful, and it seemed highly unlikely that the villain would be bold enough to attempt murder while two hundred of London's most elite looked on.

Still, he'd feel better if he knew where Beth was.

"Newton's heading toward the refreshment table," Darby said. "I'd better go and make sure he doesn't slip anything into the champagne. I'll meet you back here in an hour."

Alex gave him a grateful slap on the shoulder as he left. "See you at half past eleven."

As he scanned the ballroom below from left to right, a glimpse of red drew his eye.

Beth.

She stood in a small circle comprised of two women in light-colored gowns—her sisters, if he had to guess—and a Templar knight.

Alex studied the man, finding something familiar about his athletic stance and confident bearing. And then he placed him—Richard Coulsen.

He recalled the conversation he'd had with Darby at the pub a week ago. Coulsen *did* stand to gain a dukedom if Alex died. Was Alex being naïve to think that his cousin was above suspicion?

But his gut told him Coulsen wasn't a threat to him—at least not in a physical sense. Honorable and hardworking, his cousin presented a different sort of threat, perhaps more dangerous. Because he seemed less interested in Alex's title and fortune than he did in Beth.

But surely Alex's worries were unfounded. It was true that he'd been consumed with finding his would-be killer, but Beth understood that and would wait for him.

Swallowing his doubts, he flicked his gaze to Haversham. Good God. The gypsy that the marquess had been fawning over for much of the night stroked his long, fake beard, and the two were slyly making their way toward the tall doors leading out to the verandah.

The skin between Alex's shoulder blades prickled. What if Haversham only *pretended* to be drunk? What if he was using the gypsy as an alibi for nefarious activities that were underway at this very moment? Alex had to follow him.

He took one last, long look at Beth, willing her to look up him so he could give her a sign that he was thinking of her. So she'd know he was counting the minutes until this godforsaken ball was over so that he could go to her and tell her what he should have told her yesterday.

That he wanted to marry her.

Haversham and the gypsy staggered toward the verandah, laughing.

Please, Beth, look at me.

Time was running out. Even now, the marquess and his companion slipped outside, disappearing from view.

Damn it. Beth couldn't know he was up there on the mezzanine, but he desperately wanted to believe that she heard his silent plea. *I'm here. Don't give up on me. Believe in us.*

Just as he was about to leave and chase after Haver-sham, Beth turned her face up, gazing at the chandeliers, the silk bunting draped along the mezzanine railing—and finally, at him.

He nodded his head and held his breath, waiting for some form of recognition. A signal that all was well with her—and with them.

She froze momentarily, then timidly raised her hand and waved.

Smiling, he exhaled. "This is real," he murmured, hoping the words echoed in her heart.

He lingered one more moment before striding toward the verandah.

Beth's belly fluttered as she watched Alex walk away. For one second, while he'd smiled at her, the music had silenced, the dancers had paused, and the revelers had stilled. In the midst of the bustling ballroom, she and Alex had found each other.

Hope blossomed in her chest.

Julie jabbed an elbow into her side.

"Ow," she mumbled, glancing at the faces around her. Both of her sisters stared at her, eyes narrowed, as though they were starting to piece the puzzle together. Mr. Coulsen's gaze flicked to the now empty spot where Alex had stood and back to Beth.

And she thought she'd been subtle. Blast.

"Mr. Coulsen asked you a question," Meg whispered.

"I beg your pardon," Beth said. "It's difficult to hear above the orchestra."

Julie rolled her eyes. As if Beth didn't already know how pathetic her excuse was.

"I wondered if you might like to take a turn about the room," he said smoothly.

In spite of herself, Beth glanced at the mezzanine again. Alex was preoccupied with his investigation—as he should be.

Mr. Coulsen was a gentleman, and she admired him—in the same way one might an older brother. Spending a few minutes in his company certainly couldn't hurt. On the contrary, it would allow her to pass the time *and* to escape her sisters' questions about the duke, which were coming just as surely as she stood there.

"I'd be delighted to." She smiled as she took the arm Mr. Coulsen offered. He made a polite bow to her sisters, who glared at her as though she had much explaining to do. Beth made a mental note to avoid them for as long as possible.

Mr. Coulsen's arm was solid—if not quite as hard as Alex's—and his manners were impeccable. They strolled around the perimeter of the room, avoiding the clusters of guests and enjoying a respite from the merriment.

"It was very kind of the dowager duchess to invite me tonight," he said, his blue eyes earnest. "I'd concluded my business here and had planned to return to Kent yesterday but couldn't turn down the opportunity to attend such a grand event . . . mostly because I wished to see you."

Oh dear. Beth swallowed and looked at the toes of her gold slippers peeking beneath the hem of her blue gown. She hated to hurt Mr. Coulsen's feelings, but it wasn't fair to raise his hopes.

"I am honored that you would say such a—" she began.

"It's true."

She stopped near the corner of the room, where they had a modicum of privacy, and sighed regretfully. "While I hold you in the highest esteem, I feel obliged to tell you that . . . that my affections are elsewhere engaged."

He didn't flinch, but his shoulders sloped ever so slightly. "I was afraid of that. I saw the look you exchanged with Blackshire. You care for him?"

Beth ignored the question. "I'm sorry. And I do hope we may remain friends." The words seemed so inadequate—almost trite—and yet she meant them with all her heart. She had few friends beyond her sisters and the seventy-something-year-old duchess. It would be nice to count Mr. Coulsen among them.

"Of course we may," he said sincerely. "I won't pretend that I'm not disappointed, however I cannot say that I'm surprised. Someone as kind and beautiful as you *should* have a bevy of suitors."

"It's not like that," she assured him. "This . . . attachment . . . well, it developed rather spontaneously, when I least expected it." Lord help her, *why* was she divulging these details to Mr. Coulsen? "In any event, I have reason to believe that the, ah . . . gentleman returns my affections." Heat crept up her neck. She might as well come right out and tell Mr. Coulsen that only yesterday her *suitor* had ravished her in his wine cellar.

"Any man who didn't return your affections would be a fool," he said matter-of-factly.

For some reason, his blunt declaration brought tears to her eyes, and she sniffled. "Thank you."

"I hope that you believe me, Miss Lacey—Beth, if I may."

"Of course." It seemed harmless enough.

"I strongly believe that you deserve someone honorable and true," he said. "And I suppose that's why I feel obliged to divulge information that I've recently learned."

A chill ran the length of Beth's spine, and her stomach roiled. "What do you mean?"

"There's something you should know about the Duke of Blackshire."

Chapter THIRTY-FIVE

Beth fought the urge to flee from Mr. Coulsen and the ballroom entirely. What could he possibly know about Alex that she did not?

"If you are referring to the duke's notorious reputation," she said coolly, "I can assure you I am already aware of it."

"No, that's not it." He propped his hands on his hips, thoughtful yet fierce, looking every inch the noble knight. "I fear that the news may trouble you, and yet, I feel I must disclose it."

She doubted that he referred to the fire or Alex's parents or even the attempts on his life. Instead, she had the sense that Mr. Coulsen was about to tell her something far more personal.

"Please," she said softly. "Whatever it is that you must tell me . . . just say it."

He let out a long, slow breath, as if the revelation would pain him too. "After we spoke at Lord and Lady

Claville's ball, I found myself dwelling on our conversation, specifically the part where you told me that you and your sisters were known throughout the ton as the Wilting Wallflowers. Once I recovered from my shock, I couldn't help being appalled . . . and angry."

His outrage on her behalf warmed her. "I appreciate your concern for our reputations. But we've learned to ignore the vicious barbs and superior stares. You needn't fret on our account." Still, it was nice to know someone did.

"I made some inquiries," he said. "To try and discover the source of the ridiculous label. I was determined to confront the scoundrel. Anyone who would treat three young ladies so cruelly and callously deserves to be called out for his behavior."

Icy dread filled her veins. "What does this have to do with the duke?"

Mr. Coulsen's jaw clenched. "*He* is the one who gave you and your sisters the name, Beth. *He* dubbed you the Wilting Wallflowers."

She blinked, dumbfounded. It simply couldn't be true. Alex would never have been so malicious. Mr. Coulsen was probably just maligning him in order to gain favor with her. Perhaps he was jealous of Alex or held some sort of grudge.

"I . . . I don't know what to say." Suddenly chilled, she rubbed the tops of her arms.

As though privy to her thoughts, he said, "I wouldn't blame you for doubting me. And I won't deny that I had hoped to further our acquaintance. Of course, I'm disappointed to learn that your affections are otherwise

engaged, but I tell you the truth only so that you may
be armed with the facts."

"I understand," she said numbly—even though she
understood *nothing*. Mr. Coulsen had essentially accused
the man she loved of causing her and her sisters years
of untold pain. Her heart simply refused to accept it.

Snippets of intimate conversations with Alex echoed
in her head.

*Promise me something. The next time someone calls
you a wallflower, see yourself the way I'm seeing you
right now . . . Don't give that word an ounce of power
over you. Don't let it define you.*

She swallowed the painful knot in her throat. No, *no.*
He'd defended her. He'd helped her break free from the
name. He *couldn't* have been the one to launch the horrible, hateful name that had haunted her and her sisters
for the last three years.

"I appreciate your candor and do not doubt that you
are well-intentioned," she said stiffly. "However, is it not
possible that you were misinformed in this instance?"
After all, the ton had been incorrect about Alex's reputation as the prince of rakes. They could be wrong about
this too, couldn't they?

"I don't think so," Mr. Coulsen said regretfully. "The
person who confirmed the fact for me is a close friend
of the duke's—none other than Lord Darberville. He
happened to be present on that dubious occasion. You
may ask him yourself if you'd like."

Beth didn't want to hear any more. Alex trusted Lord
Darberville more than anyone. And if he claimed that
Alex had done it . . . Oh, God.

It must be true.

The ballroom tilted, her fingers went numb, and a low buzz started in her ears. "I think I require a bit of time to consider all you've said."

"Of course." His forehead creased in concern. "Forgive me if I've spoiled your evening. Shall I return you to your sisters?"

Her mouth turned dry as burnt toast. "No . . . thank you. I think I shall take a moment to freshen up. Please excuse me."

Her heart galloping, she fled toward the nearest door, amazed that her wobbly legs carried her out of the ballroom. Once in the hall, she hastily shrugged off the red cloak that seemed to be choking her, slumped her back against the wall, and gulped air.

She *mustn't* swoon. Closing her eyes, she willed her heart to slow and the floor to cease rocking.

It worked. After a minute she no longer felt like she might faint . . . but it took every ounce of self-control she possessed to keep from bursting into tears.

How could she have been so terribly wrong about Alex? Had she been so desperate to believe that someone needed and cared for her that she'd fallen into bed with the first man who'd paid her a compliment or two?

She'd thought that what they'd shared was real. But he'd lied to her. Perhaps, as they'd made love, he'd been chuckling at the irony of it all. He'd dubbed her a wallflower and then bedded her.

And if he'd been bold enough to lie about this, who knew what other falsehoods he'd told? He might have exaggerated the story about his parents' death to gain her sympathy. He might have seduced her so she'd cooperate with his plan to move his grandmother to the country. And at every turn, she had willingly, nay, eagerly taken him at his word.

He could have confessed the truth and she most likely would have forgiven him. But instead, he'd played her for the fool.

Now, in the wake of Mr. Coulsen's revelation, she felt beyond humiliated.

For only the most naïve sort of person would ever believe in dragons.

She swiped at her eyes. Whatever magic the masquerade had once held for her was lost. She had no wish to return to the ballroom, but she had little choice in the matter. The dowager would be looking for her, as would her sisters and Uncle Alistair, and she couldn't worry them by disappearing for the rest of the evening.

The worst part was that, in spite of his betrayal, Beth couldn't completely turn her back on Alex either.

His deception made her question everything . . . but tonight, she'd do what she could during the ball to help expose his would-be killer.

Because while he might not deserve her love, he did not deserve to die.

She would go to her bedchamber, splash a bit of cold water on her face, and gather herself for no more than a quarter of an hour. Then she would return to the ballroom and carry on, pretending that she wasn't hollow inside—and that her foolish heart hadn't shattered into a million tiny pieces.

After spending much of the last hour watching Haversham and the gypsy engage in drunken amorous activities on the verandah, Alex felt the need to scrub his eyes. Or at the very least, have a strong drink.

But he could not let down his guard, especially as the evening grew late and the guests grew more raucous. At that very moment, the killer could be drinking his champagne, gliding across his dance floor, or, God forbid, talking with his grandmother.

Moving briskly, Alex stalked to the meeting spot on the mezzanine and immediately scanned the throng below, sure that he'd be able to spot Beth from that vantage point. But he saw no sign of her bright red cape. He gripped the railing tightly and checked again. Surely, she wouldn't have left the ballroom.

Her sisters were both on the dance floor. Her uncle viewed the festivities from one of the chairs along the wall, not far from where Alex's grandmother also sat. But Beth was not beside either of them, so where was she? And who was she with?

Swallowing the bitter taste in his mouth, he scanned the crowd again, this time looking for Coulsen. Alex had defended him to Darby, but the way his cousin had been looking at Beth made Alex want to punch something— or someone. Maybe he'd been too hasty to dismiss him as a suspect.

Alex spotted the knight with a group of other young bucks near the refreshment table. He stood slightly apart from his companions and wore a somber expression that Alex hoped resulted from being soundly rejected by Beth.

But Alex no longer trusted him.

He checked his pocket watch. Darby was five minutes late, and neither he nor Newton seemed to be in the ballroom, which meant he'd likely followed Newton somewhere, and Alex needed to find both of them—quickly, just in case Newton was up to no good.

There were five ways to exit the ballroom. Alex could eliminate the verandah as a possible point of departure, which left the main doors, the side door, the tea room, and a back staircase.

He left the mezzanine and headed toward the back staircase, looking for Darby's black scarf—and any sign of trouble.

Chapter THIRTY-SIX

Beth's legs still felt shaky, but she no longer feared she'd burst into tears. She pushed aside thoughts of Alex's betrayal. There'd be plenty of time in the days, weeks, and months to come to dwell on the pain he'd caused her family.

For now, she needed to focus on keeping Alex, his grandmother, and all the guests safe.

Thus far, she'd had little time to do any investigating, a matter she intended to rectify as soon as possible. But first, she would see how the dowager was faring.

Beth found her sitting on the side of the room, tapping her foot in time to the music.

"I'd wondered where you'd gone," the duchess said, without a hint of censure. "I'd rather hoped that the handsome Mr. Coulsen would claim you for a dance."

"Sorry to disappoint," she said lightly. "I was merely fetching your fan." Beth handed it to her and sat beside her.

"It has grown rather stuffy," the dowager commented. "But then, every successful ball is." She smiled smugly, her merry eyes crinkling behind her spectacles.

"Shall I bring you some lemonade or champagne?" Beth glanced at the refreshment table and happened to notice Lord Newton and his wife, dressed as a monk and nun, slipping out of the ballroom and into the tea room, which the footmen were using as a staging area for the drinks and hors d'oeuvres.

Odd, that. There was no reason for guests to wander in there . . . unless they wanted access to the food and drink before it was served. Good heavens.

"No, my dear," the duchess said. "I'm perfectly content watching your older sister dance with her earl." She sighed in a manner that suggested she'd be *more* content if *Beth* were dancing with a gentleman. Raising her chin, the dowager looked down her nose at Beth. "What on earth has become of your costume?"

Drat. She'd discarded her cape in the hallway. Fanning herself dramatically, she said, "You are correct— it's far too warm. I left the cloak in my bedchamber."

"You look rather pale, Elizabeth. Are you feeling quite well?"

"Yes, of course." Beth kept an eye on the doorway to the tea room, waiting for Lord and Lady Newton to realize they'd wandered into an area meant for the staff and emerge red-faced.

But they did not.

"If you're certain you don't require anything," Beth said, "I believe I'll help myself to a glass of champagne."

"Yes, please do. It will fortify you. And it would

please me greatly if the next time I see you, a dashing gentleman is twirling you around the dance floor."

"Thank you. Excuse me." Beth dashed off as quickly as she could without appearing impolite. She needed to instruct the staff to watch over the food and make sure that no one was permitted to add anything to the glasses or food trays.

Halfway to her destination, a hand circled her upper arm, pinching her skin. She gasped and turned to see a peasant woman dressed in a low-cut blouse and short skirt. "Lady Haversham?"

"Indeed, Miss Lacey," she said smoothly, dropping her hand. "Forgive me for detaining you."

Rubbing her arm, Beth said, "It's quite all right. How may I help you?"

The woman adjusted her blouse, displaying her impressive cleavage to its greatest advantage. "I happened to notice that you and the Duke of Blackshire shared a rather . . . *meaningful* look earlier tonight."

Blast, had they been so obvious? Mr. Coulsen certainly seemed to have noticed. Heat crept up her neck, but she tossed her head defiantly. "I'm afraid I don't know what you mean."

Lady Haversham chuckled, but her eyes were cold and hard. "You needn't be embarrassed. A look is hardly clear and damning evidence of impropriety."

The hairs on Beth's arms stood on end. "Is there a specific reason that you stopped me?"

"Yes, of course." Lady Haversham pursed her lips, suddenly looking every inch a marchioness, in spite of her hoydenish attire. "I wished to warn you about the duke. You are no doubt aware of his reputation, and I urge you—do not be taken in by his handsome face and charming smile. Many a woman has tried to tame him, and none has succeeded. Don't allow pride to persuade you that you shall be the first."

The woman's words cut Beth to the quick. Perhaps she *was* proud. But mostly she was . . . in love.

"I am certain your advice is well-intentioned," she said coolly, "but let me assure you that your concern is unwarranted."

Lady Haversham sniffed. "I only wished to spare you unnecessary heartache. The man truly is an insatiable scoundrel. Why, only moments ago, I overheard the duke entreating a shepherdess to meet him in his study at midnight."

Beth gulped. Alex wouldn't do that. He might have neglected to tell her he'd coined the cruel Wilting Wallflower name, but he wouldn't be so callous as to seduce a woman right under her nose.

Not when she was leaving London the very next day.

Beth blinked away the tears that threatened. "I'm afraid I must go now."

Lady Haversham pressed her thin lips together, her glassy eyes troubled. "I understand, dear—better than you know. Godspeed."

Beth frowned as she left the marchioness. Her husband was one of the men suspected of trying to kill Alex. But why, in heaven's name, had the woman felt the need to issue a warning and reveal Alex's plans for an assignation?

Beth wasn't inclined to believe her, but then, where

Alex was concerned, her judgment had proven fallible. Still, she had no time to dissect Lady Haversham's words.

For Lord and Lady Newton could be poisoning the guests at that very moment. She headed in the direction of the tea room, praying she was not too late.

Alex reached for the black scarf draped over the back staircase's railing, stuffed it in his pocket, and raced down the stairs. At the bottom, he peered into the butler's room and the dining room—and found both eerily dark and empty.

As he turned to check the kitchen, someone grabbed his shoulder from behind.

Alex spun around and hauled his fist back, itching to hit someone.

Darby held up his palms. "Jesus, what are you trying to do?" he said in a loud whisper.

Unclenching his fist, Alex rubbed the back of his neck. "You shouldn't sneak up on people."

"I was trying to avoid alerting our suspect." He inclined his head toward the door to the pantry. "Newton's in there."

"By himself?"

"No. His wife's with him. And if their moans are any indication, I'd say she's forgiven him for slighting his mother-in-law."

Alex dragged a hand down his face. "Let's leave them."

Darby's eyebrows shot halfway up his forehead. "You're ready to abandon the plan, then?"

"They seem far too preoccupied with each other to

be plotting anything nefarious." Alex started walking toward the staircase, with Darby on his heels. "Haversham was similarly engaged on the verandah."

Darby snorted. "With Lady Haversham?"

Shaking his head, Alex said, "The gypsy. When I left them, they were horizontal behind the hedges. And he's still too drunk to present a danger to anyone but himself."

"Either one of our suspects could still be the culprit. Maybe they've guessed they're under surveillance." As he and Alex emerged from the back stairs into the ballroom, Darby waved an arm at the barely contained mayhem. "Or they've calculated that in a crowd this size, the risk of discovery is too great to attempt murder."

"That's true." But Alex's gut told him neither Newton nor Haversham presented a genuine threat. He and Darby were on the wrong track. "I've been considering what you said about Coulsen—about him having the most to gain from my death."

"I had no idea that you actually listened to a word I said."

"Occasionally. I've been watching him tonight too." It was hard to ignore the lovesick expression on the knight's face when he looked at Beth.

And Alex hadn't seen her in some time. His stomach clenched. It would be just like her to ignore his request for her to stay in the ballroom and, instead, try to take matters into her own hands.

Cursing under his breath, he said to Darby. "Stay alert, but try to enjoy the rest of your evening. I'm going to return to the mezzanine where I can watch Coulsen's movements." And look for Beth.

"Suit yourself," Darby said with a shrug. As though another thought suddenly occurred to him, he frowned. "Speaking of Coulsen, he asked me an odd question earlier."

Alex tensed. "What question?"

"He wanted to know if it was true that you'd originally labeled the Lacey sisters the Wilting Wallflowers."

Shit. "And I presume that you told him to mind his own goddamn business?"

"Er . . . in hindsight, I guess I should have." Darby scratched his head guiltily. "But you seemed to hold him in high regard, so I told him the truth. That you had, and that you weren't proud of it."

Alex dropped his forehead into his hand. "Christ."

"I'm sorry. If you'd like, I can hunt him down and threaten him within an inch of his life, should he tell anyone."

Sighing, Alex shook his head. "No. This isn't your fault or Coulsen's. I only have myself to blame, and it will be up to me to undo the damage. If it even *can* be undone."

"Good luck. For what it's worth, I think your wallfl— that is, Miss Lacey—is worth it," Darby said, deviously weaving his way into the crowd before Alex could throttle him.

More determined than ever to find her, Alex headed for the mezzanine stairs, located on the opposite side of the room.

But he was intercepted halfway there by a trident-wielding Poseidon. "Pardon, your grace," he said. "I was asked to deliver a message to you." He reached behind his beard into his shirt and withdrew a small folded note.

Alex snatched it from his hand and read it:

Meet me in the study at midnight.—B

Poseidon had already started a conversation with an Egyptian queen, but Alex yanked him aside, waving the note. "Who gave you this?"

"I don't know." He tilted his head and adjusted his crown, thoughtful. "But she wore a red cape," he said, brightening. "She was dressed in scarlet—like Red Riding Hood."

"Thank you." Alex spun the ocean god toward his Cleopatra, shoved the message in his pocket, and checked his watch.

In ten minutes, he'd meet Beth.

And beg forgiveness.

Chapter THIRTY-SEVEN

Beth stepped into the tea room and pulled the butler aside. "Mr. Sharp, have you noticed any guests wandering in this area?"

The butler's wizened face creased. "None to speak of, Miss Lacey. But I haven't been here the whole time. Are you looking for someone?"

"No. I only wanted to relay a message from the dowager duchess. She requests that you keep guests from lingering here where the drink and food are being prepared."

Mr. Sharp pulled himself up taller. "Certainly, miss."

"Thank you." She started to return to the ballroom, then turned back to face the butler. "Could you tell me the time?"

He consulted his watch and raised bushy black brows. "Five minutes until midnight." His dark eyes sparkled. "Almost the witching hour."

"Indeed," she said, smiling in spite of the ache in her

chest. When the clock struck, the few guests who'd managed to keep their identities secret would pull off their masks, and the revelry would continue into the wee hours of the morning.

But Beth felt none of their anticipation, shared none of their exuberance.

She should make her way back to her sisters and spend the rest of the evening with them, so that she wouldn't be tempted to do something impulsive, reckless, and utterly self-destructive.

If there was one thing she was certain of, it was that she absolutely should not give credence to Lady Haversham's ramblings.

But as she weaved her way through the crowd in the ballroom moments later, she couldn't help but look for a shepherdess—and wonder if the supposed assignation between her and Alex was related to the attempts on Alex's life. Maybe Alex needed Beth.

Before she knew it, her traitorous feet were carrying her to the study.

Oh, she was no doubt torturing herself, but if she found the room empty, she would know that Lady Haversham had been mistaken. And if she was right, and Beth witnessed Alex's duplicity with her own eyes, perhaps her heart would realize the futility of loving him.

Her fingertips tingled as she slipped out of the ballroom. Listening for footsteps, she tiptoed down the corridor. No one was in front of her or behind her as she glided down the grand staircase.

The ground floor was eerily silent, but then, she wouldn't expect a couple slipping away for a tryst to mark their arrival with trumpets. And she was still a few minutes early.

Her heartbeat thundering in her ears, she paused outside the closed door of the study.

No voices came from within, and she stood there for several seconds, unsure what to do. The prudent course of action would be to return to the ballroom. But she couldn't turn back now. She had to see this through to its potentially awful, gut-wrenching end.

Swallowing her fear, she took a deep breath, turned the knob, and ventured into the dark room.

"Alex?"

No response.

She waited for her eyes to adjust to the darkness, then moved toward his desk, careful to avoid the ladders and jars of paint in her way. She'd hide behind one of the large armchairs and wait for—

Thud.

Glass shattered.

Pain split her head.

Her chest slammed into the floor.

A moan—hers—echoed in her ears.

Liquid soaked her bodice; the smell of brandy filled her nostrils.

Behind her, someone tore through the room, throwing wood, wallpaper, and God knew what else in her direction.

A momentary silence was followed by the ominous scratch of flint on metal. Oh, God. Beth forced her eyes open and saw the spark ignite the paper. A small flame leaped to life, revealing a woman wearing a red cape. *Her* cape.

The woman dashed to the door and swiftly closed it behind her, leaving Beth sprawled on the floor behind the desk.

She tried to move, but her limbs refused to obey.

She tried to call out, but the words came out as a whisper.

Help me, Alex.

Don't let this be the end.

I love you.

Across the room, the door lock clicked, and a chill skittered the length of her spine.

Smoke burned her eyes.

And blackness descended.

Just before midnight, Alex surveyed the ballroom.

Beth's sisters chatted with each other animatedly. His grandmother conversed with an innocent-looking fortune-teller. Lord Haversham and the gypsy had returned from the verandah and taken to the dance floor—each with a different partner. Alex shrugged—to each his own, he supposed.

Newton stood by himself near the potted ferns, brooding.

But all seemed to be well, and Alex could count on Darby to watch over the ballroom while he met with Beth.

Eager to see her and loath to keep her waiting, he walked to the door leading to the back staircase. Though less direct, the route would help him avoid most of the guests and slip out, sight unseen.

Or so he thought.

Just a few paces away from the exit, Newton suddenly

stepped in front of Alex, effectively blocking his path. Their chests bumped, and Alex instinctively raised his fists.

Newton held his ground. "We need to talk," he said menacingly, the effect somewhat spoiled by his pious monk's robe.

"It will have to wait." If, as Alex suspected, Beth had discovered he'd labeled her and her sisters the Wilting Wallflowers, he needed to beg her forgiveness and re-assure her. And being late to their meeting wouldn't help his cause. He started to walk away, but Newton shot out a hand and grabbed his shoulder.

"This won't take long," he said evenly. "Please."

"Fine. What do you wish to talk about? Shall we compare injuries from our boxing match? Or perhaps review *the rules*?"

"Not here," Newton snapped. "We'll talk on the ve-randah."

Alex suppressed a sigh. He'd spent more time on the verandah this evening than he had during the entire last year. But Newton's sense of urgency told him that the conversation would be enlightening. Suspect or no, Alex would risk being alone with him for information that might help him solve the mystery.

So he wouldn't have to hold the people he loved at arm's length.

So he and Beth could begin a life together, free from worry.

Following Newton outside, Alex kept an eye on his hands. Any number of weapons could be concealed be-neath the folds of the monk's robe. If Newton carried a pistol, the knife in Alex's boot would be useless.

They walked through the doors, and the sounds of the ball faded behind them. Alex flexed his fists as he faced the sullen viscount, ready to fight if necessary. "Speak your mind, Newton."

The monk planted his hands on his hips and stared at the slate stones beneath his boots. "You let me believe that you'd bedded my wife. Why?"

Good God. Whatever confrontation Alex had been expecting, it wasn't this. Shrugging, he said, "You were going to believe what you wanted to, regardless."

"Perhaps." The viscount began to pace, his brown robe fluttering behind him. "But if there was any doubt in my mind as to your guilt, I might have spared your knee during our boxing match." He paused and looked over the hedges at the garden. "My wife told me the truth tonight. That you'd never seduced her. That she told the falsehood to make me jealous."

Alex snorted. "It worked."

"Don't be an ass, Blackshire. This isn't easy for me."

"*What* isn't easy? Admitting that you've been trying to murder me?"

The viscount blinked and stared at Alex, dumb-founded. "What in God's name are you talking about? I'm trying to apologize for falsely accusing you. But Jesus, a kick to the knee never *killed* anyone."

Damn it. Newton was far too perplexed to be lying. Which meant that a would-be murderer could be in his ballroom right now.

Or in his study—with Beth. Holy hell.

"I have to go," Alex said.

"Wait." Newton scratched his head. "Someone's been trying to *murder* you?"

Alex shook his head. "Forget I mentioned it."

The viscount crossed his arms. "If there's something I can do to assist, please let me know. I would like to make amends for my behavior at the boxing match."

"Not necessary," Alex said. "If I thought someone had seduced my wife, I'd have done the same."

Newton arched a sardonic brow. "Never say *you* plan to take a wife. Surely that would signal the end of days."

Alex inclined his head. "Then you may want to prepare for—"

He stopped and sniffed the air. The hairs on the back of his neck stood on end. "Do you smell that?"

Newton raised his chin, inhaled, and narrowed his eyes. "Smoke?"

No. It couldn't be. No, no, *no*.

Alex had to find Beth.

He was running for the ballroom when the first screams from within pierced the air. "*Fire!*"

Chapter THIRTY-EIGHT

As Alex tried to enter the house, scores of guests stampeded out of the French doors and spilled onto the verandah, frantic to escape the smoky ballroom.

He shouted above the commotion. "Not this way," he said, guiding the throng backward. "There are no stairs off the verandah. Gentlemen, escort the ladies through the ballroom and through one of the other exits. Quickly make your way outside and move away from the house."

He squeezed past the guests and moved to the center of the ballroom, where smoke floated toward the high ceilings, filling the room like a dreary London fog. Several footmen scurried to and fro.

"George," he called to one of them. "Where's the fire?"

The young, gangly man swallowed. "The ground floor, your grace. Mr. Sharp just ordered Richard to sound the alarm and send for the fire brigade."

Shit. His study was on the first floor, which meant Beth . . . dear God.

"Spread the word that everyone—staff and guests—should meet in the square across the street," Alex said. "Make sure all are accounted for."

"Yes, your grace."

The footman dashed off, and the butler strode over. "I've asked Thomas to check every room on the second floor," he said, stifling a cough. "And Richard is doing the same on this floor."

"I'll take the ground floor," Alex said, already moving toward the exit. "Have you seen my grandmother?"

"Yes, your grace. The dowager seemed a little shaken but otherwise fine. Miss Lacey was helping her down the back stairs."

Alex halted in his tracks. "Miss Lacey was with her?"

Mr. Sharp blinked. "Yes. Wearing her red cape. She had her arm around your grandmother."

Alex blew out the breath he'd been holding. Relief flooded his veins. "Thank you. I'm glad to know they're safe." But he'd feel better when he saw them both for himself. "I'm going to do a sweep of the ground floor, then we'll all meet outside and wait for the brigade."

The butler's jowls trembled. "It's a tragedy, your grace. First your parents and your uncle's house . . . and now this. I'll have the staff save what we can—the silver, paintings, some of the furniture. Is there anything in particular you'd like us to fetch?"

Alex considered the question. His heart tripped in his chest as he thought about his father's beloved desk, his mother's antique ring, and the portrait of his parents—the only one he possessed—that graced the wall in the front hall. The more practical side of him thought about bank notes, ledgers, and jewels.

But in the end, none of those things truly mattered—especially if a life was lost.

Alex clasped the butler's shoulder. "Let's ensure everyone makes it out safely. Then we'll do what we can to save the house."

Mr. Sharp gave a dutiful nod and coughed again. "The fire seems to be located in the front of the house—probably in your study. The main stairway is filled with smoke, so I'm directing everyone toward the back stairs."

"Well done. Now you go outside too. Find my grandmother and Miss Lacey and instruct them to wait in the square. Under no circumstances should they—or anyone—return to the house. I'll meet you there shortly."

"Understood, your grace."

Alex ran toward the main stairway. He needed to be sure that no one was left there, either overcome by smoke or paralyzed with fear.

As he descended the stairs, the cloud of smoke thickened and his eyes stung. It couldn't be a coincidence that Beth and he were supposed to meet in the study at midnight—just as a conflagration began there. He'd thought he'd managed to stay one step ahead of his mysterious adversary, but he'd been outmaneuvered once again.

Alex stepped into the front hall, ducking to keep his head below the heaviest haze of smoke, and turned around. "Is anyone here?" He called out. "You need to leave the house at once!"

The only reply was sputtering crackle coming from the direction of the study. Grey ghostly tendrils emerged from beneath the closed door, greedily reaching out and up.

He stalked to the door, tried to turn the knob, and found it locked. And warm.

Holy hell. As he pounded the door with his fist, he reminded himself that Mr. Sharp had seen both his grandmother and Beth making their way outside. Surely, they were safe.

Perhaps one of the staff had wisely closed the study door to slow the spread of the fire. They would have checked the room before locking it—to be certain no one remained inside.

But Alex needed to be sure.

He pounded again and shouted. "Is anyone in there?"

"Alex!"

No. The voice, feminine and husky, sounded like Beth's. But it couldn't be.

"Beth—is that you?" Fear and dread sliced through him, nearly ripping him in two.

"Help!" she said, coughing violently.

Dear God. "I'm coming!" He took a step back then charged at the door using his shoulder as a battering ram. The door rattled on its hinges but didn't open.

He tried again. The lock held.

Jesus, how could this be happening?

Desperate, he looked around for something to smash the knob and grabbed a walking stick. He swung the handle at the knob like a sledgehammer, but the stick snapped in two.

"Hold on, Beth!"

Lord help him, he had to reach her *now*. Smoke could already be filling her lungs. Flames could be licking at her skin. Every second mattered.

With strength fueled by fear, he kicked the knob with

the heel of his boot, over and over, until it hung limply and the door cracked open.

Waves of smoke and a wall of heat assaulted him, and he squinted as he peered inside. The largest flames were in the center of the room, on and around his desk, and around the windows, where the blaze consumed the heavy curtains.

It was frighteningly similar to the fire that had taken his parents.

Hell if he'd let it take Beth from him.

"Beth!" he called above the roar.

No response.

He took one more deep breath of air near the doorway and rushed into the room, running through the flames, over the piles of wood and paper. His nose and throat burned. His heart pounded as it had when he'd been a boy of six, terrified and clinging to his father.

In the midst of the suffocating heat, the realization hit him. Any six-year-old would have done the same. He wasn't responsible for his parents' deaths. Not really.

Besides, he was no longer that boy, and Beth was counting on him.

He found her on the other side of the flames, curled in the corner next to the bookshelves.

Dropping to his knees, he took her face in his hands. "Beth, it's me. I have you, and I'm going to carry you out of here."

As he swept her into his arms, her limbs dangled lifelessly. Her gown was singed around the hem, and her cheeks were smudged with ash. She looked peaceful, almost like she was sleeping. But she was pale and still.

So, so still—like his mother had been. Dear God. Don't let him be too late.

His own breathing grew labored. His lungs burned. He gasped for air.

I'm taking you out of here, Beth. And you're going to be all right. You have to be.

He counted down in his head. *Three, two, one. Go.*

Holding her close, he raced through the flames, out of the study, and through the main hall. He yanked open the front door and trotted down the steps, coughing and hacking. His arms shook as he laid her gently on the walkway in front of the house. "You're safe," he whispered into her hair. "I'm with you. Don't leave me now. I need you."

A few people who must have seen him emerge from the house shouted and ran toward him, but he didn't take his eyes off Beth. After all they'd been through, it couldn't end like this.

Desperate for a sign of life, he pressed an ear to her chest.

And heard the faintest of beats.

He thanked heaven . . . but her breaths were shallow, and in the pale moonlight, her lips had a blueish hue.

No, the heartbeats weren't enough. He *needed* to know she would be all right. Frantic, he gently shook her.

"Beth." He cradled her head in his palm—and felt something sticky. Wet.

His stomach fell like a rock. Please . . . don't let it be.

But it was. Her hair was matted with blood.

Chapter THIRTY-NINE

Beth's throat burned, and her tongue felt as dry as the sawdust that littered the floor of Alex's study.

The ache in her head radiated, invading her limbs like poison.

And though she could feel cool air on her skin, she couldn't breathe it in. It was as though someone had bound her chest with a hundred yards of cloth and cinched the ends with Herculean strength, so that she couldn't possibly inhale.

She should be fighting. For air, for consciousness, for life. But her body refused to obey her commands.

In the distance, she heard pleading . . . and her name.

She focused the last scrap of her energy on that voice—deep, rich, and heartbreakingly familiar. Alex.

He sounded uncharacteristically sad. Frightened and vulnerable. And she knew, deep in the pit of her belly, that *she* was the cause of his distress.

Dear God. He *needed* her.

Not for what she could *do* for him or even to *fix* things. He needed her for who she *was*.

And she couldn't leave him—at least not without a fight.

So she struggled harder. For him, for her, for the life they could have together.

She strained against the bands around her chest, stretching them. Expanding them by just a hair. And then another.

Her strength nearly sapped, she made one last desperate attempt to inhale deeply. If she could only manage a proper breath, she'd be able to find her way back to Alex. Surely, she would.

Ignoring the pain and the burning and the fear, she gasped and gulped, coughing until blessedly clean air flooded her lungs.

Her head throbbed.

Violent spasms racked her body.

The horrors of the night bombarded her—the blow to the head, the burning study, smoke everywhere . . . and the discovery that Alex had not been forthright with her.

But he was there, holding her head on his lap. Promising her that he would take care of her and that everything would be all right.

How she wanted to believe him.

"Someone bring water!" he shouted over her head. Leaning closer he whispered, "I have you now, Beth. And I'm never letting go."

She forced her eyes open and gazed into his earnest, devastatingly handsome face. She wanted to tell him that she loved him. But when she tried to speak, only a croak came out.

He pressed a cool ladle to her lips, and she drank gratefully, even though the water tasted like smoke.

"You're injured," he said softly, as though he regretted having to deliver the bad news. "I've already summoned the doctor, and you need to remain still until he arrives."

She nodded, wincing at the pain in her head.

"Who?" he asked, low and lethal. "Who did this to you?"

"I don't know," she rasped. "Someone wearing my cape."

He blinked and looked up, like he was trying to piece the parts together. Worry flicked across his face, alarming her once again.

"Alex?"

Gazing intently at her, he asked, "Were you with my grandmother after the fire started?"

Was she? The events of the night jumbled in her head, and the throbbing in her temples muddled her thinking. "I don't think—"

"Beth!" The frantic cries of her sisters pierced the intimate cocoon of her conversation with Alex.

"My God, we've been looking all over for you," Meg blurted. She fell to her knees beside Beth and grasped her hand. "What's happened to you? Are you all right?"

"I was hit on the—"

"Sweet Jesus, Beth!" Julie crouched on her other side, her beautiful face ghostly pale. "You're bleeding all over the—"

"That's enough," Meg snapped at their younger sister. She exchanged a look with Alex, then turned back to Beth. "Save your strength, darling. We will unravel it all later. For now, you must rest."

Alex tugged off his cravat and gently wound it around her crown.

Julie removed her cloak and tucked it around Beth like a blanket. "There," she said soothingly.

Beth's heart raced. Being treated with kid gloves was a thousand times more frightening than the blood.

But she needed to focus. Something still wasn't right.

"Where is your grandmother?" she asked Alex.

His forehead creased in concern. "She's probably with all the staff and guests, across the street. I asked Mr. Sharp to look for her."

"I didn't see her in the square," Meg said.

"The last time I saw her, she was in the ballroom," Julie mused. "Moving toward the door with Beth."

"It wasn't me," Beth choked out. "Someone else has been wearing my cape." She looked at Alex. "You need to find your grandmother."

He frowned. "I will, just as soon as the doctor arrives."

"Meg and Julie will stay with me. You must go," she urged. "Find her before . . ." *the unthinkable happens.*

"You should go," Meg agreed. "We'll care for Beth."

Julie nodded vigorously. "The Lacey girls stay together. No matter what."

Hearing their old mantra—the one they'd clung to after their parents' deaths—made Beth want to cry all of a sudden, but she swallowed back a sob and smiled at Alex. "I shan't go anywhere. Promise."

"Very well," he said reluctantly.

He reached for the folded blanket that a footman offered and tenderly tucked it under her head as a pillow,
replacing his thigh. The blanket was softer, and yet . . .

"Take care of her." He spoke to Meg and Julie, but
the adoration that shone in his eyes . . . that was all for
Beth. "And please do not go anywhere, because before
the night is through, there are two matters I wish to discuss with you ladies."

Meg arched a brow. "Do you?"

"With us?" Julie squeaked.

Alex drew himself up to his full, considerable, height.
"Indeed. I must first issue an apology, and second . . .
I'd like to seek permission to court your sister."

Beth's heart fluttered. Though she was dizzy and
sprawled on the sidewalk with the devil of a headache,
a seedling of hope sprouted in her chest.

Because the shocked expressions on her sisters' faces
said that just now, her relationship with Alex had crossed
over from the realm of fairy tales into a world that was
indisputably, incontrovertibly, and gloriously . . . real.

Alex had to wrench himself away from Beth, and although he hated to leave her, she was right. His grandmother was likely in danger.

He sprinted to the square across the street, grateful
that the bucket brigade had already arrived and begun to
work. Darby barked out orders, quickly organizing the
mob of volunteers into a line stretching from a well
one block away to the front door of Alex's house. Men,
women, and children—some of them neighbors wearing robes and slippers, some guests still dressed in their

costumes—started passing buckets of sloshing water up the line.

They'd prevent the fire from spreading to his neighbors' homes. They might even save his house.

But his town house was the least of his worries.

Alex spotted Mr. Sharp in a grassy area, distributing blankets to a pair of older women dressed in Egyptian garb. "Please accept my apologies for the disruption in the festivities," his butler was saying—as though the out-of-control fire was comparable to an unscheduled break by the orchestra. "We shall round up some refreshments at the first available opportunity."

"Mr. Sharp," Alex called.

The butler made his apologies and hurried over. "Your grace, I am glad you're here. I've been asking all the guests about the dowager duchess—and none of them has seen her since she was in the ballroom. I could have sworn that she and Miss Lacey were making their way outside. But I saw that you rescued Miss Lacey . . . is it possible that the dowager is still in the house?"

Alex's heart pounded, and he prepared to charge back into the flames. "It is possible. Or she might have made it out and left with someone. Are all of our guests accounted for?"

"I believe so, your grace. Though I'd feel better if I had a list. We asked a member of each party to confirm that everyone in their group made it to safety. Some are helping the brigade. Others, anticipating a long night, have left to fetch supplies for the volunteers."

Alex clutched his head, desperate to think what clue he might have missed. Newton and Coulsen had both shed their costumes, rolled up their shirtsleeves, and joined in the fire-fighting effort. Haversham sat against the trunk of a tree, passed out.

If his suspects weren't responsible for the fire, who was? Beth had said her attacker was a woman . . . and so was the person who'd sent him the note asking him to meet in the study.

"Are any of the guests wearing a red cape—similar to Miss Lacey's?"

"Not that I'm aware of, your grace. Although, now that you mention it, I recall seeing a red blanket . . . draped over Lord Haversham."

"Holy hell." Alex ran to the drunken marquess, snatched the cape off him, and examined it under the lantern Mr. Sharp held aloft. "It's Miss Lacey's," Alex said, dread turning his blood to ice.

"Haversham," he shouted, shoving the marquess with the toe of his boot. The man groaned and squinted as though he already suffered from the king of all hang-overs. Alex shook the cloak in his face. "Where did you get this?"

"Jesus, Blackshire. What kind of host are you? First you endanger our lives with a fire, and then—"

Alex reached the end of his fuse. He grabbed the marquess by his magician's robe, hauled him to his feet, and slammed him against the tree. "Where," he seethed, "did you get Miss Lacey's cape?"

Haversham's face turned mottled red. "My wife covered me with it," he sputtered. "Before she left."

Good God. *Lady Haversham?* "Where was she going?"

The marquess shrugged. "The devil if I know. She's been rather . . . unhinged as of late."

A chill slithered down Alex's spine. "Unhinged . . . *how*?"

"Spouting nonsense. She's fine one moment and promising all manner of vengeance the next."

"Vengeance against whom? For what?" Alex demanded.

Haversham sighed and closed his eyes, weary. "I don't know. You know what flighty, unpredictable creatures women can be. I rarely listen to her babble, much less give any credence to it."

"*Think*." Alex slammed him into the tree again. "Try to remember."

The marquess groaned. "She's intent on making me jealous. She claimed she'd take London's greatest lover to her bed—and if she couldn't have him, no one else would either. But it's all gibberish, Blackshire. She's easily confused—hasn't been herself for the last year or so."

Shit. Alex released Haversham, and the marquess landed on the ground in a heap before retching all over the grass beside him.

Unsympathetic, Alex said, "Your coach. Is it here?"

"Aye." The marquess spit and wiped his mouth with the back of his sleeve. "I presume that's my invitation to leave."

Alex snorted. "Do whatever the hell you want. I'm going after your wife."

He charged toward the queue of coaches at the end of the block, praying that he found his grandmother—before she suffered harm at the hands of a madwoman.

Chapter FORTY

Huffing and short of breath, Alex stopped in front of the line of carriages. Only five remained, as many of the ball guests had no doubt headed for their beds. "Where's Haversham's coach?" he called to a driver slumped on his seat.

The startled man spat out his pipe and sat up straight. "It was right in front of me, my lord, but left."

Damn it. "When?"

The driver shrugged. "No more than a quarter of an hour ago."

Alex walked closer. "It's crucial that I know who was in that coach."

"Lady Haversham, for certain," he replied, rubbing his chin. "But not the marquess. There was an older lady with her."

Alex's stomach dropped. "Did she wear glasses?"

"I don't recall, my lord, but she was dressed in a silver robe and cap."

"That's what I feared," Alex murmured. Louder, he said, "Which direction did they head?"

The driver frowned. "You know, I thought it rather odd, but Lady Haversham instructed her driver to take them to the Westminster Bridge."

Dear Jesus. Alex climbed onto the coach and planted himself on the seat beside the driver. "Take me there. Now."

"I can't," the driver protested. "Lord Newton and his wife expect me to wait for them here."

"Then wait for them. But I need your coach now." He reached for the reins, and the driver balked.

"Who are you? Er . . . if you don't mind me asking."

"The Duke of Blackshire. Look, Newton won't mind. My grandmother is in danger."

"You should have said so, your grace." The wiry man fumbled over himself as he snapped up the reins. "Who would want to harm a grandmother?"

"Lady Haversham," Alex said grimly. "Let's go—we may already be too late."

Newton's driver whistled to the horses and slapped the reins, urging them into a trot, then a gallop. The coach wasn't built for speed, but the driver navigated the dark streets and twisting turns as fast as he dared—just short of flipping the carriage on its side.

But it wasn't fast enough for Alex. With each minute that passed, his panic rose.

He'd managed to save Beth, but if he couldn't save his grandmother . . . he'd never forgive himself. She'd been by his side during the darkest days of his life . . . and now, the one time she truly needed him, he wasn't there for her.

The streets were largely deserted at that early morning hour, and moonlight bathed the city in an eerie, blue glow that made Alex's hair stand on end. "Hurry," he urged.

"The bridge is just ahead," the driver shouted. "And that must be Haversham's carriage."

"Stop there," Alex ordered, and before the coach had stopped moving, he jumped off. "Lady Haversham!" he called into the night.

No response.

He ran to her coach, parked at the river's edge, flung open the door, and found the cab empty. The driver had gone too.

Alex raced onto the bridge.

"Hullo!" A man in livery—Haversham's driver?—ran toward him, waving his arms frantically.

"Where's Lady Haversham?" Alex demanded. "Is the dowager duchess with her?"

"She's a duchess?" The man gulped. "The marchioness told me to drive her here. And then she and the older lady—the, ah, duchess—walked onto the bridge. I heard arguing, so I went to check on them, but then there was a scream and a . . . a splash."

No.

Alex tore to the edge of the bridge and leaned far over the side, searching the shadowy, dark water. "Grandmother!"

The surface of the Thames was calm. Too calm.

Choking back a sob, he ran to the opposite side. His torso slammed into the stone wall as he scanned the water there. He needed something to go on. A splash, a cry . . . a sign.

Downstream, a glimmer caught his eye. A piece of fabric floated ominously, an underwater ghost.

His grandmother's silver cape.

Shaking with rage and fear, he shrugged off his jacket, pulled off his boots, and climbed onto the ledge of the bridge. The distance to the water had to be forty feet. His grandmother could have survived the fall. She *had* to. Now he just had to pull her out of the Thames.

Before it was too late.

He focused on the spot in the water—the spot where her cape had been. But it was already sinking, being sucked into the cold, murky depths.

Closing his eyes, he drew in a long breath and—

"Alexander Benjamin Savage," a scolding voice called out.

Good God. "Grandmother?" He spun around to find her strolling toward him, hands propped on her hips.

"Step off that ledge at once, young man," she ordered. "What in heaven's name do you think you're doing?"

"Saving you?"

She held out her arms. "Do I *look* like I require saving?"

Relief turned his legs to jelly, and he collapsed on the ledge, sitting so that he faced her. "You're not in the river," he said stupidly.

"No." He could almost hear her eyes roll behind her spectacles.

"And you're not harmed." He slid off the wall, gently clasped her shoulders, and examined her at arm's length, from the top of her silver cap to the toes of her sensible slippers.

"No, my dear," she said, pulling him into a hug. "I am fine. But Lady Haversham . . ."

"*She's* in the river?"

"I'm afraid so. She was quite troubled, rambling on about how you'd rejected her and how she must be the only woman in London who you hadn't bedded and how you refused to forgive her husband's debt."

Alex shook his head and leaned against the wall. "I think she's been trying to kill me."

"Oh, she's definitely been trying to kill you," the dowager said. "She admitted as much. She said she'd tried to kill Elizabeth too, but you spoiled that. So she had no choice but to kill *me*."

Alex blinked at his grandmother's matter-of-fact tone. "So what happened?"

"I told her I'd rather not ruin my pretty silk cape and asked if I could remove it before she threw me into the water. She agreed, and I tossed my cloak over her head and pushed her to the ground."

He stared at his sweet, delicate grandmother, stunned. "You didn't."

"I did. And I ran, calling for help. But I hadn't made it very far before I heard the splash. She must have decided that throwing herself into the Thames was preferable to spending the rest of her days in Newgate."

Aghast, Alex turned toward the water again. "There's a rowboat on the shore. Maybe I can pull her out of the river."

"It's too late for her," his grandmother said firmly. "I don't believe she survived the fall, but even if she had . . . she's been in the water for far too long. Leave it to the authorities to recover her body in the morning. Right now, we need to return to the house—assuming it hasn't burned to the ground—and ensure that Elizabeth is well."

Alex scooped up his jacket and draped it around her shoulders. "It's been a horrid night, but now that I know you and Beth are all right, I feel like the luckiest man alive."

"What a sweet sentiment." His grandmother patted his cheek as though deeply touched. "You should marry her, you know."

Alex chuckled. "Trust me. I'm working on it."

When Newton's coach pulled up to Alex's house, the bucket brigade was still hard at work, but smoke no longer billowed from the ground floor windows. Only wisps and puffs remained.

As Alex helped his grandmother disembark, Mr. Sharp ran over, jubilant. "Thank goodness the duchess is safe. The fire is contained, your grace. The study is destroyed, but the rest of the house has only minor damage . . . we were extremely fortunate."

Alex should have been celebrating the news, but he could only stare at the spot on the ground where he'd left Beth.

The now empty spot. "Where's Miss Lacey? Is she all right?"

"She seemed well enough, considering the nasty blow she suffered. Her sisters took her home—to their uncle's house."

He couldn't blame her sisters—she'd be safe and comfortable at her uncle's. But damn it, she belonged with *him*. "I'm heading there, right now."

His grandmother placed a hand on his arm, her grip surprisingly strong. "Give Elizabeth some time," she said. "She had a tremendous shock tonight."

"Yes, but I need to see her. I need to tell—"

"*She* needs her rest." She glared at him from behind her spectacles. "You may tell her whatever you need to say tomorrow—when she will be in a better frame of mind to receive it."

His grandmother's maid rushed over, beside herself with panic. "There you are, my lady! I've been looking all over for you. I'm so relieved to see you are well."

"You'd never know a madwoman nearly threw me off the Westminster Bridge, would you?" the dowager remarked.

"Oh my stars," the maid said, clucking her tongue, but clearly not believing the dowager's tale. "Come. Your neighbor Lady Brandham invited you to spend the night there, and stay as long as necessary. I'm going to send for tea with a spot of milk, just as you like it, then settle you in her guest chamber for a good night's sleep. You'll feel more like yourself in the morning."

His grandmother smirked at Alex as the maid whisked her off, scolding her for losing her elegant cape and for being out of doors without so much as a shawl. "Tomorrow," the duchess said to him, pointedly.

Sighing, Alex turned back to his butler. "What time is it, Sharp?"

The man consulted his watch. "Half past three, your grace."

At least Alex didn't have long to wait.

Chapter FORTY-ONE

Beth's younger sister, Julie, answered Lord Wiltmore's front door and addressed Alex through a one-foot opening. "I'm afraid my sister's not receiving," she said, her tone chilly.

He'd expected a little resistance and was prepared. "Miss Lacey," he said to her, earnestly, "I suspect your sister would make an exception if you were to inform her that it is I. And that I'm here, on her doorstep, desperately concerned about her well-being." He flashed his most charming smile—the one that had never failed him.

The door opened a few inches more, revealing the eldest Lacey sister, Meg. "Beth knows," the countess said, arching a brow. "And she's *still* not receiving."

Apparently, his charming smile was rendered powerless by sisterly loyalty. Though neither woman was particularly large or menacing, he'd have better odds penetrating a Roman fortress than their front door.

But he wasn't above pleading. "I only want to see how she's faring. To apologize for the entire night, and for . . . well, for . . ."

Meg raised her chin. "For dubbing us the Wilting Wallflowers?"

Cringing, he nodded. "She told you about that?"

Julie shot him a chillingly evil grin. "We tell each other *everything*."

Dear God. He hoped that *everything* didn't include their time in the wine cellar. "I regret it more than you know. I wish I could take back that thoughtless, cruel label. Especially now that I know Beth . . . and both of you, through her."

Meg frowned. "So, it was fine before you knew us? Did you think we were dolls made of wax? Or stuffed with straw? That we wouldn't feel the sting of those words?"

Beside her, Julie crossed her arms and pressed her lips into a thin line, awaiting his answer.

He opted for honestly. "Look, I was an idiot. And an ass. I'm trying to make amends. Even if it takes a lifetime of groveling."

"I cannot argue with any of that," Meg said with a shrug.

"What did the doctor say about her head?" Alex asked. "Is she in much pain?"

Meg's face softened, as though she'd decided to take pity on him—at least a modicum. "Her head aches a bit, and she's tired. The doctor said that's to be expected. He wants her to remain in bed for at least three days."

"Without *any* visitors," Julie added pointedly.

"Three days?" He had barely managed to refrain

from scaling the trellis beneath her window last night. How would he last for three days without knowing if she was truly all right? Without knowing if she'd ever be able to forgive him?

Without telling her how he felt?

"Julie and I are taking turns staying at her bedside," Meg assured him. "You needn't worry. We shall take good care of her."

"I know," he said, deflated. "But selfishly, *I* wanted to be the one to take care of her."

"You *had* your opportunity," Julie said, narrowing her eyes. "That little experiment ended with our sister bedridden and heartbroken."

Ouch. He supposed he deserved that. "How am I supposed to fix things if I can't see her?"

"You'll have to employ some creativity," Meg said. "Put forth some effort."

Julie snorted. "Or you may follow your normal course of action and seek solace in the arms of an actress, widow, or courtesan."

Meg gasped. "Julie!"

"It's all right." Alex smiled wryly. "But I hope you'll both believe me when I tell you this—your sister is the only woman for me. If I have to wait three days, three weeks, or three years . . . she's worth it."

"Very touching," Julie smiled—too sweetly. "Now believe me when I tell you this. I still have Artemis's bow and arrows handy, and if you harm my sister again, I *will* use them."

Alex flashed his charming smile once more, confident it wouldn't fail him twice. "If you're going to use arrows, maybe you could borrow some from Cupid?"

Both women rolled their eyes. "Good-bye, your grace."

"Call me Alex," he said—just as the door slammed in his face.

From the settee in her uncle's parlor, Beth had listened to the entire exchange between Alex and her sisters. His deep voice set her pulse racing, and his words left her breathless.

She longed to see him, but her sisters were adamant. If she made a peep while Alex was there, they'd confine her to her bedchamber for the next two days.

At least she knew he was safe. She'd already heard the rumors regarding Lady Haversham. According to the gossip, she'd started the fire and kidnapped the dowager duchess . . . then thrown herself off a bridge. A tragic ending, but perhaps the marchioness thought it preferable to spending the remainder of her life in an asylum or Newgate Prison. Beth suppressed a shudder.

When she heard the door close, she quickly laid her head on the pillow and returned the compress to her head, lest Meg scold her for flouting the doctor's orders.

Julie stalked into the parlor wearing an uncharacteristic scowl. "Your duke is gone."

"For now," Meg added. "He seemed duly apologetic."

"How did he look?" Beth asked anxiously. "Was he injured or tired?"

"He looked handsome," Meg admitted. Julie snorted. "And rather desperate to see you."

"I know you're both cross with him," Beth said. "But I do wish you'd allow him to visit—even briefly."

"He claims to be devoted to you," Julie said with a shrug. "Now he shall have the chance to prove it."

Beth's chest warmed at her younger sister's show of loyalty. "I feel obliged to point out that he walked through fire for me."

Julie sniffed, unimpressed. "It's a start."

Smiling, Meg sat on the edge of the settee next to Beth and patted her leg. "It's a very good start," she amended. "But you must follow the doctor's instructions."

"He ordered rest, not a quarantine." Beth closed her eyes and sighed.

"I know," Meg said soothingly. "But you have been through much in the last few weeks, and you're still reeling from the events of last night. Take a bit of advice from your older sister, and use the next three days to determine what's truly in your heart . . . and give him the chance to show you what's in his."

Three days. Surely their relationship could endure the test—if it was real.

"Very well. I must admit that you're fairly wise," Beth teased. "One would have thought you'd have proven to be a better governess."

"I was horrid, wasn't I?" Meg laughed.

"You were the best. And you should return home to your doting husband and daughters. Julie will see that I remain abed, a prisoner in my own home."

"You may refer to me as the warden," Julie stood at attention, saluting.

"Keep me informed," Meg said. "I have the feeling there will be plenty to report."

Later that evening, on the first day of Beth's confinement, a package arrived. Beth tore off the brown paper to reveal a familiar book—*Mythological Creatures*. Between pages 278 and 279, which contained a description of Ladon, she found a bookmark with a single sentence written on it: *Dragons are real*.

On the second day, she received another delivery. It was a box containing a lovely bottle of sparkling wine and a note: *From our wine cellar*.

On the morning of the third day, a messenger brought her a large flat package. Julie held it while Beth unwrapped it.

Julie tilted her head and made a face at the half-scorched painting. "What is *that*?"

Beth swallowed the lump in her throat. "It's a horse."

Her eyes stung as she read the note tacked to the back: *Phyllis misses you*.

And then she burst into tears.

Uncle Alistair ambled into the room, his tufts of white hair waving. "There, there, dear." His forehead creased in concern. "Don't despair, Elizabeth. I come bearing good news. We've received an instigation to a dinner party this evening—at the Duke of Blackshire's residence."

Beth turned to Julie, deciding she wasn't too proud to beg her little sister. "Please, may we go?"

Julie's gaze flicked from Beth's tear-stained face to the misshapen horse painting and back again. "Your duke has eccentric tastes, it would seem . . . but when it comes to you, he could not have chosen better."

Beth hugged her sister tightly, not trusting herself to speak.

"Of course we may go to the dinner party. And we'll send word to Meg that she and the earl must attend too. I'm certain she'd never forgive us if she missed it."

Happiness blossomed in Beth's chest. The quarantine was over.

She and Alex would soon be together again.

Chapter FORTY-TWO

Mr. Sharp welcomed Beth, Julie, and Uncle Alistair into Blackshire House, apologizing profusely for the faint smell of smoke that hung in the air, and whisking them past the closed door of the study, which was tarnished with soot.

"Allow me to escort you and your family to the drawing room, Miss Lacey," the butler said, his kind eyes crinkling at the corners. "His grace, the dowager duchess, and Lord Darberville await you, as do Lord and Lady Castleton."

Beth swallowed nervously. While she'd worked for the duchess, Mr. Sharp had always treated her warmly—like a daughter. But this evening, his tone was different.

Perhaps the shift was due to the lovely gown she'd borrowed from Meg. Pale pink silk and trimmed with sparkling crystals, the dress floated around her legs like a whisper. Or perhaps the butler was merely relieved that the blow to her head hadn't been as grave as he'd feared.

Either way, Mr. Sharp addressed her not as a lowly companion. Rather, he spoke to her as though she were . . . an esteemed guest.

The butler ushered them into the drawing room and announced Beth, Julie, and their uncle like they were royalty.

Only vaguely aware of the other guests, Beth locked her gaze on Alex. Dressed in a midnight blue jacket that hugged his broad shoulders and buckskin trousers that were molded to his muscular legs, he took her breath away. And when his handsome face broke into a broad smile, one she knew was just for her, well . . . her belly spun cartwheels.

"Beth," he breathed. As though he'd forgotten about the half dozen other people in the room.

"Alex," she replied—because it seemed less awkward than addressing him as *your grace.*

He went to her—in front of his grandmother, her uncle, his best friend, her sisters, and her brother-in-law—and raised her hands to his lips.

"I confess that I'd planned to make a speech during dinner. It was supposed to charm you and entertain the gentlemen and make all the ladies reach for their hand-kerchiefs. But now that you're here, I don't think I can wait to say it, and I don't think I can manage much beyond the raw, simple truth."

"The truth is good." She gave him an encouraging smile.

"The first truth is that neither you nor your sisters are

wallflowers. And I'm sorry that, years ago, I dubbed you as such."

"Bloody hell," the earl barked. "How dare you, Blackshire?" He flexed his fists, itching to defend his wife.

Meg linked an arm through her husband's and patted his sleeve soothingly. "We accept your apology. Do go on."

Alex focused on Beth once more. "The second truth is that I am not a rake—not even remotely. Rumors of my, er, prowess are unfounded."

Perched on the sofa across the room, the dowager fanned herself. "Mr. Sharp, I require a drink at once!"

Lord Darberville sank into the nearest chair and dragged a hand through his hair. "I believe I'll have one as well, Sharp."

Julie blinked, incredulous. "This is the best dinner party I've ever attended," she declared.

Beth squeezed Alex's hands and arched a brow, her subtle way of letting him know that as far as she was concerned, the rumors of his prowess were *completely* founded. In fact, she could scarcely wait for the opportunity to allow him to demonstrate again.

He blew out a long, slow breath and gazed at her with something akin to adoration. "But the third truth—the only one that really matters—is that I love you. I'm not certain you can fix me, Beth. But I'm willing to let you try."

"You don't require fixing," she said softly. Although there *was* one charming lock of hair on his forehead that she would brush aside later. "I love you. Just the way you are."

Uncle Alistair coughed into his hand, puffed out his chest, and assumed a stern expression. "I do hope this is all leading to the appropriate confusion, duke."

Oh dear. "He means conclusion," Beth whispered.

Alex nodded at her uncle and gave him a conspiratorial wink. "With your permission, sir?"

Mollified, Uncle Alistair waved an arm magnanimously.

Alex turned back to Beth and dropped to one knee.

Good heavens. Her vision blurred and her heart pounded out of her chest.

"Elizabeth Lacey," Alex said. "A lot of things in this world aren't what they seem. But my love for you is true . . . and very, very real. I'd be the happiest man alive if you would do me the great honor of becoming my wife."

"Oh, Alex," she sniffled.

He looked up at her, his beautiful eyes pleading. "Say you'll marry me, Beth."

"Yes!"

The room erupted in a chorus of cheers and squeals as Alex stood and wrapped his arms around her. "God, I've missed you," he murmured into her hair.

Julie clapped her hands. "My sister is going to be a duchess!"

"My companion is going to be my granddaughter-in-law," the dowager said, dabbing a handkerchief at the corners of her eyes, behind her spectacles. "And I shall be free, at last, to spend my time rusticating in the country."

Beth and Alex froze, stunned. "The country? But I

thought you wanted to live *here*," Beth said. "Close to Alex."

"I did," the dowager said sheepishly. "But only to ensure that he became settled. Now that you're betrothed, I may finally enjoy a bit of a respite."

"Wait." Alex shook his head, disbelieving. "You need a *respite* from me?"

"No, dear." The dowager clucked her tongue. "But the numerous *accidents* of late—fires, broken balconies, and the like—have taken a toll on my nerves."

"That's all over now," Alex assured her. "There's no need to run off."

"I'm not running off," the dowager countered. "I promise to come visit often, especially once my great-grandchildren arrive."

Lord Darberville choked on his brandy and Alex shot him a death glare.

"Very well," Alex said, turning back to his grandmother, "but you cannot leave town for a few weeks, at least."

The dowager arched a brow. "Why ever not?"

"Well . . . I . . . for one thing, my study is in a shambles. You were in the midst of redecorating it, if I recall. You might at least finish the project."

"Pshaw." She waved a dismissive hand. "I have no doubt that Elizabeth can manage the task far better than I. If it weren't for her, you'd still have a horrendous painting of a llama hanging on your wall."

"That's no llama," Lord Darberville cried. "That's a horse."

"Damn," Alex muttered.

"Which means *I* won the bet." Lord Darberville smiled, smug in victory.

"My goodness," Meg said with a happy sigh. "It seems we have much to celebrate. After all, it's not every day one witnesses a proposal at a dinner party."

"I'd like to point out," Lord Castleton said wryly, "that it only counts as a dinner party if we actually *eat* dinner."

Alex chuckled and signaled to Mr. Sharp, who rang a bell and cheekily intoned, "Dinner is served."

Alex had spent much of the evening trying to devise ways to steal some private time with Beth.

He should have predicted that his grandmother would see to it.

At the end of dinner, she'd reminded Beth that most of her belongings were still there and wistfully wished for one last evening together so they might finish the novel they'd been reading.

No one, least of all Beth, had the heart to deny his grandmother, so it was agreed that Beth would stay in his house one more night.

After all the happy guests had gone home, and the duchess was settled in her bed, Beth sat beside her and began to read. But his grandmother—who'd had a few glasses of celebratory champagne—was snoring a mere two pages later.

Or, perhaps, she only pretended to.

Proving once again that she really would do anything for Alex.

Beth turned down the lamp on her nightstand and tiptoed into the hall, where Alex waited.

"Jesus, I've missed you. I thought I'd never have you to myself," he growled, lacing his fingers through hers.

"I am all yours now," she whispered. "And I've missed you too."

"Let's go. My bedchamber," he said. "Unless you'd prefer the wine cellar."

"Hmm." She laid a finger on her chin, as though she had to ponder the decision. Shrugging, she said, "As long as I am with you, I don't care where we are."

Warmed by the sentiment but tired of talking, he scooped her up and carried her all the way to his room. Once there, he pushed the door open with his foot and laid her on his bed.

Their bed. At last.

Cradling her cheek in his palm, he gazed into her luminous eyes. "God, you're beautiful." In the moonlight that streamed through his window, her pale pink gown shimmered and her chestnut curls glistened. The long line of her neck begged to be kissed, and the round swells of her breasts nearly spilled out of her bodice. He wanted to devour her.

"Is your head truly all right?" he asked.

"Yes." She smiled wickedly, tugged off his cravat, and tossed it onto the floor.

"And you've forgiven me?" he asked.

"Yes," she repeated, unbuttoning his waistcoat, untucking his shirt, and sliding a hand up his abdomen. "Shall I prove it to you?"

His mouth went dry. "Hell, yes."

She kissed his neck and slipped a hand inside his trousers, stroking him until he thought he'd—"Enough," he said panting. "I believe you."

"Now make *me* believe," she said saucily.

"Gladly." He shed his boots, jacket, and trousers before loosening her laces and tugging off her clothes. Though tempted to run his fingers through her hair, he left it piled on top of her head—so it wouldn't hide an inch of her. He plundered her mouth and caressed her breasts and touched her till she moaned in ecstasy.

"I want you," she said, winding her arms around his neck. "Now, tomorrow, always."

"I need you," he said, sliding into her. "God, I need you, Beth."

She wrapped her legs around his waist and they moved together until they both were panting and on the brink.

"Alex," she cried, "I . . . I . . . *oh.*"

He came with her, hard and long and . . . right. So very right.

Touching his forehead to hers, he savored the perfect fit of their bodies. "I love you, siren."

"I love you too," she said with a blissful sigh.

It seemed fairy tales really could come true.

And dragons . . . were most definitely real.

Thank you so much for reading *I Dared the Duke*—
I hope you enjoyed Beth and Alex's story!

- If you'd like to learn more about the *Wayward Wallflower* books, please visit my website (http://annabennettauthor.com) and sign up for my newsletter (http://eepurl.com/bTInsb).

- I can usually be found procrastinating on social media and would love some company! Join me on Facebook (https://www.facebook.com/AnnaBennettAuthor) or Twitter (https://twitter.com/_AnnaBennett).

- Lastly, reviews are a great way to spread the word about books. I'm always grateful for honest feedback from readers—even a quick rating or review on your favorite bookseller's site is incredibly helpful.

Thanks again for spending time with me and the Lacey sisters!
—Anna

Read on for an excerpt from Anna Bennett's next
novel in the *Wayward Wallflowers* series

THE ROGUE IS
BACK IN TOWN

Coming soon from St. Martin's Paperbacks

Sam managed to contain himself until Wiltmore left the parlor—then leaped out of his chair and slid onto the settee beside Juliette. "What the *devil* were you thinking, volunteering me as your uncle's apprentice?"

"Shh," she said, casting a nervous glance at the door. "He'll hear you."

"You should have discussed the idea with me beforehand," he sputtered.

"It popped into my head at the last moment. And I think it was rather brilliant." She leaned back against a worn cushion, beaming with triumph.

Sam closed his eyes and imagined being cooped up in the old man's stuffy study for hours on end, listening to tedious lectures concerning God only knew what—the digestive systems of mollusks . . . the mating habits of beetles . . . He broke into a cold sweat. "I can't do it. I was never a very apt student."

She picked an invisible piece of lint from her skirt. "I cannot say I'm shocked. But a short apprenticeship is hardly cause for alarm. Heavens, you'd think I'd enlisted you to fight with the British army."

"Enduring enemy gunfire might be preferable to deciphering scientific formulas," he muttered, raking a hand through his hair.

Smiling with false sweetness, she said, "You are most welcome to join the cavalry any time you wish."

He moved closer, forcing her to meet his gaze. "You'd like that, wouldn't you?"

She shrugged her delicate shoulders. "I certainly wouldn't attempt to stop you."

"And the moment I stepped foot outside this house, you'd no doubt barricade the door."

She tilted her head, pretending to consider his words. "It's difficult to predict what I would do. However, if you'd like, we can put your theory to the test."

Damn, she was beautiful—and too stubborn

by half. Her full lips were pressed into a straight line, and her captivating eyes sparked with defiance. But she knew very well that he wouldn't walk out the front door. He wouldn't shirk his responsibility or fail his brother—not this time.

"I'm afraid you won't rid yourself of me that easily . . . Juliette."

Her composure fled instantly, and her cheeks flushed pink. "I-I have not given you leave to address me by my given name."

True, but Miss Lacey sounded too prim and starchy. Juliette, on the other hand, perfectly captured her grace and passion.

He stretched an arm behind her, resting it on the back of the settee. "I shall be living here—assisting your uncle, apparently—for several days at least. Given the circumstances, I see no reason to stand on ceremony. Besides," he said glibly, "we're cousins."

"*Cousins?*" she repeated, incredulous. "Apparently you've lost track of where your falsehoods end and reality begins. Have you forgotten that our *supposed* mutual relation—your dear great aunt Harriett—is a figment of your imagination? Merely one of the many lies you told my uncle?"

Sam swallowed. No, he hadn't forgotten.

And he sure as hell wasn't having cousinly thoughts at the moment.

Juliette was so close that the citrusy scent of her hair enveloped him, and the slight pulse beating at the base of her throat entranced him. Though she may have been his adversary, all he wanted to do was to brush aside the errant chestnut curl that skimmed her shoulder and press his lips to the satin skin of her neck.

Maybe a few days trapped in this house wouldn't be as torturous as he'd feared.

She leaned toward him, giving him an excellent view of her round breasts straining against the confines her silk gown. "Have you heard a word I've said?" she demanded.

He lifted his eyes to hers. "I have. You don't want me to address you as Juliette."

"And you will respect my wishes?" she asked warily.

"Of course." He stretched out his legs and crossed them at the ankles. "But since I'm averse to addressing you as Miss Lacey, I shall have to think of another name for you. Something more fitting."

"Your manners are beyond the pale," she said, seething.

He rubbed his chin thoughtfully. "Don't fret. I've already conceived of the perfect name."

With a toss of her head, she sniffed. "Congratulations, but I have no interest in hearing it."

"No? Suit yourself than . . . *spitfire*."

Julie gasped, indignant. "How *dare* you?" She'd had the upper hand for all of two minutes before Lord Travis had managed to wriggle under her skin again.

"Forgive me." Despite a valiant attempt to keep a straight face, his eyes crinkled in a vexingly charming manner. "Like it or not, we have an arrangement of sorts. I thought we should be on more familiar terms."

"We do *not* have an arrangement," she countered, even as she dragged her gaze from his impossibly muscled thighs.

"Fine," he amended. "We are working together for our mutual benefit."

"No, we're perpetrating a lie because you've placed me in an untenable position."

"I wish it didn't have to be this way." His fingertips brushed against her shoulders—incidentally perhaps . . . it was difficult to be sure. Either way, the slightest touch had made her body thrum. "But we might as well make the best of the situation . . . *vixen*."

"Stop that at once," she snapped.

"I was only jesting," he said, grinning.

But he did have a point about their temporary alliance, blast it all. Regrettably, they would be spending an inordinate amount of time together, and until she could prove that Uncle Alistair was the rightful owner of this house, she had no choice but to trust Lord Travis. With one careless action or word, he could ruin her. Indeed, the shattering of reputations was all in a day's work for an unapologetic rogue.

But she had no intention of falling victim, either to him *or* his charms.

"I am willing to form a truce with you," she said, careful to keep her voice icy.

"Excellent," he said smoothly. Hopefully. "There's no reason we can't make the next few days . . . pleasurable."

Oh dear. "I'd prefer *amicable*."

"Why split hairs?" he said, as if there were no distinction at all. "In any event, allow me to extend the first olive branch and make a gesture of good will. Simply tell me what you would like me to do."

"Very well." She sat a little straighter and folded her hands in her lap. "You may begin by acting the part of a gentleman."

"Happy to oblige." He pulled in his legs and

squared his shoulders. "How am I doing so far?"

She cast a critical eye over him, from his mop of sandy brown hair to the toes of his expensive boots. "Marginally better. However, there is still the matter of your cravat. I'm certain I don't need to tell you my sister's embroidery cloth is hardly an acceptable substitute."

"You are correct," he intoned formally. "I shall remove the offensive garment at once."

Good heavens. As he grasped the cloth from behind his neck, she reached out with both hands to hold it in place. After all, a makeshift cravat was better than none at all. "That won't be necessary," she said quickly—but it was too late.

As he yanked the cloth free, it slid from beneath her fingers, leaving her palms on the tanned, warm skin of his neck and chest. Lord help her.

Stunned, she momentarily froze while Lord Travis lightly circled her wrists with his hands and tugged her closer.

"I'm trying to act like a gentleman," he said hoarsely, "but it's damned difficult in the face of so much temptation." He stared at her lips like a starving man . . . and her traitorous heart leapt in response.

"It wasn't my intention to tempt you," she whispered—but made no move to pull away.

"Perhaps not," he breathed, "but you have earned yourself another name nonetheless . . . temptress."